Slightly
Mad
Scientists

A Book of Short Stories

J.F. Smith

Trafford rev. 06/10/2015

 www.trafford.com

North America & international
toll-free: 1 888 232 4444 (USA & Canada)
fax: 812 355 4082

INTRODUCTION

Attn: Office of Future Mad Scientists

Are you a slightly mad scientist? Do you have the desire to rule the world; or at least to control the destinies of your colleagues and neighbors?

If so, this book is for you. It contains useful information that will help you get started on your career as a fully sanctioned mad scientist. It's packed with valuable ideas, unorthodox concepts and unbelievable scientific inventions.

You may already be working on such a device or invention; in that case this book will show you just how you can turn it against mankind.

Think of this book as a training manual for the up and coming mad scientist. Herein are fifty slightly mad short stories penned by an author who breaks all the rules of science fiction; enough ideas to enlighten the novice mastermind with helpful ideas and suggestions for building that invention or device that you've always dreamed about.

There are also few stories about alternate dimensions; time traveling con artists, death rays and alien visitors just to keep you entertained. The stories are short, to the point and fun to read; a fine madness from a writer who never quite exceeds the speed limit of the Twilight Zone.

This book is dedicated to
The Billster,
for helping me figure out all
those time travel paradoxes.

TABLE OF CONTENTS

COLONY SHIP

Colony Ship Odyssey
Captain's Log: 2368 AD

300 years have passed since our historic launch from Earth orbit. Only the quantum engineer's know how much time has elapsed back on Earth, traveling at half the speed of light and skirting giant gravity wells has surely slowed ships' time.

As I read the pass-downs from each crew as they turned over the ship I can't help but feel saddened, for I fear this might be the last log entry.

I've made the decision not to awaken the next crew due to our dire situation. Every system on the ship is malfunctioning. We've performed exhaustive testing, run countless diagnostic programs and gone over every schematic in the manuals trying to isolate the problems, to no avail. For no apparent reason the ship is shutting down, systems are going off line. I fear for the passengers in cryogenic sleep, if that section of the ship fails all is lost.

The Captain was interrupted by a knock on his cabin door.

"Yes, come in" he said.

The First Officer entered and said, "We're getting a strange message on the Crew Alert Annunciator Panel sir."

They returned to the bridge.

AWAKEN CREW 26

"Does anyone know who Crew 26 is?" asked the Captain.

"The computer interface is being very vague about it sir. They were part of the original crew at launch but they weren't actual crew members, by which I mean they didn't have crew assignments," said the navigator as he scrolled through the ship's ancient records.

"They seem to be a collection of scientists, physicists, researchers, some engineers, a few inventors and writers; science fiction writers to be exact, whatever that is."

"So they weren't the Founding Fathers?" asked the Captain.

"No Sir," said the navigator. "But they must have known them. They've been in deep sleep all this time; they must have been recruited by the founding fathers and put on board for some reason."

"Wake them up then," said the Captain.

Crew Mess Hall:

When the Captain arrived in the mess hall, which also served as a briefing room, Crew 26 was dressed and busy questioning the First Officer.

"So we've been in space how long?" asked one of the Crew 26 members.

"It has been approximately 300 years since we left Earth," answered the First Officer. "But I believe you were placed in cryogenic sleep along with many other passengers, some 30 years before that."

"Oh yeah, the paying customers," said another. "That was one of the ways they funded the project; wealthy donors forked out millions to be part of the first off-world colony."

"Geez," said Fred, a physicist and one the newly awakened crew members. "All the people we knew are long dead now."

"Hey, we knew that going in, right," said Albert, one of the engineers in the group.

The Captain joined the First Officer.

"They're all old guys, in their 60's, maybe older," he said. "They might well be the original founding fathers." His spirits began rise.

"I wouldn't get my hopes up sir," warned the First officer. "I was curious as to what the letter H after each of their names on the crew roster designated and I was told it stood for Hippie. It's kind of an inside joke they said. The computer records define the term as a generation of dreamers and pacifists from the late 20th century, it didn't elaborate."

The Captain was introduced to the group.

"I'll get right to the point gentlemen, for some time now the ship's power and several critical systems have been failing or intermittent." Almost on cue the lights in the mess began to flicker as power from one system was shunted to another.

"We can't figure out why. All of our troubleshooting and testing hasn't come up with any answers. We thought we caught a break when the computer alerted us with an automated message telling us to awaken your group from deep sleep."

"Have you tried replacing the Dilithium Crystals?" said Larry Niven, one of the science fiction writers in the group.

"Pay him no mind Captain, he's just joking," scolded Fred.

"What are these Dilithium crystals?" asked the First Officer.

"They're a fictitious power source on a make-believe Starship from a television show from our time. The show had many groupies, called Trekies. Larry was one of them in his younger days."

The Captain was beginning to lose his patience. "So you aren't the Founding Fathers, or even their designated representatives?"

"The Founding Fathers?" asked Fred. "You must mean NASA, the National Aeronautics and Space Administration; the builders of this vessel. No, we're just passengers like all the others. We were culled from a generation of science fiction movie goers. We grew up believing in space travel. All the pseudo-scientific terminology and nonexistent tech was an integral part of our culture, we ate it up. I'm sure I speak for everyone in our group that we feel lucky to have lived long enough to see it come to pass."

"But you have no idea how to fix the ship fix the ship," he said.

They all shrugged.

The Captain lowered his head. "Then I'm afraid all is lost."

The First Officer spoke into his ear. "Keep them talking sir I think they're onto something. I've been doing some research into the history just prior to launch, and it might shed some light on why the founding fathers chose to include this group of hippie scientists in the crew."

"Go ahead," said the Captain.

"Early in the 21st century astronomers discovered several star systems orbited by potentially habitable planets; planets of roughly Earth size orbiting G-type stars like our own within the Habitable Zone," said the First officer.

"According to the records of the period the earth's population was doubling at an impossible rate of every 25 years. The planet's resources couldn't keep up, add to that the catastrophic climate changes that were being caused by greenhouse gases and you had the formula for an extinction level event."

"Harsh conservation measures were instituted on a global scale but that alone couldn't stop the inevitable famines and mass migrations caused by flooding and droughts. Earth's leaders finally decided to go "all in" and build colony ships to take its burgeoning population to the stars."

"What is this "all in" reference?" asked the Captain.

"I think it's a poker term sir, you know the card game, when you push all your chips into the pot. The human race was putting all their chips into the game."

"Go on," said the Captain.

"It was estimated the ship would take well over 30 years to build, and most of the systems that would be needed weren't even on the drawing boards yet. Yet every industrial country in the world contributed their dwindling resources to the project, which someone dubbed Project Odyssey and it stuck. Countries that were once sworn enemies collaborated with each other on ship designs, ideas for propulsion, force field generation, communications and cryogenics," he continued.

"The worlds' best and brightest were recruited to work on the project and ultimately join the colony passengers when the ship launched."

"Even though numerous systems were still in the developmental stages the builders went ahead anyway believing they'd come up with the answers to the problems as they came to them. They needed a ship that bad; the *Earth* needed a ship; a seed if you will, to take mankind's germ to another world," he concluded.

"That still doesn't explain why this group was brought aboard," said the Captain.

They were approached by the group of hippie scientists who had obviously been listening. "I think I can help you with that," said Joe.

"Like we said before our generation grew up believing that space travel was not only possible but inevitable; hell we believed almost anything was possible, time travel, teleportation, warp speed," said Joe enthusiastically.

"I think someone on that original design team factored our unshakable belief into the equation; they realized that they had too many unproven and untested systems so they added some star-gazing hippie dreamers to the mix. They recruited us from different disciplines and kept us around for the design and manufacturing stages; whenever they hit a snag they would call our team in for consultation and the problem would resolve itself. Then we were put us on ice until launch day; we weren't getting any younger. Most of us were pushing 70 by then," he added jokingly.

"Wait a minute," said the Captain. "Are you trying to tell me that the science that controls this ship; that propels it through space is only possible because you guys are on board? That's preposterous!"

"Not just us; the entire passenger compartment is full of believers; space flight is second nature to them. They wouldn't have gotten on board if they didn't believe it would make it to their new home. That unwavering belief in space travel is a factor, a component if you will, in its very success."

Larry chimed in. "Think of it as a variation of quantum physics, the simple act of observing a given experiment has an effect on the outcome. In this case the simple act of wanting space travel to be possible has an effect on its outcome. Take the Higgs-Boson/Fusion Drive that powers the ship; you've studied the manuals, you know the theoretical principles involved, but do you really understand the physics? Not really, but you believe it works. And so it does."

"That's not how physics works," said the Captain shaking his head.

"And I believe that is why the ship is failing; as each new crew is awakened and the belief in space flight is stretched a little thinner, the ship is responding by breaking down," said Joe triumphantly.

"That's the most absurd theory I've ever heard. This discussion is getting us nowhere," said the Captain exasperated. He stormed off to join the First Officer on the bridge.

The First Officer motioned him over to the control panels. "The power is coming back sir."

Across the board malfunctioning systems were coming back to full power, red lights were turning green; bridge personnel were enthusiastically getting back to the business of flying a starship.

The Captain shot a look down the passageway he had just left, was that group of old hippie scientists responsible for this sudden change in fortune?

"It couldn't be that simple," he thought.

Within an hour every failing system was up and running and the group of scientists from the past were invited onto the bridge.

"I can't even begin to understand what has happened but I'm not going to question it. Be it providence, luck, wishful thinking, quantum physics, or maybe a little of each; the Founding Fathers knew and that's good enough for me. On behalf of the crew of The Odyssey and its sleeping passengers I thank you."

He shook each of their hands in turn.

The First officer interrupted the joyous moment.

"We have another problem I'm afraid," he said.

"Navigation, like so many other systems was off-line for so long we don't know our present location in the cosmos let alone the coordinates to our destination star system. We know its approximate location in the spiral arm, but as you can see there are literally millions of stars out there."

Fred turned to Haldeman, one of the science fiction writers. "Well Joe you were always the star-gazer; put all that astronomical observation of yours to good use; find us our new world."

The small group of hippie scientists stepped up to the observation bubble; the spiral arm of the galaxy in all its magnificence spread out before them, a breathtaking view.

Wow was all anyone could say.

After a while Joe pointed to a group of very bright stars lined up in a straight line.

"How's that line go? "Second star to the right and straight on till morning," he quoted.

"You heard the man Helmsman," said the Captain. "Set a course for that star, full speed ahead."

The First Officer smiled, it would seem the Captain has become a believer too.

As they stood at the observation bubble looking out at the vastness of space, the Captain asked, "When we get to our new world do you think it will be hospitable?"

"I gotta believe it will be," answered Fred.

"You know, I do too," said the Captain.

BOB AND TOM'S TRAVELING HOLOGRAPHIC ARMY

15ᵗʰ Century Normandy

A light rain was falling as the King was led to a makeshift pavilion in the middle of the battlefield.

"This way Sire," said the rebel leader.

"Have a seat. Before you is a decree that states you will no longer control the people of this land by force of arms, you will levy no more unfair taxes, and you will not wrongfully imprison its citizens. You may retain your castle and possessions, and you will still be our King; but a parliament will be appointed to govern the people. Sign the document and the revolution will be over."

The King had no choice but to sign. Around him stood an army of rebels and mercenaries his generals estimated at 60,000 men strong. A force so overwhelming they could not stand against it.

"But how did you raise such an army?" asked the King.

The leader of the rebels looked over at Bob and Tom standing in the corner of the tent, "We had divine help, Sire."

The King signed the document, and the rebel leader held it up for everyone to see. A great cheer went up all over the land.

"Well, how much did we get this time?" asked Bob as they packed up their equipment.

"A few thousand in gold and jewelry, maybe more if we can sell some of this stuff to a museum," said Tom.

"I have to admit this wasn't such a bad idea after all."

The idea; conceived in Bob's wily imagination, was *Bob and Tom's Holographic Army.*

"Need to scare away some powerful enemies? Maybe intimidate a ruthless tyrant to ease up on the taxes? We can put an army at your disposal."

Bob and Tom were two out-of-work scientists from the 27ᵗʰ century. They didn't exactly invent the holographic equipment they were using but they'd found some unique and original ways to use it.

Bob was a tall and athletic type, with short blond hair and deep blue eyes. Tom was his opposite; short, slightly over-weight with long, scraggy brown hair.

"Come on Tom, it'll be the adventure of a lifetime," Bob suggested one day back in their lab in the future.

"With our present holographic technology we can broadcast a realistic army up to three square miles, that's a pretty threatening army."

Tom went along, as usual.

"But what if they're not scared off and decide to fight?"

"Well then, we get the heck out of there," said Bob.

"Let's make sure we're never very far from our time machine, agreed?" Tom insisted.

"Agreed," said Bob.

Bob and Tom traveled to many lands and many times. With their holographic army they persuaded attacking armies to retreat, convinced hordes of Huns to take alternate routes, and made would-be usurpers to lay down their arms. Along the way they made a few friends and a whole lot of money. It really had been quite an adventure.

After a couple of close calls in 12th century Mongolia they decided to call it quits; Bob figured they'd pushed their luck as far as it would go; it was time to retire. Before they went back to their own time in the 27th century they decided to check up on the rebel friends in the 15th, just to see if everything had worked out.

When they arrived they found the King up to his old tricks; the peasants were shackled with even higher taxes and most of the rebel leaders were imprisoned.

Bob and Tom immediately set up their equipment and started broadcasting small groups of mercenaries arriving from three miles away. By evening a formidable army surrounded the castle.

To give their army a realistic look they programmed eating and sleep periods. Their army didn't just stand around, they interacted; with occasional fights breaking out between factions. Section leaders rode horses, some men carried swords, some spears and thousands were archers. It was a very sophisticated program; that was Tom's specialty. In the morning they would issue their demands to the King.

As night came and most of the camp was in sleep program, the King sent a small group of his best men to scout out the enemy. They slipped past the sentries and caught Bob and Tom in their tent with the holographic equipment.

"What manner of devil's work is this?" exclaimed the King's officer.

"Uh oh," said Tom.

It wasn't long before they were in chains and hanging from the dungeon walls.

"I hope you're happy," said Tom. "I should have known we'd end up like this. Why did I listen to you?"

"Don't worry I'll get us out of this. Maybe we can convince the King to hire us as his sorcerers or something," said Bob.

"You're really something you know, nothing fazes you. We're hanging from the dungeon walls here!" yelled Tom.

"They'll probably boil us in oil or something equally horrible and you're planning our next employment opportunity. How do you do it?"

"It's a gift."

Late that night, the King's daughter Princess Glenda, stole down to dungeon by secret passage to get a look at the strange warlocks.

"So you are the magicians my father is going to put to death in the morning," said the princess.

"I knew we were going to be executed," Tom muttered.

"Where are you from?" she asked.

Neither of them answered.

"You are from the future aren't you?"

"How would you know that?" asked Bob.

"I sometimes have dreams of what people will look like in the future; with your short hair and clean-shaven faces you look exactly like what I've imagined."

She got up close to Bob and pulled on his chin. "What's that smell?" she asked.

"After shave, your ladyship," said Bob.

"After you shave, you put on this fragrance?"

"Yes."

"It's very pleasing. Does everyone do that in the future?" asked the princess clearly attracted to Bob.

Bob was a devilishly handsome dude; almost everywhere they went, women threw themselves at him.

"Just about," said Bob.

"How did you get here?" asked the princess.

"We have a time, I mean, a vehicle hidden in the forest near the castle," said Tom.

"If I release you, will you show me the future?" she asked.

Bob and Tom looked at one another; they couldn't believe their luck.

"Of course," they both shouted.

"I will release only one of you at a time," she announced. "I am not fully convinced that you are not the demons they say you are."

She released Bob of course. He took the princess on a whirlwind tour of the future. He showed her all his favorite times.

They visited Renaissance France, Elizabethan England, the 1960's of the old United States, the African Restoration of the 23rd century, and of course his own time in the 27th century. Glenda was mesmerized by what she saw. They returned at the exact moment in which they had left and stole back into the castle to release Tom.

Tom couldn't believe the transformation. Glenn (as she wanted to be called now, not Princess Glenda) was suntanned, she had a Billy Jean haircut and she was wearing a mini-skirt from the 1960's; she looked great.

"How will you defeat my father this time?" she asked as they all went back to the time machine in the forest.

"He won't fall for your trickery again. Your, what did you call it, holographic machinery has all been destroyed."

"I'll think of something," said Bob as he got back into the time machine and disappeared, leaving Tom and Glenn standing there.

Barely a minute elapsed and he returned. He had a week's growth of beard and all sorts of weapons; flintlock muskets from the 18th century, M16's from the 20th, mortars and shells, and a dozen bazookas from WWII.

"You can't bring all this stuff here and use it. It's a historical anachronism of epic proportions!" exclaimed Tom.

"We'll bring it all back when we're done," said Bob.

"What if they won't give the weapons back?"

"We'll tell them the stuff is black magic or something. Do you want to win this thing or not?" asked Bob.

"Well of course I do," said Tom.

"Then stop worrying about the details," said Bob.

Over the next week or so they rounded up what rebels were left and trained them in the use of the magical firearms.

At dawn, two weeks after their incarceration, they once again surrounded the castle and began a bombardment with mortars, bazooka and rifle fire. The rebels weren't particularly accurate but then they didn't have to be, the overall effect was enough. After hours of knocking holes in the castle walls and picking off the King's soldiers from the parapets, the King finally surrendered.

The rebel leaders were released from the dungeon, replaced there by the King and his retinue. And there they would stay until a proper government could be assembled.

The rebel leaders were beginning to think these two crazy looking travelers truly were magicians and wanted them to help with the transition to parliamentary rule.

Bob and Tom recused themselves. They did write down a few suggestions for the rebel leaders to mull over; things like freedom of speech, freedom of the press, freedom to cheat on your taxes; stuff like that.

They found Glenn waiting for them at the time machine.

"Now that your father has been overthrown what will you do?" asked Bob.

"Return to the future with you of course," said the princess.

"But, but you won't be a princess in the future; you won't be able to order people around up there in the 27th century," said Bob.

"I'll be able to order you around," said Glenn.

"Yes dear," said Bob.

Tom had to snicker to himself as they all crowded into the time machine with the weapons.

"Bob has met his match," he thought.

And not a minute too soon, he'd had enough adventure to last a lifetime.

OUTSIDE

"And yesterday I was about to get on the Express Tube and I couldn't. Just the thought of being in such a confined space made me sick."

"That's when I called you. What's the matter with me doctor?" asked Rodney Fellows, an enigma, a modern day contradiction. A man afraid of his own shadow, living in a time when fear and anxiety as well as all other forms of mental illness had long been eradicated from the human psyche.

"It sounds like claustrophobia to me, but I haven't heard of any case of the fear of confined spaces for over a hundred years," said the doctor.

"How long have you been coming to me, Rodney?"

"Oh, about two years now doc," said Rodney.

"And in that time you've complained of your fear of heights, your fear of the dark, your fear of flying, your fear that the neighbors are spying on you, even your allergy to your girlfriend's cat; have I missed anything?"

"My fear of spiders," said Rodney.

"I didn't include that one because we're all afraid of spiders Rodney. Have you ever heard of hypochondria?"

"No, is that what's wrong with me? Is that a fear of something?" asked Rodney.

"It means there's nothing really wrong with you, you just worry too much. There's no reason that I can think of that you should be experiencing these fears. I'm going to prescribe a radical treatment. I don't know if it's appropriate in your case but I don't know what else to do."

"I read a psychology paper a few months ago about how mankind had been *inside* so long we've lost touch with the real world."

We live in temperature-controlled, esthetically pleasing City Domes; we travel via underground transit tubes and we venture off world in luxurious cruise ships. We never go outside.

"It might be causing some of our citizens to feel shut-in, confined, even trapped. I think you should go outside the dome Rodney. Take a day off from work and go for a walk. I hear it's very beautiful out there. The wide open spaces and fresh air should do you good."

Before he left the doctor's office he was given a map of the city. A few miles from his apartment in the city there was an exit to the outside of the dome. Of course everyone knew about the outside, but no one ever went there. He'd have to think about this awhile.

He thought about it for about a week, even went down to the south exit a couple of times but couldn't go through the door. Finally, when he couldn't stand it anymore; he went to the South Exit and pushed the airlock button.

The door slid open with a hiss. There was a small corridor and then another door. Rodney closed his eyes, took a deep breath and pushed it open. He was outside.

"Wow, it's wonderful," he said when he opened his eyes. What lay before him were beautifully manicured parks, clean rivers and pristine forests, all kept up by an army of mechanicals.

His fears and anxieties completely forgotten, Rodney stepped out onto the path.

"Can I help you sir," asked a passing mechanical.

"No, I'm just going for a walk."

"Have a nice day," said the mechanical and moved on.

Rodney was wading waist deep in a creek when the head groundskeeper, Robot R2626, arrived on the scene. "What are you doing sir," it asked.

"Just wading, the water looked so inviting I couldn't resist," said Rodney.

"Is there some reason you're out here? Is this a surprise inspection?" asked R2626.

"No, I don't work for the city. I'm just an ordinary citizen out for a stroll."

"A stroll?" inquired the groundskeeper.

"Yeah, you know a walk. I've got to hand it to you guys; I mean you robots, you really keep it looking nice out here."

"Well, thank you sir. We work very hard at it," said R2626 who was obviously very proud of his custodial duties.

"Would you like a tour?"

"Yes," said Rodney.

He was shown meticulously pampered gardens and precisely sculptured hedgerows. Everything was very neat and orderly.

"May I come for a visit tomorrow?" asked Rodney.

"By all means," said R2626.

The next day R2626 found Rodney sprawled out in the middle of a meadow, the leftovers of his picnic lunch scattered all around him. Some of the debris had taken flight on the breeze and several mechanicals were in pursuit.

"What's happened here?" asked R2626.

"Just a picnic," said Rodney.

"Don't you have to get back to your job sir?"

"I'm kind of on an indefinite leave of absence," said Rodney.

"Exactly what kind of job is that?" asked the groundskeeper.

"It means I don't have to go back to work till I want to."

R2626 could only raise his mechanical eye sockets towards the heavens and ask for guidance. His only hope now was the human would eventually tire of the outside world and return to the dome.

But each day the human returned and made a bigger mess. Keeping up with him was causing delays and backups in work schedules. R2626 knew he had to find a way to get rid of this nuisance before it got out of hand. But a robot can't harm a human being, they were created to serve the humans; even nut cases like this one.

R2626 put in a call to the City Authorities. What they suggested was a departure from his usual programming. He was unable to execute the order. A visit from the city's chief robotics scientist took care of that glitch though.

"That should do it, R2626. How do you feel?" asked the robotics scientist.

"I don't feel any different," said R2626.

"Let's try something." The scientist purposely knocked over a flask of dangerous lawn chemicals.

"Clean that up," demanded R2626.

"But it's toxic; I could be harmed," said the scientist.

"Well you should have thought of that before you knocked it over," said R2626. "Did I say that?"

"You certainly did. I'd say your new programming is fully integrated," said the robot scientist proudly.

The next day when Rodney made his usual mess he was handed a rake and told to clean up. When he started to protest he was handed this notice:

Rodney Fellows,

You have been re-assigned to the Park Service. Please report to R2626 for your work assignments from now on.
 And good luck at your new job.

And so it was that the first human began working outside again. Of course many would follow.

THE CHIPPER

It was a brisk autumn morning in a small Virginia suburb where the local tree-pruning company was cleaning up a neighborhood's leaves and branches after a big storm.

Pat Smith, the youngest member of the crew was feeding branches into the chipper, which ground them up into mulch. He was asleep on his feet and not paying much attention when suddenly he felt a sudden tug on his arm. A branch had caught his shirt sleeve and it was pulling him into the gaping maw of the chipper.

Now Pat was fully awake; he fought the pull of the machine with all his might and was just able to hit the cut-off switch in time before it pulled him inside.

"What's the matter, something stuck?" asked Tim, the crew chief.

"Didn't you see what happened?" said Pat. "It tried to pull me in. This thing is possessed just like Joe says; it tried to eat me."

"Not you too," said Tim. "It's just a machine kid; your sleeve got caught that's all. You've been listening to too many of Old Joe's stories about these things. He's got you spooked; you just gotta be more careful."

"But Joe says his whole crew got chipped when he worked for Columbia Township?" argued Pat. "They were part of some secret test project to see if the new machine worked as programmed. And it obviously did, they had to bury sixteen bags of chips because they couldn't separate the people from the shrubbery."

"You don't really believe that story do you? That's just Joe ranting. He's a paranoid; a burned out Vietnam vet who thinks everybody is out to get him," said Tim.

"But you don't know the whole story," Pat continued.

"He said he used to be a scientist or something working on that covert government project. The government is redesigning lots of ordinary machinery like this into lethal robotic mercenaries, for who knows what evil purpose."

"That's ridiculous," said Tim looking at his watch.

"Our Joe, the guy who only comes to work when he feels like it, told you he was a scientist working on some Top Secret government project?"

"Yeah," said Pat.

"And now he's on the run from the Feds because he knows too much? Come on kid, can't you hear how crazy that sounds?"

"Well, it sounded believable to me," said Pat. "He knows lots of facts about the government, and how sneaky they can be."

"Well, believe what you want, now get back to work."

"When am I going to get a chance in the bucket?" asked Pat. "That's where I want to be, up there in the treetops like you."

"You'll get your chance someday kid," said Tim. "Everybody starts with the chipper."

Later that evening, Pat climbed the fence to the maintenance yard where the chipper truck was kept. He started it up and jumped in; raising the bucket up as far as it would go. He swung it back and forth getting a feel for the controls, and then he sat back and relaxed looking at the stars overhead; imagining the day when he'd be the tree trimmer and not just part of the clean-up crew.

Suddenly the machine lurched; the bucket spun around and tipped over. Pat was just able to grab the safety bar. He watched in horror as the doors on the top of the chipper opened exposing the deadly chipper blades. The crane wouldn't allow the bucket to get any closer but now it began to bounce up and down trying to shake him loose. All he could do was hold on and stare down at the spinning blades of death.

"Old Joe was right, this thing is alive," he thought.

"They'll never find my body. I'll just be so much mulch in somebody's garden."

"Grab my hand kid." A familiar voice came from above.

Pat looked up to see Joe hanging from the roof of the control cab. "Joe, it's you. What are you doing here?"

"I live in that shack over there," said Joe. "I've been keeping an eye on this contraption; making sure nobody gets chipped late at night, if you know what I mean."

"No, actually I don't," said Pat.

"Never mind kid, just grab my arm and jump."

Pat jumped, his feet missing the swirling, demonic blades by mere inches.

"God, that was close. Thanks man, I owe you my life."

"Come on kid, we've got to go underground. They'll be looking for both of us now," said Joe.

"Who are they?"

"Haven't you been listening to me kid? *They* are the secret society that's behind everything that's evil in this country. *They* are the ones that get us into wars we have no reason to be in, *they* took out Jimmy Hoffa, probably with a machine just like this one. *They* are the ones that make the traffic lights turn red even when there isn't anyone coming the other way."

"Oh no, here he goes again," thought Pat as they hurried to Joe's hideout.

Somewhere downtown:

"Well, at least we got the old one to come out of hiding," said the federal agent.

"Do you think the kid believes him?"

"Probably not, but it doesn't matter, they both know too much. They'll have to be eliminated. We'll make our report later; I'd like to give the old vet a head start if you know what I mean."

"I do, I'm a veteran too you know. Let's get some breakfast, I'm starved."

They left their office in the basement of an inconspicuous federal building downtown. On the door was a small plaque that read:

FBI - CHIPPER DIVISION

HUNTING PARTY

Four hunters made their way up a steep trail in the mountains of Southern Alaska; make that one experienced hunter and three weekend warriors on an Alaskan Adventure Big Game Hunt.

The three novice hunters were all scientists at the Lawrence Livermore Facility in the San Francisco. They didn't think of themselves as nerds but you could tell they weren't exactly outdoor types either.

Their guide, a Native American named John Tenkiller, was born and raised in this wilderness; the newbies were having trouble keeping up with him.

"I can't keep up this pace. What's the big hurry anyway?" complained Harry Jensen.

"Oh stop whining Harry," said Pete Wilcox.

"If you remember this expedition was your idea."

Up ahead of them on the trail, John paused to let the others catch up. He was standing on a high bluff overlooking the breathtaking majesty of one of the last great wilderness areas on Earth.

Everything was green and fresh at this time of year. He could think of no other place on Earth that he wanted to be.

As he waited a blast of cold wind whistled by; a storm was coming.

"Looks like we're in for some bad weather," said John when they finally caught up.

"I know of a cave not far from here where we can go for shelter."

"But don't bears live in caves?" asked Fred Cummings, the last in the group.

"Not at this time of year," John laughed. "But if there is, I think we've got enough firepower to scare him off."

He looked around at his hunting party; each of his charges was carrying the latest in high tech weaponry. They had enough armament to take on a small army.

Before they reached the cave the storm hit. It was ferocious; wind and rain pelted them mercilessly. They had to struggle just to keep their footing. Not even John had experienced a storm this violent before.

When they finally made it to the cave no one ventured very far from the entrance, just in case Fred's suspicions were warranted.

They were still getting out of their wet gear when a tremendous; almost primordial lightning bolt struck near the mouth of the cave. The light was blinding, and the thunderclap was immediate and deafening. Electricity literally filled the air.

"Was that the mother of all lightning bolts or what?" shouted Harry, who'd been knocked down by the pure energy of the thunderclap. He got up and turned on his flashlight, pointing it around at the group.

"Fred, look at your hair," he laughed.

"Mine, look at yours," said Fred.

Everyone's hair was standing on end. John's long black tresses looked like a fright wig. They all stood there laughing at each other.

They were almost giddy with relief; they knew that was as close as one could get to a lightning bolt and still survive.

After the laughter died away, they began to hear noises coming from deep within the cave.

"Sounds like someone whispering," said Harry. "Is anybody in there? Come on out, we're harmless."

John went to investigate. He lit a lantern and went into the cave; the others followed. What they found was straight out of a grade school history book; a group of primitive men, women and children were huddled around a small fire. Their garments were made from animal skins; their weapons were spears and clubs. It was like looking at a museum display of early modern man, right down to the cave drawings.

"Now I've seen everything," said Harry.

"Who are these people?" asked Fred. "Is this some kind of cult?"

Both groups just stared at each other for a couple of minutes and then John suggested they back out slowly.

"Whoever these people are; this is obviously their home and we are trespassing," said John.

The storm passed and everyone loaded up their gear and began the long hike back to camp. No one spoke of what they had seen back in the cave.

When they finally got to the campsite everything was gone; the tents, the canoes; even the fire pit. It was like their camp had never been there.

"Is this the right spot?"

"Yes," said John. "I've been bringing hunters to this area for years. Someone turn on a radio."

Peter tried his radio, nothing but static.

"Try your cellular phone."

It was the same, nothing but static. Harry tried his phone too, nothing.

"We're just out of range," said Harry.

"No, I called my broker from this very spot just this morning," said Fred.

"Well something strange is going on here," said Harry.

Pete, a biology professor at Stanford before he joined the staff at Livermore, was the first to venture an explanation.

"I don't know how to break this to you guys but I don't think we're in Kansas anymore. Did you notice the change in flora on the way back to camp? It's different, more ferns and mosses, and hardly any hard wood.

"The weather has changed too; it's gotten much colder," added Fred.

"So what are you trying to say?" asked Harry.

"I'm saying, I think the energy from that bolt of lightning somehow ripped a hole in the timeline and we stepped through it. I know that sounds like science fiction but it would explain a lot.

Maybe events like this happen all the time but no one's ever been that close before. We were just in the right place at the right time; or the right place at the wrong time, depending how you look at it. I'm guessing it's a temporary phenomenon too; I doubt we can get back that way."

He looked around at the shocked faces of his friends.

"Hey, that's just one theory. If anyone has a better explanation for the cold, the change in vegetation, the missing camp and those people up there, I'd be glad to hear it."

"That's the craziest thing I've ever heard," said Harry.

"There's no way we've gone back in time. We all know that's impossible. There's got to be a more plausible explanation," said Harry.

"What are we going to do?" asked Fred.

John interrupted. "We can sit tight here and wait for the plane; it's due back in a week. Or we can hike out." "We're only about one hundred miles north of Anchorage. It would take some time and we'd have to hunt for food along the way, but we could make it. Of course, if Anchorage isn't there anymore we'd have walked a great distance for nothing."

"I think the answer lies in that cave up there," John continued.

"We should camp here tonight and in the morning go back and try to communicate with those people. If they are primitives, then they're my ancestors. I'd like to make their acquaintance; maybe we can help each other."

"Make their acquaintance? Help each other? Have you guys all gone nuts?" shouted Harry.

"You're talking about joining up with a bunch of savages, no offense John."

"None taken," said John.

"If we have gone back in time and I still don't believe we have, then we've got a lot more important things to worry about than a bunch of natives. Our supplies are going to run out in about a week and then we're screwed!"

"Not necessarily," said Fred. "We've got guns and I don't know about you guys, but I brought enough ammo to bring down a hundred mastodons."

"Plus we've got compasses, maps, knives, water purifiers, radios, cell phones, ipods, even a lap top," said Pete.

"I know some of that stuff seems useless now, but we've all seen McGyver; nothing is useless.

"And we've got enough trinkets like mirrors, pens, toothpaste, cigarettes and lighters to dazzle the natives," added Fred.

"It's not quite the adventure I had in mind when I called the travel agent but what choice do we have?"

"But wouldn't us giving all this modern stuff to the locals change their future?" asked Harry.

"Well let's see, we pretty much wiped the Native American off the face of the Earth in our time; I don't see how we can make things any worse than that," said Pete.

The next day they hiked back to the cave and into history.

December 16th, 1620:

The Mayflower weighed anchor off the coast of the New World. Captain Christopher Jones and a small group of passengers and crew paddled to shore.

On the shore they are greeted by a group of colorfully dressed dark-skinned natives. Captain Jones had been briefed back in Southampton that they might encounter some aboriginals upon arrival in this new land, but he wasn't expecting this.

"Greetings travelers and welcome; your arrival has been foretold for many generations. We have food and lodgings prepared for you. Come this way."

The captain and the rest of the landing party looked at each other in puzzlement. They spoke English; a strange dialect to be sure, but it was English.

So they followed the natives up the beach. They came to a narrow wooden walkway cut through the dunes and followed the winding thoroughfare to the other side. When they emerged on the other side they could scarcely believe their eyes.

"What is all this?" asked the captain.

Brightly lit buildings rose to staggering heights and strange flying vehicles filled the air.

"Oh, those are personal flyers. And that over there is a shopping mall where you may obtain all your daily needs; your womenfolk will love it. And next to the mall is a Casino."

"If you have passengers on board your ship who are ill please get them off your ship first, we have medical personnel waiting to help them," added another native.

"There are lodgings waiting for everyone on board, we call them motels. You need just sign the ledger and we'll show you to your rooms."

"What is that strange music we're hearing," asked one of the ship's crew.

"Oh that; that's Rock and Roll, our ancestors said you might like it. Of course, the musicians who wrote this music have not yet been born; but that's another story," said their Native American guide.

"Not to worry, we will explain all to you in due time. Let's get you settled in first."

Captain Jones halted the party. "But we haven't enough money to pay for all this."

"Not a problem," their guide assured them.

"I'm sure you'll be able to get a line of credit; using your ship as collateral of course."

DREAM GAME

Monday, September 12th, 2026:
Native American Park, Maryland

Week 1

Red Walters, the beleaguered head coach of the Washington Native Americans, sipped his coffee as he made his way to the film room.

This was the hardest part of the week, reviewing Sunday's game film. They'd just received a humiliating defeat at the hands of their archrivals, the Texas Sodbusters. The score was 55 to 0; the worst trouncing the team had taken in this century. Red wasn't looking forward to watching that again.

When he got to the film room he found one of his assistants already there.

"Hi coach," said Mike Westbrook, the receiver's coach.

"I couldn't sleep so I came in early. I couldn't shake the strange feeling I had during and after the game. Something wasn't right. I've been going over the film and I've found a lot of plays that just couldn't have happened."

Mike rewound the tape.

"Look at this pass in the first quarter. That must be 85 yards in the air. We had that guy in camp last year; I know he can't throw the ball that far. Hell, nobody can!"

Mike fast-forwarded the tape a little.

"And this catch in the second quarter, the receiver jumped six feet in the air, made the catch and still came down in bounds. Even in slow motion it's hard to see how he did it. And that sixty-five yard field goal at the end of the half? Come on! There was more going on yesterday than just a football game. It was like we were all in a trance."

Dallas Super Mall

Week 2

Chad Pitt, star receiver for the Texas Sodbusters, waited with a suitcase full of money while a wizened old man got out of a taxi, paid the driver and hobbled over.

"It worked perfectly professor," said Chad. "We creamed them."

"I don't concern myself with the machinations of such meaningless pastimes. I need money to continue my research so I am forced into this clandestine activity. I will probably go to jail someday because of it, but I feel my research is worth it," said the old scientist.

"Whatever old-timer," Chad said. "I'll be a needing the machine again next Sunday. We're playing the New York Metropolitans."

"As you wish," said the professor.

The machine Chad referred to was the professor's latest gadget.

It was based on the *Dream Parlor* technology already available in Europe and Canada; patrons of those *Dream Parlors* reclined in a chair and mind-linked with a pre-recorded adventure of his or her choice. They were in complete control of the dream; anything they wanted to happen would happen.

The professor simply expanded on that technology. He upgraded the device so it could be focused outward, aimed at a group of people, in this case an entire stadium; allowing the dreamer to bring everyone into his dream. And like a dream in a Dream Parlor anything the dreamer can imagine is possible. He can make fantastic catches and have others do equally heroic things just by wishing it.

Week 15

After the embarrassing loss to the Texans the Native Americans went on to have a pretty good season.

They won enough games to qualify for the playoffs as a wild card team; but the memory of their encounter with the Sodbusters in Week One still haunted Coach Westbrook.

He asked for and was granted a leave of absence and went to Tom Landry Stadium for the Sodbusters last game, a Monday Night affair.

It was like before, a dream world. Everyone seemed to be moving in slow motion, except the Sodbusters. It was difficult to stay focused on the task at hand. He felt there had to be some device that was causing this effect.

He had a hunch it must be in the rafters, high enough to encompass everyone in the stadium. It took him most of the game to find his way up there. As the game drew to a close he spotted a machine that looked like a TV camera being operated by a little old man.

"So what's all this?" asked Mike.

"Huh," the startled old man jumped up and put his hands over his head, "I guess you've come to take me to jail."

"Not exactly," said Mike. "But I would like you to explain what you're doing."

The professor was only too happy to show off his invention.

"You've daydreamed haven't you?" asked the professor.

"Well sure, everyone does," said Mike.

"That's right we all do," said the professor. "We can be sitting at our desk at work, walking in the park or waiting for a light to change and for no reason our mind wanders off on its own."

"These daytime fantasies usually only last a few seconds, they may seem longer but the duration is usually very short. Our conscious mind snaps us back to the real world at the first distraction."

"My machine stimulates the dream centers of the brain; it allows young Mr. Pitt down there to daydream all he wants. Of course he has to stay focused on the game; it requires discipline; it wouldn't do if he were to grab a cheerleader and go swinging through some imaginary treetops. But until I turn off the machine there will be no distractions to snap him out of his daydream."

"It doesn't give him a dream; that comes entirely from Brad's imagination and he makes it up as he goes along. The machine does offer thousands of bits of useful football trivia and historical sights and sounds of the game that he may use to enhance the dream. And because everyone in the stadium is in the machine's broadcast range we see what Chad dreams up. We become part of his dream."

"What about television? How can it be recording a dream?" asked Mike. "That doesn't seem possible."

"It is amazing isn't it," bragged the professor.

"The brain is a very powerful thing. While Brad is dreaming he believes what is happening is real. That conviction is amplified by my machine and projected to everyone here. It's like a mass hallucination; even the TV cameras are fooled."

"That power of conviction could explain things like miracles and other unaccountable events in which thousands of people claim to have witnessed things that others (who weren't there) have a hard time believing. I'm doing a research paper on that very subject."

"Very impressive Professor," said Mike.

"I would like to think it is important work," said the professor.

"Tell you what, I won't get in the way of your research if you do something for me," said Mike.

Mike explained his plan to the professor, who readily agreed. It turned out he was a bit of a football fan after all, and he'd always disliked these Texas Sodbusters.

Back in the nation's capital, Mike was trying to explain to the coach what he had discovered.

"So you're saying that there was some kind of hocus pocus going on in that first game," said Red. "And that's why the Texans have won all their games."

"Yep," said Mike. "But don't worry I've convinced the inventor to re-focus the machine on one of our guys once the game starts. I just have to let him know who."

"Well if you think it will work, I know just the guy," said Red.

NFC Playoff Game:

"Glad you could join us for today's game between the (9-7) Washington Native Americans and the (16-0) Texas Sodbusters at Tom Landry Stadium in Dallas today folks" said the TV announcer.

"Well Frank, it looks like Red has decided to go with his third-string quarterback. That's a bit of a surprise."

"It sure is John. This kid hasn't played a down all season. I wonder what old Red is up to?"

Down on the field young Gus Frerotte III was getting a last second pep talk.

"OK son, I want you to go out there and believe you can do anything; and I mean anything! You're the greatest football player that ever lived. Go out there and do anything you want."

Gus figured that was just "coach talk" as he ran out onto the field, but soon he was caught up in it. He threw a pass that sailed too high for the receiver to reach but at the last second the ball descended right into his hands. He wished for big holes in the line for the running backs and big holes he got.

Halfway through the first quarter he took the hike and scrambled to his left, right into the path of an on-rushing linebacker. "Oh my God!" he thought. But as the defender dove at him Gus leaped high into the air, a slow motion hurdle that would have made an Olympic high jumper envious. He never looked back. He let the dream take him to pass diving tacklers all the way to the end zone.

Later in the half he caught sight of a wide open receiver well out of his range, but threw the ball anyway; the ball sailed 82 yards and hit his man in stride. His teammates were getting into the dream too; they were running faster and making plays all over the field.

"John, are you seeing what I'm seeing?" said Frank astonished by the performance of this 3rd string QB.

"I'm seeing, but I'm having a hard time believing; it's like another team. I wonder where they've been hiding these guys all year?" said John.

Gus was dodging tacklers like Fran Tarkenton, throwing bullets like Dan Marino and running for first downs like Michael Vick. He could do no wrong.

It was the greatest single game performance since Sammy Baugh in the 1937 playoffs.

The Washington Native Americans beat their arch-rivals that day by a lopsided score of 52-10; poor Chad Pitt never figured out what happened. The Washington Native Americans went on to Superbowl LXII.

But of course you already know that part of the story.

THE KITTILSTADS OF VALLEY FORGE

"I've got bacon and eggs or waffles and syrup; I'm not making both," said Winnie from the kitchen.

"I'll take bacon and eggs," Bill called out from somewhere in the house.

No reply from the living room. Her husband was oblivious to the outside world when he was reading the morning paper, especially when the Eagles were in a slump.

It was a typical Sunday morning at the Kittilstad residence. Owen Kittilstad (Kit to everyone who knew him) was in the living room reading the Inquirer; his wife Winifred was in the kitchen and their youngest son Bill was in the basement working on his latest science project.

"OK, I'm making bacon and eggs," said Winnie. "That's what I'm making."

She listened for a reply but got none.

Not until breakfast was on the table and they'd all sat down did Kit speak up.

"Doesn't anyone want to know what I want?"

"OK Dad what did you want?" said Bill.

"Well, waffles would have been my first choice," said Kit.

"Too bad Dad; you snooze you lose" said Bill.

Kit looked at his youngest a little annoyed, "When did you say you were going back to school?"

"I'm working on my thesis here at home; you can do that now. It's not like when you were in school, they give us a lot of leeway," said Bill.

Actually, he was suspended at the moment because of a lab experiment that had gotten way out of control, but he didn't need to explain that to his parents just yet. He'd set up shop in the basement and was trying to figure out what had gone wrong.

It was like this most every Sunday at the Kittilstad residence on Stephens Drive in Valley Forge, PA. That was about to change.

The first indication that something was amiss came about a half an hour later. Kit was sitting at the kitchen table having a second cup of coffee, Winnie was cleaning up the breakfast dishes and Bill had retreated back to the basement; when the lights began to flicker, and then the power went out completely.

"Power lines must be down," said Kit as he threw on an overcoat and headed out to the shed to start up the auxiliary generator. Moments later the muffled sound of the generator throbbed through the house and the power and heat came back on.

"It's really coming down out there," said Kit as he shook off his coat and hung it back up.

"I can't even see the Henderson place it's snowing so hard." In fact, as he looked out the living room window, he couldn't see any of the houses on the block.

He was about to put his coat back on and go investigate when the first explosion rocked the house; something loud and close had struck in the backyard. Kit ran back to the kitchen just in time to see another explosion tear up a large patch of lawn; a gaping hole smoldered in the middle of the blanket of snow that covered the yard.

"Good Lord, we're being bombarded!"

"Is it terrorists?" Winnie wondered out loud.

"More likely some nut job has commandeered one of those old cannons at the Park and is firing randomly into the neighborhood," said Kit.

The south ridge of Valley Forge National Park overlooked their housing development.

"But aren't they supposed to be plugged with cement or something?" asked Winnie.

They were crouched down in the kitchen wondering what was happening when another explosion hit the house knocking them both to the floor.

When they came around they found themselves on the sofa in the living room and armed soldiers were pointing muskets with bayonets at them.

At first glance it looked like some kind of reenactment ceremony gone terribly wrong. But upon closer inspection of the uniforms they were wearing and the general appearance of the soldiers it was plain to see this was no reenactment; these were real soldiers.

Their uniforms were filthy, they had bandanas and rags wrapped around their heads and feet and their boots were covered with mud. They'd been exposed to the cold a long time, they looked haggard and worn out.

"Who are you people and how did this house get here?" asked one of the soldiers.

"We live here," said Kit. "Who are you?"

"We're militia in the First Continental Army; Colonel Mulchaney's brigade, and this house wasn't here yesterday."

Another soldier came running through the door.

"The Colonel is coming to question the prisoners," he said.

"Prisoners?" thought Kit and Winnie looking at each other in amazement.

"Alan Funt had better come through that door and say *Smile your on Candid Camera* soon," thought Kit.

The Colonel entered the house with a small entourage. He looked curiously around the living room, his gaze stopping at the television set. He seemed fairly young for a man of such high rank. But when he spoke his rich British accent hinted at a well-educated upbringing.

He wore a dirty overcoat over his military uniform.

"My name is William Mulchaney. I command the brigade entrusted with defending the outer fortifications of our encampment here at Valley Forge. May I ask your name sir?"

"Owen Kittilstad," said Kit getting up from the couch to shake the colonel's hand. "U.S. Air Force retired."

"Air Force, what's that?" asked the colonel.

"Long story," said Kit.

The colonel didn't pursue it. "Do you have any idea what's going on here?" he asked instead.

"No, we haven't the slightest idea what's happening here," said Winnie angrily. "We've lived on this block for over twenty years. Your men are trespassing on our property, calling us prisoners and asking us strange questions. You say you're in the military but no one has worn uniforms like that in a great many years. We should be the ones asking you people the questions."

"What's a block?" asked the colonel.

"You know a street, where people live," said Winnie. "What kind of question is that?"

The snow had stopped falling. Kit went over to the window and looked out. As he had suspected earlier all the other houses on the street had disappeared. Their house stood alone in the woods. Their driveway was still there but instead of connecting to Stephens Drive it simply ended at open pasture.

"Uh oh," said Kit. "You're not going to like this Win"

"What's happened to our street!" exclaimed Winnie.

Kit was the first to put it together. "What year is this?" he asked the colonel.

"Why it's 1776 of course, we're fighting a war against the British."

"I think I know what's going on here but it's pretty outlandish. Before I tell you would you and your men like a cup of coffee and a pastry?" asked Kit.

The soldiers looked to the colonel anxiously. The tantalizing smell of breakfast still lingered in the air.

"Very well," he said. "I guess you're not spies."

"Come on into the kitchen," said Kit.

On the way to the kitchen the Colonel asked about the lights. "These lamps have no flame, no wick or oil. How do they work?"

"It's called electricity," said Winnie. "Why wouldn't you know about electricity?"

They all looked at her with blank faces so she explained. "Electricity comes into the house through power lines from a power generating plant in the city."

While the coffee heated up Winnie gave the soldiers a guided tour of the kitchen and its gadgetry. "Electricity runs all these appliances; the toaster, the refrigerator, the microwave and the stove."

The men were enthralled as she demonstrated the operation of each kitchen appliance.

The Colonel stood back and observed. Kit nudged his elbow and whispered, "If you should run into Benjamin Franklin, tell him he's on the right track."

At this juncture the Colonel was having trouble collecting his thoughts; these nice people were speaking English, but the words they spoke made little sense.

After they had all been served coffee and muffins they went back into the living room.

"I'm deeply sorry about firing the cannons at your house; but when it appeared out of thin air just outside our encampment it panicked the men. I'm afraid we overreacted. You were going to tell us your explanation of how you arrived here?" asked the Colonel."

"Oh yeah," said Kit. He picked up the TV remote and switched on the boob tube. The set came to life startling the soldiers, but there wasn't any signal, just fuzz.

"Just as I suspected," said Kit. "You're going to find this hard to believe but we're from the year 2015. Somehow this house and its occupants have been transported back in time. I have no idea what would cause such a phenomenon but as implausible as it sounds it seems to be the only explanation."

The colonel and his men were momentarily dumbfounded, looking at this elderly couple dressed in strange clothes, standing in this cozy living room, in a house like no one had ever seen before.

The colonel finally said, "Back in time you say."

"Yes," said Kit.

"The General isn't going to like this."

"General Washington?" asked Kit.

"Yes," said the colonel.

"What year did you say this was again?" asked Kit.

"1776," said the colonel.

"What month and day?" asked Kit.

"Why it's December 23rd," said the Colonel.

"But shouldn't you be on your way to the Delaware for your surprise attack on Trenton?" asked Kit.

"Attack Trenton in the middle of winter, that would be folly," exclaimed the Colonel.

"No," said Kit. "According to history in 1776 on the day after Christmas you crossed the Delaware, completely surprising the Hessian troops guarding Trenton. You took back the city and went on a successful campaign that ended with your victory at Saratoga. It was the turning point of the war."

"How do you know all this?" asked the Colonel, thinking maybe these two were spies after all.

"It's all right here," said Kit going over to the bookshelf and taking down a book about the Revolutionary War. He flipped through the pages and there was Valley Forge, the Battle of Trenton and Morristown, and the famous rendition of George Washington crossing the Delaware.

"Are you saying we won this war?" asked the Colonel.

"Oh yes, the British surrendered at Yorktown on October 19th, 1781." Kit handed the book to the Colonel.

He slowly turned the pages of the history book, tears welling up in his eyes. He stopped at the picture of Cornwallis surrendering at Yorktown. "I never thought we had a chance," he said.

He looked at the back cover of the book; it was dated 08/1999 USA.

"What is USA?" asked the Colonel.

"The United States of America," said Kit proudly.

The Colonel thought about that for a moment. "I'm not going to pretend I know why this is happening, but if by some act of divine providence we're being given prior knowledge of battles we have not yet fought I will not question it. I will take this information to General Washington with my recommendation that we move on Trenton immediately."

"Keep the book. It might help you convince General Washington," said Kit.

The colonel signaled to his men to move out. Kit and Winnie followed them outside.

"I guess you'll be staying here," said the Colonel.

"Yes, we must. If the phenomenon which brought us here reverses itself we need to be right here when it happens." The lights in the house had already started flickering.

"Well then I guess we'd better be on our way. Thank you Mr. Kittilstad," said the Colonel shaking Kit's hand.

"Call me Kit."

He turned to Winnie.

"And thank you Mrs. Kittilstad," he said kissing Winnifred's hand.

He got on his horse and rode off with his men.

As soon as they disappeared over the ridge full power came back on in the house. It started snowing again, and good old Stephens Drive reappeared along with the rest of their neighborhood.

Both Kit and Winnie let out a sigh of relief. Kit headed for the backyard to see how much damage had been done to the house. And

Winnie suddenly remembered Bill in the basement and ran to the top of the stairs.

"Bill, are you alright?"

"Sure, what's been going on up there anyway; I heard a lot of strange noises."

"Bill? What have you been doing down there?" asked Winnie as it now dawned on her who was responsible for this strange occurrence. "Not another one of your strange experiments?"

"Nothing unusual, just your normal run-of-the-mill time experiment," said Bill.

"Well stop it right now! Do you realize what just happened?" And she went down to scold her son who was always doing something unlawful with laws of physics.

SLIGHTLY MAD SCIENTIST

"This had better work," said Harold Darby, freelance inventor, to Spot his loyal companion as he soldered down the last circuit board in his latest invention.

"If not, it's the bread line for us."

He looked around his workshop, "What a clutter it of discarded gadgetry. I'll have to do something about all this stuff when I get back," he thought.

"Some good ideas here though," he thought. "There's just not enough time or money to finish them." That would all change when he put this new scheme in motion.

"How had it come to this?" he wondered.

He had once had a promising career working for American Electric, inventing numerous household conveniences that everyone took for granted.

AE had convinced him to sell the patents to them; which he did believing the company would compensate him when he reached retirement age. But times had changed; instead they'd laid him off to make way for automation.

There was no need for a craftsman in a world of assembly lines and mass production and where individual achievements were quickly forgotten.

He tried to teach physics at the university for a while but got bored with the world of academia in short order. He was an inventor and a damn good one; that's what he did.

Now that he was getting on in years the realization that he had nothing put away for retirement worried him. These last couple years he'd devoted exclusively to get-rich-quick schemes.

First, he came up with the money duplicator. You put a $10 bill in this end of the duplicator, pushed a button, and two $10 bills came out of this end. Brilliant, the only problem was the duplicates were too good; they didn't wrinkle or get wore out. He got funny looks from merchants when he tried to spend them. They were perfect in every way, they just looked too new. You couldn't even crumple them up. He tried rubbing them in the dirt, even washing them in the washing machine, but they came out just as fresh and brand new as before. He was afraid some shopkeeper would call in the Feds and they'd figure out the serial numbers were bogus.

So he tried something else; The Coal Compactor; which compressed ordinary coal into diamonds. It worked perfectly, alas too perfectly; the diamonds had no flaws. Diamond experts wouldn't touch them with ten-foot tweezers.

This latest invention, a Teleportation Machine, was his most promising project to date. He'd spent almost a year working on it and used up all his savings. This was his last chance to get rich. If this didn't work it was Walmart Greeter for him.

On this first test he would teleport into the First National Bank, (inside the vault after hours) help himself to a few thousand dollars and then teleport out again.

He'd calculated the distance from the vault to his lab here in his basement down to the millimeter. The whole thing had been quite exciting, like a bank robber casing the joint.

He felt not the slightest bit of guilt at what he was about to do. If society could sweep him aside like an outdated invention, he felt no remorse in exacting a small portion of revenge. It wasn't like he was going to take millions.

"Wait here Spot. I'll be back with more money than we can count."

Spot had heard that before.

Harry made the jump. Like all of Harold's inventions the machine worked to perfection. He found himself surrounded by neatly stacked piles of money in all denominations. He took only ones, fives and tens. They probably wouldn't even know the money was missing until their next audit. His next Bank Job he'd take enough for a good long vacation in the Bahamas, and some badly needed test equipment.

"Time to go," he thought.

He pushed the return button on his backpack mounted teleportor but instead of returning to his lab in the basement of his house, he'd materialized in a strange white walled expanse, like an underground garage or something. The room had no windows or doors and the floors and ceilings seemed to go on forever. As he stood there contemplating the nature of the universe and how badly he'd misjudged the physics of teleportation he finally noticed that two men in white lab coats sat at a table about a hundred feet in front of him.

One of them was gesturing him to come forward. He did.

"Please sit down Mr. Darby."

Harry looked around and there was a chair directly behind him.

"Who are you?" he asked as he put the money down and took a seat.

"Who we are is irrelevant," they said. "We can't let you get away with this."

"I'll put the money back," Harry started to say.

"Not the money, your invention," they said.

"The human race isn't ready for teleportation technology yet. It would cause too many social and economic problems."

"Who are you guys again?" Harry asked.

"We are from the far future. We keep an eye on mankind, in its infant stages."

"Time travel is possible?" Harry interrupted.

"Oh yes, it was perfected in the late 25th century. Now as we were saying, we make sure civilization moves along at the proper pace. We've determined that your invention would be dangerous if introduced at this time, so we have decided to suppress it."

"Oh you've decided to suppress it huh? And what gives you the right to do that?" asked Harold.

"We have every right. We live in your future, when you people make a mistake it affects us," said one of the future guys a little annoyed.

"I'll give you an example; a carburetor that gets 150 miles to the gallon was invented a few years before your present time. The introduction of this superior carburetor meant better gas mileage yes, but it would have prolonged the use of fossil fuels, which would lead to more pollution and the failure of your society to invent new and more efficient power sources. We had no choice but to suppress it."

"So you're saying we have to be forced to invent new stuff," said Harold.

The future guy nodded his head. "Sad but true, the human race is lazy. Only when faced with complete depletion of carbon based fuels will you move on to better ones. The introduction of fuel conservation would have slowed down the process of change. We need you people to go on using fossil fuels at your increased and quite alarming rate; only then will you see the need to go to alternate fuel sources."

"Us people? So what other inventions have you suppressed?" asked Harold.

"Solar power comes to mind," said the other future guy.

"What's wrong with that?" asked Harold.

"We've determined it to be a scientific cul-de-sac. It would waste too much time needed in finding the right fuel source for your future."

"Well then, what is our next power source?"

"We can't tell you that Harry," they both said.

"What about cold fusion?" he asked.

"Another dead end I'm afraid."

Harry was perplexed. "Are there any other things you've had to suppress for our own good? How about soy burgers that taste good?" he asked.

"Actually we did suppress those," said one of the future guys.

"Soybean products that taste like meat don't accomplish anything. Mankind needs to completely separate himself from meat and meat by-products if they are ever going to reach the level of sophistication they are capable of. Eating the flesh of other animals or even vegetable products that taste like flesh has been determined as the root cause of Mankind's violent nature. At some point you will realize this and move on to a healthier diet and a more peaceful existence."

Harold could see where all this was going and it was really pissing him off.

"Well it's not right and I'm not going to let you get away with it. I'm turning you in," he shouted.

They weren't fazed by Harold's threats.

"It's our standard practice to put you and your invention where you'll do the least damage; so we're dropping you off in the 23rd Century where teleportation is a common form of transportation. So long Harry."

"Now wait a minute, you can't do that! What about my dog Spot?"

They aimed something that looked like a channel changer at him and he disappeared.

When he reappeared he found Spot leashed to his teleportation machine. They were in a beautiful park, surrounded by a futuristic city; skyscrapers of marble and glass reached to staggering heights. People glided past them on moving sidewalks and flying cars sped by overhead. Harry was truly impressed.

"What do you think Spot, should we let them get away with it?" he untied his friend and they went for a walk.

"It's easy to see what they're up to. They drop us off in a great place like this so we'll forget about what they're doing back in the 20th century."

"Nice try, but it won't work. It's my duty to the other inventors and scientists in the world to blow the whistle on those guys."

"Nope," said Harry shaking his head. "They're not getting away with it."

And so Harold Darby, master inventor, immediately set himself the task of inventing a time machine, which would work perfectly of course, after all, he was the slightly mad scientist.

OUTLAW IN TIME

Chapter 1

Prairie Flat, South Dakota: 1867

The sun was just coming up over the eastern foothills as Jake Spivey and his gang rode into town. They were a rag tag group; some were dressed in traditional cow hand attire, others still worn remnants of their old confederate uniforms. There were nine outlaws in all, including Jake. They hitched their horses in front of the town's saloon and gathered in front of the doors waiting for Jake to give them a cue. Jake knew they were thirsty and tired but he wasn't sure a beer or whiskey this early in the morning was a good idea. Still, they needed something to take the edge off. He nodded for them to go in.

He stepped over to the railing and surveyed the town, not much had changed since he had passed through here a month ago. A man stirred on the bench outside the bar; sleeping off a drunk from the night before but otherwise the place was deserted; that was how Jake wanted it.

He turned and spat on the boot of a passing citizen. The outraged man looked up in anger but then quickly scurried away when he got a look at Jake.

Jake was a mountain of a man. He had a mop of dark ringlets tucked under his hat and an unkempt beard; a natural born killer and someone you should try your best to avoid.

"A town full of cowards," he thought.

"We'll ride into town, have a drink at the saloon; then we'll rob the bank," he said to his men just outside of town where they'd spent the night.

His men agreed; it was a good plan.

Jake's right hand man, a wild-eyed former Confederate soldier who went by the name of Travis, was the first one through the door. Travis was always the first through the door. He walked with the swagger of a gunman who'd never met his match. He was armed with two Colts;

one holstered and another in his belt. As he stepped through the door he drew them both.

"Hands up folks; that's right this is a holdup. Nobody tries being a hero and I'll see that nobody gets hurt."

The actual hold up took only a few minutes but when they came out of the bank they were caught in a cross fire of buckshot and bullets, wounding one of the gang and forcing them back into the bank.

"Well, I guess the sheriff noticed us after all," thought Jake.

"No sweat," he thought. "We've been in tighter spots than this."

His men began returning fire through the bank's front windows. This went on for some time, glass breaking and bullets ricocheting off objects inside the bank but pretty much a stalemate. The sheriff seemed to have the advantage outside the bank but he was shorthanded; Jake could see he had only two new deputies. The locals were staying behind closed doors.

"Someone go look for a back way out of this place," Jake yelled over the shooting.

"Ain't one boss, it's a bank," said one of the gang. "What are we going to do?"

"Shut up a minute, I'm thinking," said Jake.

It got real quiet inside of the bank; the bandits had stopped returning fire.

"Hold your fire men," said the sheriff.

"Do you think they've run out of ammo?" asked one of the deputies.

"I doubt it," said the sheriff.

"Hold your fire sheriff, we're coming out." A voice called from inside the bank.

"Throw out your weapons first; then you all come out with your hands up," said the sheriff.

All manner of weaponry was tossed out onto the dusty street. Then one by one the gang members streamed out of the bank and were immediately pushed to the ground onto their stomachs by the sheriff and one of the deputies. The other deputy stayed hidden behind a wagon with his rifle trained on them.

Travis was the last to emerge from the bank and just stood there admiring the scenery when told to get down on the ground.

"I said get down or so help me I'll cut you in half," said the sheriff pointing his shotgun at the bandit's midriff.

Travis stood there with his hands high in the air. His keen eyesight could see the sheriff's finger slowly tightening on the trigger of deadly double-barreled shotgun.

"So, just three of them," he thought. "This will be easier than I thought."

It was moments like this that brought the outlaw's unique talent. The world around him slowed down; he could see a bead of sweat slowly making its way down the sheriff's forehead and into his eye. The sheriff blinked. And in that half second his eyes were unfocused Travis made his move. He reached behind his back and drew the revolver he'd put there before leaving the bank.

Neither the sheriff nor his deputy could react fast enough to the sudden appearance of the revolver; he shot both of them.

Then he dove to the ground and sent a couple of shots into the other deputy's kneecaps. When the unfortunate young man staggered out Travis put a bullet between his eyes.

"Damn you're fast," said Jake brushing himself off.

"Someone go back in the bank and retrieve the money."

"Now there's no need to go racing out of town is there?" said one of the gang members. "We can go over to the saloon and have another drink."

"Yeah, the sheriff has done us a favor. I'm tired of sleeping out on the prairie; we can hole up here in town for a while," said Jake.

"The townspeople can bury their dead and get on with their lives, a little poorer, but at least they've got their health." His men laughed.

University of South Dakota
Science Lab - 2516 AD

Gary 7-MP39 (Gary 7 to his friends, Professor to his students) emptied his pockets onto his desk; carefully placing his ID/Credit Card and the keys to his flyer where they could be found if he didn't return. There was good reason to believe he wouldn't.

"I guess that's everything," he thought.

He was a regular looking guy in his early thirties with long black wavy hair. He was tall and rather slight of build; at first glance one might describe him as frail, but he kept himself in good shape.

He climbed into the University's Time-Displacement Machine and flipped on the power switch. He was anxious to get under way; he'd been planning this expedition for a long time. His heart pounded as he set the coordinates into the chronometer: June 16th, 1867.

There was always a danger when travelling back to lawless times in history but this trip was particularly dangerous; the other visits had been mere excursions into the past to observe and gather data, this time he would interact with the inhabitants, become one of them. He was bringing a firearm to protect himself; from the data he had collected the gunfights were numerous and fatal more often than not. He wasn't going to pick a fight but if challenged to a duel he wouldn't back down, he was confident he was up to the task.

"No sense in dawdling," he said out loud.

"Dawdling, that's a funny word," he thought, his finger hovering just inches above the energize button.

That was one of the words he'd extracted from the ancient texts written about the era. He'd always been fascinated with the past, especially the Old West of the late 1800's, the age of the "Gunfighter".

He'd memorized lists of words like "hey" and "yonder" and "mosey" in preparation for this trip. The English language had changed drastically in 600 years. He was afraid he'd give himself away with his 26th century speech patterns.

Authentic clothing had been a real problem. Cotton didn't exist anymore so he'd had clothes made from synthetics that closely approximated cotton; but they just didn't look the same. The trick was to fade into the crowd not look like a tourist.

"I must be crazy," he thought. "I'm a prominent historian at a major university; one of few select number of historians allowed to travel back in time. I'm endangering my own future and the university's reputation by embarking on this personal project."

He sat there in the time machine bathed in the lights from the control panel wondering again why he was going through with this.

Boredom was the main reason; and a life without adventure. In his many visits to observe the past he had witnessed many exciting events.

He wanted to be part of that. It would be dangerous, but it beat the techno-paradise in which he lived now.

His own world had become antiseptic and automated. People were content to let the machines do all the work and make all the decisions for them; there were no risks, no dangers; and no excitement.

He had tried on several occasions to enlist in the Space Corps but they said he wasn't fit enough to stand the rigors of space travel.

So he found a hobby. His fascination with the Old West led him to an illegal gun club. They met secretly in remote areas and held target practices and quick draw contests.

He had turned out to be a natural; out-dueling everyone in the club.

"If you get any faster Gary we'll have to re-calibrate the equipment," a friend at the dueling club had remarked.

Of course it was hard to miss with laser-guided, heat-seeking bullets; but at just getting the gun out of the holster no one was faster.

The gun club wasn't enough though; it had only served to whet his appetite for more. His fascination turned to obsession. He longed to participate in the real thing, pitting his skills against those of the real gunfighters of the past, with death to the loser.

Now he was about to steal the University's only Time-Displacement Machine. They'd come after him of course but he didn't care. This was his destiny, what he'd been born to do.

Gary 7 looked around the classroom one last time and then pushed the energize button.

June 16ᵗʰ, 1867

A few miles north of the mining town of Prairie Flat, South Dakota

The machine materialized in a remote area of South Dakota. He'd been here before and had a hole dug to hide the machine. A small mining settlement was located a few miles to the south. When he finished burying the machine he headed that way.

It was a cool summer morning in the high desert. Gary had brought only a few items from the future, a canteen of water, a pouch full of gold to pay for things, a brand new Colt 45 holstered at his side and some ammo. He felt the gun at his side now as he walked; it was reassuring to know it was there.

As Gary neared the town he could hardly contain his excitement. For the first time in his life he felt alive.

His mind raced. First he'd find a hotel and get a room, then go mingle with the inhabitants.

Later that evening Gary sat in the back of a crowded saloon.

"Evidently the town is quite prosperous," he thought.

The place was full of miners; drinking, gambling, smoking, spitting, and just having a good time with their new found wealth.

The place reeked.

"It would seem no one cares much for personal hygiene in this era. This will take some getting used to," he thought as he leaned back and took in the whole scene.

He noticed that everyone carried a weapon of some kind. Most of them looked like they had only a cursory knowledge of its use, but a group of men in the corner of the saloon had the look of men whose knowledge of weapons was their stock and trade. They had all manner of firearms concealed and displayed, and were given a wide berth by the other occupants of the establishment.

"That must be what's known as a gang of desperadoes," thought Gary.

The evening passed without incident; there were a few scuffles, but no one got shot. Gary retired to his room with mixed emotions. Tomorrow he would go buy a horse and see if he could learn how to ride it.

At the livery stable the next morning he was able to purchase a horse. It was a magnificent animal, a pure white Arabian.

When the proprietor saw he was paying in gold he threw in a saddle. He also warned Gary about Jake and his gang.

"I wouldn't spend much time in this town if I were you mister." the proprietor warned and went on to tell him about how Jake had killed the sheriff and taken over the town.

After he'd finished his transaction the Blacksmith walked away leaving Gary with his horse. He tried a few awkward attempts at mounting the creature but wasn't having much luck. The Blacksmith's helper, a Native American was watching and having a good laugh at Gary's expense.

He finally came over and showed him what he was doing wrong. "You never ride horse before?"

"No, this is my first time," said Gary.

The Native American showed Gary how to mount, dismount and ride without falling off.

"You should ride around here in corral for a while till you get the hang of it."

After a short time Gary was getting the hang of it. The horse seemed to anticipate his actions which made it easier. It was a very intelligent animal. That was never in the history books.

"Thank you. You're a Native American aren't you?

Giving Gary a strange look, "I am a native, yes. But town people would never call me an American."

"You are not from here?"

"No, I come from very far away," said Gary.

He didn't want to be rude but he was curious about this man's heritage, this being the first Native American he'd ever met. Their race had not survived to the 26th century.

"Do you live in town? Gary asked.

"No, I work and live here at here at stable but I'm not from this town. My people live on the Reservation. I am not allowed to go into any places in town.

"Why not?" asked Gary.

"The town people, they don't trust my people."

Gary had read about such prejudices in books but of course had never encountered it.

He liked this man. He had a quiet strength about him; he too carried a sidearm as well as a mean-looking knife in his belt.

He thanked him and gave him some gold for his help.

Later that morning, after a breakfast of eggs and various meat products, he headed for the general store.

"No wonder these people don't live very long", he thought. "They eat like the Romans."

He decided he would need different clothes; the looks he was getting from the population meant he hadn't gotten the styles right.

"I'd like to buy some new clothes," Gary told the shopkeeper.

"Certainly sir, right this way. May I ask where you got the clothes you're wearing?" asked the shopkeeper.

"Back east," said Gary.

"Styles certainly are different back there."

"Oh, this is the latest in Western clothing, but I need something a little more comfortable."

"I understand sir. When you've picked something out you can change in the back."

He was in the back of the store changing when three of Jake's men came in and immediately started trouble.

Stepping out of the backroom he discovered the shopkeeper on the floor and his wife in a state of undress.

"Leave these people alone," he said in the meanest voice he could muster.

"Who invited you to the party," said Travis as they spread out in front of him, their intention clear.

"Oh my God," thought Gary. "This is it."

"It's not happening the way I had imagined it, but then nothing here is as I had imagined."

"Leave this to me," said Travis to the other gunmen. They immediately relaxed and moved away smiling.

"This should be fun to watch." said one of them.

"You're not from around here are you mister?" said Travis.

Gary could sense the supreme confidence in this outlaw. He noticed that he wore his holster on his left side but positioned it so he could draw with his right hand.

"Here was a man who must be very good with a gun," he thought.

He was probably outmatched. Of course there had to be outlaws who were good with a gun that no one had ever heard of.

"Just my luck," thought Gary.

"What are you waitin' for mister, a written invitation?"

The outlaw was toying with him, like prey. Then, in a blur, he went for his sidearm.

Something happened at that moment that took Gary by surprise. He had never drawn against a real person but the rush of adrenaline, caused by the very real fear of death quickened his already practiced draw. In a flash the gun was in his hand and he was firing.

The outlaw was knocked backwards by the force of the bullets, a look of astonishment on his face.

The other two gunmen immediately went for their guns but Gary dropped them where they stood. All three gang members were dead a few moments after they hit the floor.

"Solid projectiles fired at this range were usually lethal," thought Gary.

He stood there for a long moment frozen with fear, the sound of the gunshots still ringing in his ears and the smell of cordite in the air.

It had all happened so fast. A moment ago he was a tourist in a strange land, now…

"Had he changed the future by killing three lowlifes?"

He thought not. But still, he wasn't supposed to be here. He had altered time even if just slightly. Now he too was an outlaw.

After a minute or so he snapped out of it, holstered his gun and excused himself to the shopkeeper and his wife. He knew that Jake and rest of the gang would be looking for him. He needed time to think.

In his hotel room the consequences of his actions were just sinking in. Somehow he'd taken on an entire gang, a gang that didn't fight fair. There'd be no gentlemanly contest of skill out on the main street like he'd read in the books; they'd simply hunt him down and kill him. He needed a course of action but his usual scientific judgment had deserted him.

Later, in the general store Jake surveyed the carnage. He was angry; damn angry, but he also had a feeling something wasn't right. Some stranger had come into town and done this. It certainly wasn't one of these sheepish townspeople.

"This wasn't no ambush," thought Jake. "It looked like a stand up fight, three against one. And Travis was the fastest gun he'd ever seen. Whoever this stranger was, he was good."

"What's the plan? Should we spread out and find him?"

"No, I've got a better idea," said Jake.

Gary paced his hotel room, going over his options. He knew he should get on his horse and ride out of town. He'd had his gunfight and been victorious. Mission accomplished right? But there hadn't been any thrill in the victory, only the feeling that he'd started something that he knew he'd have to finish.

"But why should I?" Gary thought. "I don't owe these people anything. I don't even know them, to continue this folly would be suicide."

His analysis was cut short by a knock on the door.

"They couldn't have found me already," he thought. He drew his gun and opened the door carefully. It was the shopkeeper of the general store.

"They've taken some of the townspeople to the saloon; they say they'll start killing them if you don't come. One of them is my wife mister; you've got to do something!"

"Do you have a weapon?" Gary asked him.

"I've got a shotgun," said the shopkeeper.

"Get it and meet me downstairs."

The usually crowded street was completely deserted when Gary stepped out of the hotel. The sun was at its zenith; a slight breeze was causing small dust devils in the earthen street. He felt surprisingly calm, considering the situation; he stepped down onto that ancient roadway.

In his many travels he'd walked the Apian Way, stood in the Parthenon and the streets of Pompeii but they didn't compare to this ordinary dirt street. There he had been a tourist, this was for real.

"I must be in shock," he told himself as he walked up the street towards the saloon. He could swear he could see the faces of the townspeople watching him from behind drawn curtains. He wanted to turn and run, but for some reason he kept walking.

The shopkeeper soon joined him clutching his weapon; Gary made a point to walk just a little bit behind him for fear it might go off accidentally.

Jake and his men were reposing in various states of slouch on the steps of the saloon. They stood up and spread out as Gary approached.

He counted six of them. The hostages were positioned on the steps directly in front of the gang members. Gary stopped well short of the saloon in the middle of the street.

"Nice of you to be so prompt," said Jake. "My name's Jake Spivey; damn good shooting back there in the general store; how is it I've never heard of you?"

Gary didn't answer; the fellow seemed to be enjoying the moment. It was clear he wasn't going to move the hostages out of the line of fire. That took the shopkeeper out of the equation; he would surely hit one of them with his scattergun at this range.

"Better move back, you can't do much with that shotgun from here," Gary told him.

As the storeowner moved out of range he reassured Gary.

"You can take them mister, I've seen you draw, you're fast."

"I hope your confidence in me is warranted," said Gary as he surveyed the group in front of him.

Apparently they all preferred their handguns as weapon of choice. No one had a rifle and for that he was thankful.

He stood there thinking, "Six bullets, six targets, I can do this," when he noticed that one of the desperadoes was wearing an apron under his holster. That meant that either the bartender had decided to join Jake's gang, which was highly unlikely, or that Jake had drafted him to throw off the count. And that meant that one of Jake's men was concealed somewhere and probably had him in his sights at this very moment.

"Damn," he'd underestimated this Jake fellow and it would probably cost him his life. His only chance was to make himself a moving target, but before he could dive for cover a shot rang out and a bullet ricocheted in the dirt near him.

When Gary looked up the body of the bushwhacker fell into sight, behind him stood the Native American he'd met earlier in the day. He nodded to Gary as he wiped the blood off his knife.

Gary nodded back. The whole scene had played out in only a few moments and now Jake, realizing he'd lost his trump card, made his play.

Five more shots rang out that day, five bullets found their marks. When the bartender opened his eyes he was relieved to see he was surrounded by dead gang members, he alone was unharmed.

"Well, now these people have a story to tell their grandchildren," thought Gary. "A legend has been born."

But even as he thought it he realized that this gunfight in a small mining settlement in South Dakota must never be more than a legend, a myth; if the account ever found its way into actual history books his whereabouts would be discovered by future historians.

So instead of staying to receive the congratulations of a thankful town, he climbed awkwardly onto his horse and rode away.

As he rode he wondered if anyone would discover his little secret. Each bullet he'd fired was a small miracle of modern technology; each contained the micro-mechanisms which guided it to its target. He figured his secret was safe; nobody would bother to open them up to inspect the insides. They'd simply melt them down for their intrinsic value; for each bullet was made entirely of silver.

His new friend joined him along the trail. Gary was glad to see him. He had a feeling he might need a guide and confidant on this amazing adventure, especially since he had no idea where he was going.

"I didn't catch your name my friend," Gary inquired.

"Tonto," was all he said.

Chapter 2

Nebraska - Six Months Later:

Gary and Tonto rode across an endless expanse of prairie, not so much as a tree broke the vast openness.

Many months have elapsed since the shootout in the small mining community in South Dakota; there have been many more since. And because Gary could not allow his actions or even his countenance to be recorded in history for fear of detection by future historians, he'd taken to wearing a crude mask over his eyes whenever they went into a fight.

"I've grown weary of all the crime and violence we've encountered my friend," said Gary. "The books I read about this era romanticized the Old West; but there is nothing exotic about it. It is a harsh, cruel period in American history. We've tried to stop what crimes we could but because I have to remain anonymous, we too are considered outlaws by the authorities."

Tonto had grown accustomed to Gary's strange way of talking; but once again knew just what to say.

"We go to my village, you need rest. You will like it there," said Tonto.

His people were usually nomadic but since the last treaty they had settled along the banks of Deer Creek in the Platte River Valley. As they rode down into the valley Gary was overwhelmed by the beauty and serenity of the place.

He was introduced to the chief and given lodgings. The villagers brought him food and blankets and made him feel welcome. For the first time since traveling to the past he was able to relax.

He was invited to go on hunting expeditions with the younger braves and sat around the campfire at night listening to the elders tell stories of the old days, before the coming of the white man. Soon all the violent memories of the last few months began to fade.

Gary learned their language as quickly as he could and tried to respect their customs. One custom he soon found out about was that an eligible bachelor didn't stay single for long. It seemed like every unmarried girl in the village was flirting with him. He found it very embarrassing.

Tonto tried to explain, "If you don't have a mate, it's considered unnatural; all the animals in the forest and on the plain have mates."

One girl had caught Gary's eye. She was stunning, and not as flirtatious as the others. He asked Tonto about her.

"Her name is Keota," said Tonto. "She is one of the chief's daughters and she is unmarried. Did you want me to introduce you to her?"

"No, I'll get around to it," said Gary.

Not long after that he got to meet her. Gary would get up very early each day and sneak down to the creek to avoid bathing with an audience. One morning when he showed up Keota was already at the creek bathing.

At first he was a little hesitant about getting undressed in front of her, but then he thought, "Well, when in Rome" took off his clothes and dove in.

They got to know each other very well that morning. Afterwards they lay on the grassy bank talking.

"You are very beautiful," said Gary.

"Thank you," said Keota.

"You speak English?" asked Gary.

"A little bit, Tonto is teaching me," she said.

"Alright Tonto," said Gary.

They met every morning after that. Gary thought it was their little secret, but of course everyone in the village knew of their rendezvous and left them alone.

It wasn't long before he was head over heels in love and decided to ask her father for her hand in marriage. He only hoped he wouldn't have to perform some kind of life-threatening tribal ritual.

He never found out. The next morning he was awakened by the sound of gunshots. When he emerged from his tent he was met with the butt-end of a rifle and knocked unconscious. When he woke up the village was in flames; dead or wounded villagers were lying everywhere.

He ran as fast as he could to Keota's tent and found her lifeless body lying with those of her family. He carried her body away from the flames and laid her down on the banks of the creek.

He found Tonto shortly after that, alive but mortally wounded. There was nothing he could do for his friend; he died in his arms an hour later.

Gary was filled with rage, "Why would anyone do this?"

He got on his horse and rode, following the trail the gunmen had taken out of the village.

He soon had his answer, the trail lead directly to a railroad construction site, about twenty miles east of the village. The train tracks were heading straight across the reservation.

"Why waste time re-negotiating treaties with savages, just kill them and make up some official story later," he could imagine them saying.

He wanted to ride into their camp and kill as many of them as he could but that wouldn't help the village.

So instead he rode north, back to South Dakota, back to his time machine.

Along the way his mind raced; he had no idea if what he was about to do was even possible.

It took him three days to reach the spot where he'd buried his time machine. Once he got it working he traveled back to his lab in the 26th century, arriving late at night to avoid detection. He gathered up a few things and programmed the machine to materialize in an area near the village, one week before the attack. He waited till nightfall and then crept into the village and left a small package in front of his own tent.

Then he went back to his time machine and traveled forward a week. He still had one more thing to do.

The next day Gary came out of his tent to find a crowd of villagers standing around a package that had magically appeared during the night. There were two boxes of his special ammo, a book and a note.

He read the note.

Gary,

It's kind of weird writing a letter to myself but I have to warn you. The village will be attacked in exactly one week.

Pinkertons, hired by the railroad will ride in from the east. I've brought you more ammo and a book on *The Battle of Hastings*. You have one week to prepare yourselves.

Good luck.

Gary

It wasn't in the message but he had a feeling that in that attack, many of the villagers had probably been killed, possibly even Keota. Why else would he cause a time anomaly of this magnitude to come back and warn me; I mean himself. Wow, this was confusing. He opened the book and began reading.

Gary was already familiar with the battle that took place in Europe in 1066, in which King Edward of England, with a better equipped army, was defeated by Duke William of Normandy using mostly archers and some light cavalry. It was the tactics that he was interested in. He read all morning while the villagers watched.

When he finally put the book down he thought, "That just might work."

He had Tonto call a meeting of the Chiefs where he explained what was about to happen and his plans to prevent it. They never questioned how he came to have this knowledge of the future, but immediately went about making preparations. For the next week they fashioned as many bows and arrows as they could, dug ditches and built barricades.

One week later, when the Pinkertons rode into the village, just as predicted, they were ready. The children and elders had been taken to a safe place earlier that morning. At a predetermined spot Gary gave the signal and volley after deadly volley of arrows rained down on the hired gunmen. Every man and women who could draw back a bow had enlisted.

The Pinkertons were caught off guard, they took heavy losses before they were able to re-group and charge the barricade where the archers stood. When they did, the archers dropped down and the young braves with rifles stood up and began firing at the advancing gunmen.

Meanwhile Gary, Tonto and the remaining braves on horseback attacked from the rear trapping the railroad men in a cross fire.

The results of the attack were much different this time. Hardly any of the villagers were harmed while most of the hired gunmen lie dead or dying on the field of battle. Those who did survive rode headlong back the way they came.

Gary rode into the railroad camp; it was hours after the attack on the village. He had no way of knowing if they had been successful out there on the prairie. He could only hope. As he approached the train he counted eight gunmen in their trademark long trench coats, above them on the caboose of the train stood a man in a business suit. That was the person he needed to see.

"From what my men here tell me you pulled off an amazing feat at that Injun village, stranger. I'm very impressed," said train executive.

"But as you can see in front of you stand eight professional gunmen, I'd suggest you throw down your weapons: unless of course, you're the fastest gun that ever lived."

"Ironic," thought Gary. "That was the very thing that had brought him to the past; but at this moment it was the farthest thing from his mind."

"I've come to convince you to change the course of your train," said Gary.

"Not a chance," said the train executive.

"Kill him."

The next couple of minutes were the longest in Gary's life. He was hit but stood his ground and kept firing until he'd emptied both his gun and Tonto's. It seemed like an out-of-body experience; his senses were heightened like those of an animal that is forced to fight for its life.

When the smoke cleared eight professional gunmen lay dead on the tracks in front of him.

The train executive had disappeared. He found the man cowering inside the train.

"I'll give you a choice," Gary told him as he chambered one round in his gun.

"Either you re-route your tracks to the north along the Platte River or I kill you right here."

"I'll go north," said the executive.

"Good decision. I've heard rumors there's gold in the hills along the river up there; you never know you might get lucky."

That last part was a complete fabrication; he hoped the combination of greed and fear would keep the tracks well away from the reservation.

Badly wounded he rode back to the village. He couldn't go in of course but watched from a safe distance until he saw what he needed to see.

There was his friend Tonto, Keota and his other self; they had survived the attack. For this he was extremely grateful, but also sad, for in saving the village he had taken himself out of it.

"It's time I was getting back anyway," he thought as he rode back to his time machine. He would miss his future wife and his friend Tonto but he had made his decision; he would always have the memories.

"I've had my gunfights and I've lived to tell about it," he thought. "I wonder if the Autodoc is programmed for gunshot-wounds?"

"My career as a historian is probably over but what was it the train man had said? *The Fastest Gun That Ever Lived*; that sounds like it has the makings of a good western novel."

CAR

John Cardenas slowed down his hover car and pulled over to the side of the road to pick up a hitchhiker.

"Where you going?" he asked.

"Mexico City," said the hitchhiker.

"Hop in; I'm going that way too."

"You don't see too many people hitch hiking these days," said John.

"I don't usually hitch, but my car is in the shop being fitted with new jets and a pressure cabin. I'll be able to go to 30,000 feet and Mach 2."

John's passenger was young and obviously excited about the upgrades being done to his car.

"How fast get this old thing go?" he asked.

"I can cruise at 250 KPH," John proudly announced.

"That's all. What model is this? Is this one of those old manual vehicles? It is isn't it; you're actually driving this thing. I've only seen these in museums."

"Yeah, I guess I'm kind of old fashioned," said John.

"Why don't you get a newer vehicle? These older models only sense road conditions and relay that information to the driver. My car is completely automated; speed, guidance, navigation; the works. I just punch in where I want to go and how fast I want to get there, and it does the rest. Are you one of those anti-progressives?"

"No, I just prefer this older model to the newer ones," said John.

"Didn't these old cars use *Personality Chips*, imprinted with actual living tissue from someone who'd died or something?" asked the rider.

"Something like that; before the advent of OTGB's (organ tissue growth banks) people could donate their organs to hospitals so when they passed away or they were killed in an accident someone who needed a heart or kidney or some other organ could use theirs."

"How gross!" said John's young passenger.

"Well it saved a lot of lives in the old days. The *Personality Chip* came into being as an off shoot of organ donation," John went on.

"When the first automatic cars were being developed someone hit on the idea of imprinting the car's central processor with the DNA pattern of an actual person's donated brain tissue, thus giving the computer its own personality."

John went on. "Many other traits of that person's character were passed on as well; things like caution, anticipation and logic; traits that would prove valuable as speeds began getting faster and faster."

The car and its passengers glided soundlessly along International Route 25 to Mexico City. The air was crisp and cold outside and the traffic was light; a perfect day for driving.

John continued, "Of course, when they developed Artificial Intelligence in 2065 they did away with the *Personality Chip*. But there are still a few of these original models hanging around."

"How do you know so much about it?" asked the hitch hiker.

"I was a scientist on some of those early development teams," said John. "When my father passed away in 2060 I used some of his DNA for the processor in this vehicle. I broke a few rules, but by then I was project manager so..

A long silence ensued after that revelation.

"So you talk to this thing and it talks back?"

"Yes."

"And it's listening to us now?" inquired the passenger.

"Of course," said John.

"Car, could you speed a little?" asked John.

"We are traveling at the optimal speed for this sector," answered the car.

"I know, but could you speed up a little anyway?"

"Very well," said the car. The car sped up.

His passenger sat quietly for a long time looking out at the smooth desert sands.

Eventually the young man blurted out, "I'm sorry mister, but I've got to get out. This is too spooky for me."

John pulled over to the next way station and his passenger got out.

A little farther down the road, "Since when did you start calling me car?" asked the car.

"Sorry Dad, it won't happen again."

BAD BEHAVIOR

"Are you Jay Spencer?" asked the police robot.

"Yes," said Jay.

"My name is R226; I'm placing you under arrest for bad taste. Come with me please."

They got into the flyer and flew off in the direction of Metropolis City.

Metropolis City Court, 2097 AD:

"How can you arrest someone for having bad taste?" Jay pleaded. "Who's to say what's in bad taste?"

"The Social Behavior Laws are very clear," announced the judge as she read the charges in front of her.

"You've cut off the leggings of your tunic," said the judge.

"I call them shorts," said Jay.

"Shorts refer to undergarments," said the judge.

"Not necessarily," said Jay. "In the old days people wore shorts as outer garments on really hot days."

"These are not the old-days anymore young man, and what do you call that hairstyle?"

"It's called a crew cut. I looked that up, it's neat, comfortable and no hassle," said Jay.

"Everyone knows God gave us hair to enhance our appearance, long hair is God's way of making everyone a little different. Would you want everyone to look the same?" asked the judge.

"Well no," agreed Jay.

"You've been heard making strange noises at work and while you walk."

"It's called whistling," said Jay.

"Unacceptable; what if everyone did that? You've also been overheard telling morally offensive jokes."

"You've got me there. It's a bad habit of mine, I've been meaning to quit," said Jay.

"This court finds you guilty of bad taste; under the provision 1A of the Bad Behavior Laws you are hereby sentenced to three years at Alpha Two Space Colony to reform you of these dangerous anti-social tendencies. Take him away."

Outside the Courthouse:

As Jay and R226 left the courthouse they found themselves surrounded by a group of men wearing white lab coats; one of them had a small box, which he held next to R226's head.

"Remove those restraints from the prisoner please," he said.

"I am removing the restraints from the prisoner," said R226.

"Now walk down the street, I think I see someone jay-walking."

"I shall pursue," said R226.

"What did you just do?" asked Jay.

"If you hold a powerful magnet close enough to their electro-mechanical brains it causes them to lose their short term memory. It's a design flaw. Now get into the flyer."

Jay climbed into the waiting vehicle and they sped away.

"Who are you guys?" asked Jay.

"That's information you don't need to know," one of them said.

Since they wouldn't give their names, Jay referred to them mentally as Nerd One, Nerd Two and Nerd Three. They were a very peculiar bunch of longhaired, pocket-protector wearing eccentrics.

"Here's some advice kid, if you want to be a subversive you can't go around looking the way you do; it's too obvious," said Nerd One.

"I'm not a subversive," Jay protested.

"Oh sure, with that haircut and those clothes you've got throwback written all over you," said Nerd Two.

"What were you arrested for?"

"Bad taste," said Jay.

"And what was your sentence?"

"Three years at someplace called Alpha Two," said Jay.

"You see what I mean!" Nerd Three began to rant.

"That's crazy; it's another example of how this world's turned upside down. If this young person wants to dress like this, that's his business! We must do something before it's too late."

"No offense guys, but except for busting me out of jail what can you do?" asked Jay. "Not that I'm not grateful."

"For your information, we happen to be well respected scientists at the National Academy of Science. We have access to the institute's time machine. We've decided to go back and attempt to change all this; nothing drastic, just enough to get the world back on track," said Nerd Three.

"We've traced the origin of today's madness. It all starts getting crazy early in the 21st century when some guy named Newt Gingrich becomes president. We're going back and make sure that doesn't happen," said Nerd Three.

"Wow, you going to kill him?" asked Jay.

"No, we think we can rig the elections; it's been done before," said Nerd One.

"But how could one guy have caused all this," Jay paused looking for the right word. "All this stupidness?" asked Jay.

"Stupidness, is that even a word? You really are a throwback," said Nerd One.

"Well, according to the historical records this Newt Gingrich fellow enacted stringent rules on social behavior; apparently the entire population was glued to something called a cell phone? It was a communication device that could access music, vids, news, weather, you name it. They were so entertaining they couldn't put them down, they spent their every waking moment texting one another, taking selfies and watching funny cat vids; whatever those are? No one was paying attention to the actual world around them; and more importantly no work was being done," Nerd One continued.

"What was left of the sentient population turned to this Newt Gingrich guy to put a stop to it," Nerd One concluded.

"And put a stop to it he did; we've been stuck with all these rules and regulations ever since; they keep society from moving forward," exclaimed Nerd Two.

"You can't spit without being arrested by the behavior police."

Jay was beginning to think that Nerd Two was a bit of a hot head. He attempted to change the topic.

"Since you guys are going back in time and all, could you drop me off in the 1960's; I've heard it's a pretty cool time." asked Jay.

It was kind of exciting the way things were turning out; to think only a few hours ago he was just a kid with a bad haircut.

"Sure, if that's what you want. You don't belong in this time that's for sure. I'm not so sure if they'll accept you with that terrible haircut though," said Nerd One.

THE NEXT STEP

Sadr City, Iraq
March 2007

"Here's the world famous bomb-disposal expert taking the last screw out of the detonator's cover plate," Cpl Jorge Torres always talked to himself on the job.

He'd been disarming bombs for about six months now, ever since he'd arrived in Iraq. It wasn't something most people could do, but he had a knack and talking to himself seemed to help.

He'd volunteered for this assignment; everybody on the squad had. The Army had trained him in electronics, and though these things weren't all that sophisticated you still had to know your way around a wiring diagram.

"OK, that's out of the way. Let's see if we're getting any power here? No power at this terminal; looks like an ordinary alarm-clock timer. I'll just jump around this wire here, and cut this wire here and that should do it."

"Hmm, what's this thingamajig?"

"Click"

A very loud explosion rocked downtown Sadr City, setting off car alarms all over the city. Of course, Jorge never heard a thing.

Heaven, March 2007

"Where am I?"

"You're in the hereafter son," said a middle-aged man in a white lab coat as he shook Jorge's hand.

"This is heaven?" asked Jorge.

"Let's just say you made it to Kingdom but you're not at the Castle yet."

"So what do you do here?" Jorge inquired.

"We're God's assistants. He's pretty busy you know, running the universe, so we take care of the daily functions. The stuff most people take for granted.

Take this machine here; it controls all the hair follicles for men in North America, ever wonder why some dudes are bald and some aren't? It's that machine there. This machine here controls the weather from Tibet and Nebraska, and that one over there, the rice crop in Thailand."

The angel/assistant guided him through a labyrinth of cubicles in a seemingly never-ending office. There were people of all ages and nationalities working at computer terminals or standing by the water cooler.

They smiled and waved to Jorge as he passed.

"As you can see we've got a lot of responsibilities. You'll be assigned to a console like one of these after your orientation."

"That's all there is to the afterlife?" said Jorge.

"Oh no, this is just the next level, there's much, much more. We all work our way up to Angel eventually. But what's the rush? Why not enjoy this level for a while."

"I guess I was expecting more," said Jorge.

"Hey, don't knock it. You're a supernatural being now; you'd be surprised how rewarding it is doing God's little miracles. We make sure the trees grow and the babies are born, it's really gratifying. Let me give you a demonstration." They walked up to the nearest console.

"Hey Bob, mind if I show the new guy your set-up?" he asked.

"Go right ahead boss, I've got a good one in Kansas there," said Bob pointing at the screen.

"Oh yes, I see what you mean," he turned to Jorge and said, "Shall we take a trip to Kansas?"

He pushed a button and they found themselves on the side lines of a high school football game; no one could see them of course.

"Bob's charge is that wide receiver over there," he said pointing to the team just breaking huddle.

"His name is Joey Dillon, a back-up receiver for the Dragons playing in his first game. Our job is to make it a memory he'll keep forever."

As they watched the teams line up Jorge glanced at the scoreboard; the Dragons were losing by four points and there was only six seconds on the clock. When he looked back the ball had already been hiked, and Joey was sprinting down the sideline. The Quarterback just got the ball off before he was knocked down, and now every eye in the small high school stadium was on Joey.

"That defender isn't making it easy for him," thought Jorge. "In fact he was on him like flypaper."

As Jorge watched the angel/assistant nudged the ball's trajectory a little higher allowing Joey to snag it out of the air and dive into the end zone.

The hometown crowd went berserk. Jorge couldn't help getting caught up in the moment and let out a yell of his own. Only the angel/assistant heard it though.

"See what I mean?" he said.

"Your right this supernatural being stuff is awesome!" said Jorge.

They returned to the afterlife.

"And you can be in two places at the same time, which is pretty cool; you have all the information of the ages, unfiltered by opinionated historians I might add," the angel/assistant continued. "And, you're not confined to this world anymore either," he said proudly.

"What do you mean," asked Jorge.

"Imagine Jupiter or some far away spiral nebula and you're there."

"Wow," said Jorge.

"Everyone who ever lived is here Jorge, all the great people. You'll meet Lincoln, Humphrey Bogart and Joan of Arc. We have some terrific Christmas parties up here."

"Wait a minute," the angel/assistant stopped walking.

"I'm getting a message from the personnel department. Seems you weren't killed in the explosion after all. Half of the Downtown Market was blown up but somehow you survived. You're one lucky bomb-disposal expert."

"You are in a coma though, and you've lost several body parts I'm afraid; but you're still alive. We have to send you back; but not to worry we'll be seeing you again, Jorge. Of that I am sure."

Walter Reed Army Hospital - Post Op Ward
Washington DC

Two weeks and several operations later:

"It's the strangest case of post-traumatic stress I've ever encountered," the Army Surgeon remarked to the staff.

"Look at him kidding around with the nurses; physically he's in bad shape but he's just as happy as a person can be. I've never seen anything like it."

"You're right" said the head nurse. "Ever since waking up from the coma he's been acting like he just won the lottery or something."

DREAMERS

Joshua Cain has a gift, he can dream. Not the ordinary, fleeing, jumbled up dreams like the rest of us have, but lucid dreams; dreams so clear and vivid they can be recorded.

Josh, and few highly imaginative people like him were recruited by a hugely successful corporation to dream up new stuff. A dream chip was implanted in their heads so they wouldn't have to go into the lab anymore; they could dream from home. The dream chip or Memory Recovery Implant records all neural output while the subject is in REM status and uploads it to several super-computers.

When the program first started the dreamers had to sleep in the lab with diodes attached to their shaved heads; the lab people were in the next room monitoring them while they tried to sleep. It was awkward and impersonal, and not a lot of quality dreaming was recorded. The creation of the implant allowed the test subjects to dream anywhere; at home, napping on the Metro or sleeping in class. Joshua did some of his best dreaming in Econ 101.

Josh is dreamer #4, he's twenty-three, a junior in college and he's been in the program about two years, most of that time was spent in testing. After that he joined a select group of individuals whose dreams are so vivid and detailed they can be recorded; most people's dreams are a collection of random memories, usually coming at the end of the sleep period and hardly more than a minute or two in duration. Josh has dreams lasting over 5 minutes.

One thing he doesn't tell them is that he can remember his dreams well after he's awake. He figured they didn't need to know everything. He doesn't even know who *they* are, but they had him sign all sorts of non-disclosure forms, no talking to strangers and all that cloak and dagger stuff. They wanted exclusive rights to whatever new ideas, inventions, new designs or gadgets he thought up in one of his dreams.

There are five other dreamers in the program; six unique individuals, and once they received the implants they were cut off from direct contact with each other. He was told it was because each one of them has a specific area of expertise.

Most of the things that get uploaded from their dreams is either too hair-brained to have any practical purpose or too far advanced; like death rays and teleportation machines, to be workable. But every once in a while one of them comes up with something the corporation could use. When this occurred the corporate types would come down to the lab to thank them and tell them what a great job they're doing, and don't worry they will all share in the profits if and when an idea or invention gets patented.

On the other side of the ledger the scientists Josh worked with didn't give a hoot if the stuff he thought up was financially successful, they were just interested in the research. They'd give him scientific journals to read; architectural magazines, popular science, medical journals, and math books; even suggesting a science fiction story or two, to fill his head with new ideas to dream about.

Josh's apartment present day:

Josh woke up remembering how very cool his dream was last night; a radical new design for an office building. He made a cup of coffee, grabbed the paper and went out on the balcony to read. The sun should have been hitting this side of the building by now he thought, something was blocking it. He looked up to see that a giant skyscraper stood where there hadn't been one just yesterday; and not just any skyscraper, *his* skyscraper; the one he'd just dreamed about.

"Kind of shocking isn't it," a voice said behind him.

Josh whirled, "Who are you?"

"I'm a dreamer like you. Name's Wanda, dreamer #3; remember me."

"Oh yeah, I remember, it's been awhile. How'd you find me? I thought we weren't supposed to make contact with each other. I've tried looking for the others in the labs' computers but all I've ever found is a bunch of tech stuff," asked Josh.

"Easy-peezy, I'm a hacker, or I used to be; just one of the many skills I picked up in my sorted life," said Wanda.

"So enough chit-chat; aren't you wondering why your new skyscraper is already built when you just dreamed of it last night?"

"Yeah, how can that be?" asked Josh as he turned around to gaze up at it.

"Beats me; but it's happened to me too. I thought up a permanent cure for kidney disease only to wake up and find it's already in the medical journals," said Wanda as she stepped up beside him to look at the new building.

"Cool building."

"Isn't it, but it's not possible for it to just appear like this," said Josh.

"Something weird is happening," said Wanda. "That's why I looked you up. I'm planning to visit the other dreamers and get to the bottom of this. I've got some theories, but I want to see what the others say, you in?"

"Theories, like what?" Josh asked.

"Like that maybe we're getting too good at this. Before we'd dream up stuff and they'd take it to the drawing board and maybe a year from now it would be a reality. Now we dream it and it's a reality when we wake up? It goes against the laws of physics. The people at the lab couldn't know about this; they'd shut down the project immediately," Wanda continued.

"I need to talk to the others and see if they're experiencing the same phenomenon. Are you with me on this?"

"Yeah, I'm in," said Josh. He'd always had a thing for the Segourney Weaver/Linda Hamilton take charge type of women.

"We can't be seen together. We should meet somewhere. Somewhere we all have been; remember the roof at the Institute where we would all go to smoke? Back before they separated us?" she asked.

"Yeah," said Josh. "It's gonna be hard to get up there with all the security in that place."

"Dream yourself there; you remember it well enough don't you?"

"Like it was yesterday," said Josh wondering if what she was proposing was even possible.

"Can we do that?"

"I dreamed myself here," she said.

"This is a dream?" Josh blurted out.

"I'm dreaming, you're not," she said. "See you on the roof of the Institute at 9 tonight," and she disappeared.

Josh stood there gaping; then he quickly turned around to see if the new building was still there. It was still there.

Rooftop of the Dream Recovery Institute: Group Dream

When Joshua materialized on the roof of the institute the others were already there. He walked around checking it out.

"How is this possible?" he said. "Am I in someone's dream or are they in mine?"

Wanda came over to greet him and answered. "The way I figure it we aren't really in another's dream, we're having separate dreams, but those dreams are overlapping."

They joined the group. "Your hair is different."

"Yeah, I don't know why I dream I have blond hair, it's like some childhood memory or something; weird isn't it?"

Ralph got the conversation going. "Can anyone tell me how our dreams are becoming reality? And why the scientists don't shut down the project to investigate this phenomenon?"

"It's like little bits of our dream world are following us to the real world," said Wanda. "My guess is something about the dream chip has amplified our abilities."

"I'll bet the researchers on the project don't realize it. If we're changing reality how would they know? We only know because it's stuff we just dreamed," said Tonya, another dreamer in their group.

"Amplifying our thoughts enough to change the whole world's reality!" exclaimed Ralph. "That's not possible."

"It's got to be something else; my guess is we're still dreaming. All of us are dreaming this whole thing up."

Howard broke in. "You guys are missing the point here; if we can change things in the real world, this ability of ours is way more important than thinking up new inventions for a greedy corporation."

"Yeah, we should be dreaming up new machines that make work easier," said Tonya.

"Hell with inventions, we should dream up a whole better world." Howard exclaimed.

"How about no more wars; and how about we make people forget we ever had any wars so nobody is mad at anyone else," said Tonya.

"That's a good one," said Josh.

"How about we come up with a cure for cancer," said Sara.

"That's another good one," said Josh. "Maybe we should be writing these down."

"Wait a second people; you're talking about altering reality; shouldn't we consider whether we have the right to that?" said Ralph. "I mean we're not just talking about adding new inventions to the mix; the world itself would have to change radically to accommodate the things we're proposing."

"Let's say we dream of a world without war for example, we'd be changing humanity's very nature. It's in our DNA to fight. Every change we make will have ramifications," he added.

"OK, how about this; we change just one thing, and see how it turns out?" said Howard. "Does that sound reasonable?"

"We change just one thing, like a test; yeah. OK what should we change?"

"How about the cure for cancer?" said Wanda.

"OK," they all agreed.

The next day the world's population doubled. People in the poorer countries were starving and several nations were at war over dwindling resources, the population explosion caused by adding just the victims of cancer was too much for the world to bear.

Back on the rooftop the next day: Group Dream

"OK, that made things worse; obviously if we're going to make changes they all have to happen at once," said Howard, who was quickly becoming the group's leader.

"Right," agreed Wanda. "To end starvation humanity would have had to figure out a long time ago how to conserve and husband the world's natural resources."

"And share," added Tonya. "Bickering and petty grievances between countries will have to stop."

"What about technology? Clean water and abundant food sources are possible with affordable technology," said Ralph.

"Yeah, and no more fossil fuels, we'll need to invent a new energy source. I'm not that keen on solar power, what about fusion power?" said Josh.

"Is that even possible?" Sara asked.

"It is if we dream it," said Josh.

"Fusion power it is then." said Howard. "With a cheap and reliable source of energy we've solved a lot of the world's problems right off."

"We're all agreed on these changes," asked Howard.

They all agreed.

"See everybody back here tomorrow then."

Before they went back to their own dreams Josh raised one more question. "But what if Ralph is right; what if we're just dreaming this world-altering stuff?"

Wanda spoke up. "Josh, remember when you woke to find that skyscraper of yours, wasn't that real?"

"It sure did seem real," said Josh.

"It is real, I've seen it downtown. I have friends who work there. Dreams have a different feel to them; take this meeting place of ours, we're just dreaming we're here. I remember the door being over there and the skylight being a little that way. This group dream is a composite of all our memories of the roof; it works for our purposes but it's not exact. When I wake up at home on the other hand, that feels much different; it's clear and detailed. And I can see all the way to the horizon, I know it's real. And the changes we've made are real too."

One by one they left the group dream and returned to their own; and dreamed of a better world.

Dream Institute:

"Hey Bob, any changes?" asked Frank, the second shift lab tech, looking into the sleep chamber.

Six catatonic dreamers lay there hooked up to I.V.'s; monitoring devices were connected to their shaved heads.

"No, still sleeping," said Bob.

"Are they dreaming?" asked Frank.

"Nothing lucid; but from the readings it's clear that they're all in REM sleep and dreaming like crazy! We're just not getting it. I know this sounds crazy but it's almost like they're blocking us out somehow," said Bob.

He got up and put on his coat. "Well, I should be going; you have a good night Frank."

Bob walked to his car in the underground parking garage. As he got in he had the strangest feeling that something was different, that something had just changed; but the feeling soon passed. He started up his *fusion powered car* and drove home to a much better world.

FLIGHT 206

UPN Headline News:

"A plane carrying 32 passengers crashed and burned in the Adirondack Mountains near Bakers Mill, N.Y. today."

"Miraculously, there were no casualties. Several hikers witnessed the crash and said they saw the fuselage separate from the aircraft just before impact and float to the ground supported by parachutes. When emergency response teams arrived they found each passenger strapped into their seats by an elaborate webbing system. A few of the passengers had minor cuts and bruises but everyone walked off the plane as if they were getting off an amusement park ride. The rest of the aircraft is a pile of burning debris spread over a half mile of mountainous terrain."

"Before you run out and buy stock in this safety-conscious airline though, listen to this. All the passengers on Flight 206 claim to be from the future."

"The word our reporters got, before the FBI spirited them away, was they boarded a flight from London to New York City, at 7 PM May 21ˢᵗ, 2085. The plane went off course just as they reached landfall and crashed here in the Adirondacks. Authorities have not been in contact with any of the flight crew because, according to the passengers we interviewed, these flights are completely automated. It just keeps getting stranger and stranger."

"Stay tuned to this station for more on *The Amazing Crash of Flight 206* on the late night news."

TEMPORARY FBI HEADQUARTERS: Howard Johnson Motor Lodge, Bakers Mill; New York:

"We've interviewed all 31 passengers sir, and just about everyone is telling the same incredible story," said FBI Agent Nancy Trueblood.

"They boarded the plane in London for the 2 hour flight to New York; everything was normal until just before 8PM when the plane went into a steep dive and crashed."

"You said just about everyone. Have you spoken to someone with a different version?" asked Senior Investigator Kenneth Colbert.

"Well, there is one passenger who has a different story. He claims there were 32 passengers on board Flight 206 and that one by one they'll all be retrieved by the future and we'll have no memory of this ever happening."

"How is it he knows this, but the others don't," asked Agent Colbert.

"He claims to be a scientist from the future and wants some kind of asylum; says the crash was his idea."

"So we're dealing with either a nut or a terrorist from the future?"

"It would seem so sir, as crazy as that sounds."

"And none of the other passengers knows anything about this retrieval system?"

"No."

"I guess we'd better go talk to this guy."

The FBI agents walked down to Room 16 where they were holding the scientist from the future.

"My name is Ken Colbert, and this is Agent Nancy Trueblood; we're from the Federal Bureau of Investigation," said the FBI agent flashing his badge.

"I want asylum!" demanded a disheveled man in a business suit, sitting on the bed. He was fairly young, and fairly good looking; one might even describe him as distinguished looking.

"Well that could be tricky, seeing as how you claim to be from the future," said Investigator Colbert.

"Claim to be from the future! Look at my clothes; look at the plane; look at all the stuff in our luggage. I'm sure you've had time to go through it, it should prove we're not from this time."

"Our experts are still going over everything," said Agent Trueblood.

"We're wasting time, let me explain. I made a few adjustments to the autopilot; the plane is completely automated you know, and brought it down in this uninhabited area. I'm sorry about the wreckage but as I said the retrieval teams will take care of that in short order."

"You keep mentioning these retrieval teams, what are you talking about?" asked Agent Colbert.

"Let me start at the beginning. That plane out there on the mountainside is part of a Vacation Getaway Package. Think of it like a tour bus from the future. Actually, the plane *is* the Time Machine. Citizens from my time pay an exorbitant amount of money to go sightseeing in the past. When they arrive in New York they are met by our personnel who direct them to your tour buses and airplanes. When their vacation is over; they re-board our plane/time machine and go back to our time. The company that runs the airline at that gate is fictitious."

"You're kidding right, there's a gate at the airport in New York that's run by a tour company from the future?" asked the agent.

"Yes, personally I think it's an incredible waste of a scientific marvel but time travelling is very popular and our distinguished scientific community believes they can avert any time anomalies that might occur. They've gone way out on a limb by allowing ordinary people from my time to gad about in the past without any real precautions though, and they know it. The time travel components on that plane; were they discovered, would send irrevocable ripples down the timeline," exclaimed the alleged scientist from the future.

"That's why if anything happens in the past during one of these sightseeing excursions a team of specialists is sent in to retrieve every piece of hardware, every scrap of wreckage and every passenger. You haven't found the Flight Recorder yet have you?"

"No, but we're still looking."

"You won't find it. That's the first thing they salvage, and then the time machine components.

"Let me get this straight, you're saying there are people from the future out there going through the wreckage alongside my agents," asked the FBI agent.

"Yes, just like there are tourists from the future mingling with your citizens at your National Parks, Art Galleries and Museums," said the scientist/terrorist from the future.

"This is preposterous! This is the biggest line of bullshit I've ever heard. Time travelling airplanes, fictitious gates at the airport; there's no way Homeland Security wouldn't have found out about all this before now," said Agent Colbert shaking his head.

He stepped aside to confer with Agent Trueblood.

"Have your people found any proof that this flight was from the future?" asked Agent Colbert.

"We've found passports dated in the 2080's, books copyrighted at future dates and electronic gadgets that no one has ever seen before; and the engine and aircraft design have our experts scratching their heads. It doesn't make sense that someone would manufacture all this stuff just to crash it here. And of course, there's the 30 passengers who also claim they're from the future," said Agent Trueblood.

"Excuse me; did I hear you say 30 passengers?

"Yes, 30 passengers."

"See it's already happening; my time is running out. Soon the crash recovery people from my time will locate and retrieve every passenger from that flight; including me. They will clean up all that wreckage, and return every passenger. They can't allow anything to be left behind in the past; it might cause time distortions in the future. First they remove all the physical evidence, then they go back and revise or erase all newspaper accounts, radio and TV accounts of the event. All traces of the incident are redacted from your historical records, and eventually from your memories. The only people who remember are those individuals who actually witnessed the event and they are usually scoffed at as conspiracy theorists. It's the basis for all your so-called conspiracy theories. The incidents that a few people remember probably did actually occur, but those few eye witnesses are considered crazy people because no one else remembers the event."

"It seems a stretch that you can erase our memories by simply removing the evidence," Agent Trueblood interrupted.

"As soon as each passenger or article from the future is removed, the present timeline is readjusted. It's as if it never happened. It's not anything our people are doing; it's just the way time works."

He could see by the looks on their faces they weren't buying it.

"I'll put it another way. Time is like a rubber band. I've caused this particular timeline to stretch by allowing you to see a bit of the future when I caused this accident. An example, let's say you're headed straight at another vehicle on the motorway, but somehow at the last second you avoid that collision. On one timeline there is a terrible accident, but because you avoided the collision you're still headed down the motorway, rattled but unscathed. You've stretched the timeline but not broken it. After a short time you don't even remember it; you move on. If you thought about every near miss in your busy world you'd be nervous wreck. So if an improbable event occurs, but is erased very quickly without any proof that it ever occurred, the memory of the stretching of that timeline will also be erased."

He sincerely wanted them to understand. "Does that make any sense?" he asked.

"At this point I don't know what to think," said Agent Colbert.

"I guess my next question is why? Why did you do this?" asked Agent Colbert.

"You mentioned asylum when we first came through the door; are you trying to escape from the future?" added Agent Trueblood.

"Yes, yes finally you're asking the right questions.

There's a small loophole in the Universal Time Laws. I can claim asylum in the past if I become a citizen of that time before I'm retrieved."

"What? Just how does someone go about becoming a citizen of another time?" asked Agent Colbert shaking his head; this was getting better by the minute.

"By marrying someone in the past; preferably someone with a family," he said.

"I've read history books on this time period and they talk about a situation that they refer to as single parenthood?"

"Why yes, as a matter of fact, Agent Trueblood is a single parent."

"You are?"

"Yes. I have a thirteen year old son."

The time traveler suddenly got down on one knee.

"Would you marry me? I'm in good health. I'd be a good provider. Please say yes."

"Are you crazy? I don't even know your name," said the agent.

"The name's Patrick Kilraine, how do you do," said Patrick shaking her hand enthusiastically.

"How do you do," she said back.

"I don't see how you can even be asking me this. You just admitted to sabotaging a plane, that's a crime in our time," said Nancy, hardly believing the whole conversation.

"I know it looks bad, but in a couple of days, maybe even hours, everything will have been retrieved. It'll be like it never happened. I had to do something to get away."

"What's so bad about the future?" she asked.

"The future is a bloody bore. Our lives are completely planned out for us. We're pigeon-holed from birth. Because of overpopulation and dwindling resources every citizen must do what he or she can to make society run smoothly, which means doing what you're told mostly. We're assigned a job and social strata at age twenty and there you stay for the remainder of your working life. There's no room for individuality or creativity."

"It does sound a bit boring. You're British?"

"Yes, does that matter?"

"No. I was just wondering why you don't have an accent."

"No one does in the future, not since the advent of worldwide television. So you'll marry me?" He said looking up at her with his bright blue eyes.

"He is quite handsome, in a Hugh Grant kind of way." thought Nancy.

The FBI agent looked over at her boss.

"What should I do here?"

He shrugged and said, "It's up to you Agent Trueblood. I have to admit I'm a little curious to see what happens next. If this whole thing turns out to be a hoax you can annul the marriage and we'll throw him in prison."

She looked down at Patrick kneeling in front of her.

"Alright, I must be crazy, but I'll marry you. If this turns out to be some kind of scam, remember I am an FBI agent."

As they rushed to the courthouse Nancy asked, "What happens when the other passengers are gone and the wreckage is removed? Will I remember any of this?"

"I'm not sure, my guess is you'll have a vague memory of the crash investigation but it will fade," said the time traveler. "After that we'll have to play it by ear, is that how the expression goes?"

"Yes, that's the expression. You mean we'll have to make up a more reasonable explanation of how we met and fell in love and got married?" said the FBI agent.

"We could write all this down; get it notarized and put in a safe place for when the kids ask "How you met Dad." said Patrick.

"The kids?" exclaimed Nancy.

"You know there is a precedent for this," added Patrick trying to change the subject.

"I looked it up in the time records. Asylum has been granted on a few occasions before. The courts have to approve the transfer of course; make sure there were no time anomalies, that sort of thing."

"One case I read about involved a time traveler named Mary Magdalene, I think that's how you pronounce her name; she went back and married a fellow named Jesus in year one."

That stopped Nancy in her tracks. "You're saying that Mary Magdalene was a time traveler?"

"Yes," said Patrick. "She was the first recorded case of a time traveler being allowed to stay in the past. It caused quite a stir at the time because Jesus was killed shortly after their marriage; but the courts had made their ruling so she was allowed to stay."

Nancy was speechless.

"Could we get hitched first, then we can sit down over drinks, and I'll tell you all about it."

BONANZA

Glitter Palace Casino
Metropolis City, Planet Earth
2126 AD

"Why do we gamble Daddy?"

"Good question son. Well, it's kind of our way of life here on Earth. It's what we do. It's what sets us apart from the other planets in the galaxy. It's even written into our Constitution:

> "Whenever two or more citizens
> are gathered together, there
> will be games of chance."

"What's a constitution?"

It's the code we live by. Just look at the other planets in the Consortium, struggling to get by, at war all the time; their people starving. We used to be like that until we realized that gambling was God's gift to man. We have a knack for it.

The people of other worlds flock here with their money and valuables because they have nothing like it on their planets. Oh, they'll figure it out someday and build their own casinos; but that will take time. We know because it was the same here.

He paused to put another quarter into the machine.

"In the beginning not everyone wanted gambling; some fought it, said it was evil. But in time they all came around. No one really knows when the first casinos were built but legend has it they were built out in a great desert, far away from civilization.

The true believers would make pilgrimages to them around Christmas time. Of course, in the old days they didn't have flyers, or even reliable ground transportation. They had to get there in something called *Wagon Trains*. It must have been quite a struggle, but they made it because man was born to gamble."

"They say it's in our blood," said the boy.

Another quarter went in the slot machine.

"That's true son, little by little each country came to accept the idea that gambling was inevitable; and that's when an amazing thing happened. Soon there was no more unemployment, no more poverty, no more fighting, and no wars. Our world became the *Go-To Place* in the Galaxy."

"Look Daddy, you won!" exclaimed the boy.

"So I did. How about that, this must be our lucky day, son"

"Can we go eat now? I'm starved."

"We sure can. How about we go to that buffet I've heard so much about."

"That would be terrific," said the boy.

"Just let me play one more quarter.."

THE WISH

Sam Vincent, retired physics professor and part-time handyman at his apartment complex, sat in his car in a long line of afternoon traffic wondering if it would ever start moving again.

"I'm never going to get there at this rate," he worried. He had an appointment at his doctor's office in ten minutes.

"I wish time would just stand still till I get there," he said out loud.

And it did. The world didn't stop turning or anything like that; time just stopped. To be more precise, every clock in the world stopped.

Sam didn't notice it until he glanced at his watch and it still read ten minutes to two.

"Oh great, now my watch has stopped."

Then he saw that the big clock at the First National Bank had stopped too.

"That's strange," he thought.

It wasn't until he arrived at his doctor's office and all the clocks started up again that he wondered if maybe he had caused it.

"But that's impossible, it was just a coincidence," and he didn't give it another thought.

When he read the headlines in the morning paper the next day he did a double take.

TIME STANDS STILL FOR 32 MINUTES! WORLD'S SCIENTISTS BAFFLED! All the clocks in the world stopped yesterday, at exactly ten minutes before two o'clock, EST.

"Well how about that," thought Sam. "My silly wish came true."

And that jogged a long-forgotten memory. Forty years ago, no, more like fifty, when he was just a kid, he found a strange looking lamp at the dump. He took it home, and late that night after everyone had gone to bed, a genie had appeared to him and granted him three wishes. He remembered now that he had wished for a good report card.

"And all this time I thought I'd just dreamed that," said Sam.

"I guess that means I've still got one wish left," he said out loud, looking around the room. "Is that true?"

No answer.

"I've wasted the first two wishes so I'd better make this one a good one," he said to nobody in particular.

He looked around, still no answer.

Sam thought. "I could wish for a million dollars. But that would change my life drastically; and how would I explain how I got it?

"Oh some genie appeared to me when I was a boy and granted me three wishes. I've waited fifty years to make my final wish. They'd lock me up and throw away the key," he said to himself.

"I could wish to be young again, but I have no desire to cheat father time. I've had a good life; I don't need to live it over. This is going to take some careful consideration," he thought.

Sam considered for several days. He asked his friends what they would wish for, and got all sorts of answers. He read the newspaper, watched the world news on the TV, and finally he decided on his wish.

"I hope you're listening. I wish for a world where there's no need for insurance, no car insurance, no health insurance, no life insurance; a world where people just trust one another."

It was kind of a strange wish, but Sam had a hunch.

He woke up the next day to a kind of Utopia. People were walking or riding bikes to work instead of speeding by in cars. Everyone was smiling and saying "Good morning", no one was in a hurry.

He looked over at the freeway, it wasn't bumper to bumper like usual at this time of day, he couldn't even hear any horns. He walked to the coffee shop on the corner, bought a newspaper and read it from cover to cover. There were no wars; anywhere! There wasn't any hunger, or poverty; not even any pollution.

"Even the grass on my front yard looks a little greener," thought Sam as he returned home.

Everything was right with the world.

Trust, or the lack of it, was the one thing that had held humanity back all this time. By eliminating the need for insurance he had forced the genie to create a world in which mistrust was no longer in the human experience. Total honesty was now the norm, no one would ever think of not paying a bill or cheating on their taxes.

Yep, Sam had done alright; of course he did have a little help from a very, very patient genie.

EDDIE HASKEL VS.
THE PRINCE OF DARKNESS

The devil leaned back in his high-backed chair and called in his next victim. An elephant approached cautiously.

"What on earth did you do to wind up here?" asked Lucifer.

"I was the human's accomplice on Earth. I helped them to clear rain forests in Southeast Asia; which ultimately caused erosion, floods and great suffering," said the elephant looking down at his feet.

"But you are the most powerful creature on Earth, why would you have to do anything for the humans? You could have crushed them like bugs!"

"You don't know what they're like," exclaimed the elephant. "They're more powerful than you would think."

"I've seen these humans; they're puny, insignificant, little beings; nothing to be afraid of," said the devil.

"But you've only seen them when they're dead. A living human being can be very persuasive."

The prince of darkness leaned back and thought.

"Summons my henchmen," he ordered.

When they arrived, "You will go to Earth and bring back a living human being. I want to see one of these creatures before death has changed them."

"As you wish, sire," said the henchmen.

The devil's minions wasted no time finding a suitable subject. They discovered a human engaged in fowl deeds almost immediately.

"He'll do," they said.

As soon as the human was alone they appeared and transported him out of this world and into the next.

So it was that Eddie Haskel was brought to the gates of hell. Actually, they brought him to the outer office of the gates of hell.

Eddie hadn't changed much over the years. He was still the schemer. He'd parlayed his ability to con people into a successful business, part-time inventor, consultant, and full-time scam artist.

Eddie strolled around the office checking things out. It was very nice; thick pile carpet, leather furniture, van Gogh's and Monet's on the walls.

When he came upon a list of "the recently departed" posted on a bulletin board he noticed that his name wasn't on it. He was quite put off by this; he'd had a feeling he hadn't died yet. I mean you'd know if you'd bought the farm, right?

"What the heck is going on here," said Eddie. "I'm not dead."

The secretary looked through the computer files and could find no Edward Haskel listed.

"This is most irregular. I wonder what the Prince of Darkness is up to now," she said.

"Let me get God down here Mr. Haskel, please have a seat."

Over the intercom:

"Sorry to bother you God, but we've got a problem down here."

God arrived instantly.

"What's the devil up to now?" He asked.

"He prefers to be called the Prince of Darkness, sir," said the secretary.

"Whatever; what's he done?

"He's had a living human being brought down here," said the secretary. "I'm not sure what he has in mind."

"This man isn't dead?"

"We're sorry for the inconvenience Mr. Haskel. We'll get to the bottom of this and have you back on Earth in no time," said God.

"Sorry isn't good enough," said Eddie. "I want compensation! We're talking mental anguish, lost salary, and my family is probably worried sick wondering where I am."

"What can we do to make it right, Mr. Haskel?"

"Well, how about a few extra years added to my life."

"Done," said God.

"How about you add a few extra years to my wife and kids lives.

"Done," said God.

"I could use a million dollars?" Eddie suggested.

"Don't push your luck Eddie," said God.

"Well then, um, I want an apology from this prince of darkness guy," said Eddie.

"And you shall have it," said God.

The secretary rang the lord of death.

"We have that live human you sent for sir."

"Send him in."

Eddie entered the depths of hell. It was everything he'd heard about the place and more. Dante's Inferno, a fiery cavernous abyss spread out before him. The heat was so intense it made you put your hands to your face, even though that didn't help.

"Wow, hot as hell in here; what's the matter the air conditioner broken?"

"Very funny human," laughed the devil. "This place doesn't make you afraid?"

"I can't say I'm not impressed," said Eddie.

"So this is a "live" human being. You don't look very powerful to me."

"What was he doing when you found him?" asked the Devil.

"He was engaged in a malicious con game at his place of employment," said one of the minions.

"I was selling Cramway products on the side, that's all," said Eddie. "It's a pyramid set-up.."

"We're aware of the scheme," said the devil. "We've got lots of former Cramway sales persons down here."

He waved his hand and the heat rose a few degrees bringing more cries of anguish from the surrounding caverns.

"I've a feeling you'll be joining us down here someday puny human," said his lordship.

"But I'm not dead yet am I?" Eddie inquired.

"No."

"You had no right to bring me here. I want an apology," Eddie demanded.

"I'm not going to apologize to you. Don't you realize who I am? I'm the Lord of the Underworld."

"Yeah, I know," said Eddie cutting him off.

"If you won't apologize then I want you to take a vacation. No evil, no temptations, no bad things happening to the Earth; leave us alone for a month," said Eddie.

"You can't order me to leave you alone! It's what I do. It's taken me several millennia to get the Earth just the way I want it. I won't do it."

He looked over at God standing in the doorway and knew he would have to comply.

"Darn, I should have listened to the elephant!"

The Earth was a paradise for that next month; no wars, no hatred, no prejudice. The people of Earth actually started getting along. And that goodness spilled over into the next month; and the month after that. It turns out that virtue, morality and doing the right thing are contagious. And we owe it all to Eddie Haskel.

Of course, Eddie had to go back to his old job, his scams wouldn't work anymore.

THE SICKNESS

Dave Hill found himself sitting in the tub with the shower on; he hardly ever sat down in the tub; what had made him do that? As the cool water pelting down on him he was reminded of the summer thunderstorms he and his four brothers took joyous pleasure in when he was young; splashing around in puddles until their mother would yell at them to get inside.

"You'll get hit by lightning!"

It's funny that that memory would come back to him now after all these years.

He knew he needed to get going, he was the Vice President of a Major Corporation and they had a merger meeting today. For some reason though he felt like playing hooky.

"What's come over me," he thought. "Am I getting too old for this? Maybe he was; the 14 hour days, always in a hurry; rarely seeing the wife and kids."

Thoughts of his family filled his mind; right then and there he decided to slow down and enjoy life. What's the big rush anyway?

"I've lost track of what's really important." he thought.

When he finally got on the freeway he noticed that traffic was extraordinarily light. Any other time he'd gun the motor to make up for lost time, but today he didn't care whether he was late or not. A nice leisurely drive would do him good. It would give him time to collect his thoughts; it occurred to him that after the meeting he'd talk to John, the CEO, and propose a few changes.

"Change is good," he thought.

The conference room was only half full when Dave finally got there.

"Guess I'm not the only one late today," he thought.

"Hi Dave," said John Casey, the CEO.

"As I was saying," said John. "I really can't see any reason for us to proceed with this takeover. Let's face it, I don't do the numbers, I'm not even good with numbers. I'm not down there in the cubicles with you guys; my only job is to know when something feels right. And

100

this doesn't feel right. I mean, do we really need to take over another company?"

"Well, they've had an outstanding year, and our economic forecasts show they can do even better; with their assets and our management we could be looking at an increase in profit margin of 11%; that's 6 billion over the next three years," said Ned, who was the only numbers' cruncher to show up at the meeting.

"But wouldn't that mean a lot of lost jobs," said the CEO.

"Oh yes sir, job losses are inevitable. Once we've taken over, their employees would come under our management; personnel departments like payroll, human resources and accounting would no longer be needed. Additionally, as the parent company we would absorb only the parts of their company that are the most profitable; outsourcing some things if we need to and getting rid of considerable dead weight," said Ned a little embarrassed.

"That seems brutal. Isn't there a way to keep their people?" asked the CEO.

"Not if we want to make a profit," said Ned.

CEO Casey looked around for input. "What do you think Dave?"

"I think you should go with your gut feeling sir," said Dave. "We don't need to ruin the lives of hundreds of people just so we can make a few more bucks; last time I looked we were making plenty of money. If Allied Faucet needs cash why don't we just lend it to them?"

"Dave's right. All in favor of dropping this whole merger business say aye."

Everyone present agreed.

"Is it Ned?" the CEO asked the numbers man.

"Yes sir."

"Ned, get Allied Faucet on the phone; tell them the takeover is a thing of the past. If they need funds tell them to call me, we'll work something out."

"Well now that that's settled, got any new business Dave?"

"Yes, as a matter of fact, I thought of something on the way in," said Dave. "After the meeting if you could spare a few minutes."

"Spill the beans man; what's on your mind?" said John.

"Well, I was thinking we could experiment with a 4 day work week; employees would get the same pay as before but work a shorter work week. The quality of work would surely go up, everyone would have more time to be with their families; and us executive types could have more time on the golf course," said Dave, wondering why he hadn't thought of this years ago.

"That would mean a sharp decrease in profits sir," said Ned. "But, what the heck, it's only money."

"Now that's the spirit son," said the CEO patting the young man on the back.

All over the city similar decisions were being made. Accountants and executives alike were taking longer lunch breaks; some weren't coming back at all. The city's normal, frantic pace was shifting into a lower gear; the wheels and cogs of commerce were grinding to a halt.

Many miles above the city an Alien Spacecraft hovered.

"*THE LETHARGIC RAY* is working perfectly commander," said Chief Science Officer Loki.

"Excellent," said Expedition Leader Demus.

"Move the fleet to a higher elevation and irradiate the whole planet continent by continent."

"Are you sure sir, the sickness seems to be confined to this one country; this United States of America. Funny name for a country," said the science officer.

"There's no need to expose the entire planet to *THE LETHARGIC RAY!*"

"I'm not taking any chances," said the Commander.

"We've seen how rapidly this thing they call *Capitalism* can spread. If we aren't successful in stopping it here and now, we'll be forced to destroy this entire planet and all its inhabitants."

"We can't allow a race of greedy go-getters into the galaxy, there's no telling what kind of damage they would do."

IMPETIGO

Hi, my name is Kevin Bradley and the story I'm about to tell you is true. Because it's so fantastic I thought, why bother, no one will believe me; but it concerns world domination by an alien species so I thought I should at least try. See, you're skeptical already.

A race of intelligent parasites has taken up residence in my body; I think they've been there since that time I got frostbite as a kid. The doctor called it Impetigo. It's a highly contagious skin infection usually found in children, but it can stay with you your entire life if not properly dealt with. You fight it with topical creams and antibacterial ointments. For me none of that worked; I've heard they have stuff that kills it from the inside but I never got around to going to a skin doctor. I just itched and scratched my whole life.

Looking back on my life, I'm an old man now, I guess I always believed that somehow this parasite was keeping me alive; a kind of symbiotic relationship. I've never had any illnesses, I don't get the flu, my hips and joints don't hurt; I don't even get headaches.

Now I'm convinced that these determined little organisms that I've carried around with me all these years are trying to contact me. Through daydreams mostly; I'll be sitting at the computer or watching TV and I'll have the most unusual thoughts. Stuff I would never think up on my own. I believe they are allowing me to glimpse their ancestral past.

They arrived here in the warm bodies of visitors to our planet many eons ago. They made contact with our early ancestors and evolved along with us down through the ages. To most of the human race they're just a pesky fungal annoyance, like ringworm or athletes foot.

They are far from that. They are an intelligent space-faring species. No they don't actually live in outer space; they would die just as we would if exposed to the vacuum of space. But their species inhabits the bodies of people on thousands of planets throughout the galaxy; anywhere warm-blooded creatures can live they can too. Left behind on this primitive planet, they have long desired to rejoin the rest of their species out amongst the stars but knew it would take a very long time before mankind was ready to make that jump. So they settled in for the long wait, doing what they could to nudge our civilization towards their goal of interstellar travel.

They influenced Galileo, Da Vinci and Goddard; and they had us so close, so very close. They pushed our species to the very brink of space travel. JFK, I'm quite sure had Impetigo too.

But then we faltered, we drifted away from our dream to inhabit the stars; maybe too much reality television, I don't know. Our quest to conquer new worlds faded.

Some of their best minds went to work on the problem and they concluded that it was partly their own fault. You see they have individuals in their numbers that don't feel the need to move on. In fact these individuals are dead set against the search for new worlds to inhabit. We'll call them the conservatives; they're content to live out their lives feasting on human epidermis. Why change?

The conservatives are greedy too; they eat too much epidermis and thus cause The Itch. You see if they eat only their fill and back away from the area the host would never know of their presence. There would be no itch, the host wouldn't scratch; and wouldn't feel the need to go to a doctor for treatment.

The liberals have always believed in conservation; why contaminate the host's skin to the point that he or she fights back. Let's face it Impetigo is easily treatable with the right medicines; only people like me, who are too afraid to go to a doctor or third world counties that can't afford the medicines, are inflicted.

But being of one mind on whether their species should be seeking out new worlds to conquer isn't the biggest problem. The real dilemma they believe is that mankind (the vehicle they will ride back to the stars) is running out of time. Every civilization has a very narrow window of opportunity between when their science reaches the stage when it's ready to make that evolutionary step; leave the home planet and venture to the stars, and when that civilization starts running out of the very resources that will be needed to support that evolutionary step.

As the decades slip by it will become harder and harder to convince world governments to throw all their remaining resources to this end.

That is why they've stepped up their campaign to infect as many humans as possible; and in so doing garner support for their cause.

I don't think it's such a bad thing what they're doing. Yes, it's a form of world conquest but really they just want to hitch a ride with us to other worlds.

I'm retired now. I spend a lot of time at Airports, Train Stations and Bus Depots shaking the hands of travelers so the overlords can transfer to them. I've joined their cause to infect enough people to take over the world and force the human race to once again look to the stars.

Who knows, maybe someday I'll shake the hand of a future JFK and they'll be on their way.

YOU ONLY LIVE THRICE

TIME COURT: 2495 AD (MORNING SESSION)

"Your Honor, rule 147 clearly states that no one from the past can be removed from their timeline and brought to any other time," said the prosecutor.

"We're all aware of the statute Prosecutor Ward. Does counsel for the defendant have any extenuating circumstances to report?" asked the judge.

"We do; your honor. We'd like to offer into evidence the time log subpoenaed by our office. It's quite remarkable. I believe it will shed some light on my client's intentions," said the defense attorney.

"I'll allow it," said the judge.

"Run the vid please," said the lawyer.

Computer voice over:

"TIME LOG, BEGINNING OCTOBER 3RD 1967 - 40 KILOMETERS NORTH OF AN LOC, REPUBLIC OF VIETNAM," announced the computer voice over.

The video showed a group of infantry men (2nd Platoon, Alpha Company) on patrol in the jungles of Southeast Asia.

Computer voice over:

"A WAR WAS BEING FOUGHT BETWEEN NORTH VIETNAM AND THE UNITED STATES IN THAT YEAR. THE HISTORICAL RECORD IS NOT CLEAR AS TO THE ACTUAL CAUSE OF THE CONFLICT, BUT THOUSANDS OF CASUALTIES WERE BORN BY BOTH SIDES."

The platoon was spread out in a clearing in the jungle, some of the soldiers were sleeping; others were eating.

"Hey Sarge, are we going back to base camp anytime in this decade?" asked Pvt. Murphy, who could always be depended upon to say what he was thinking. "I've got mail to read and warm beer to drink."

That last statement got a rise out of some of the men.

"I'm afraid not Murph," said Sgt. Miller.

"HQ suspects Vietcong movement 3 or 4 klics north of here; they want us to go check it out."

"It figures! This really sucks! Why does this always happen to us?"

"Take it up with the chaplain Murphy. Everybody get up; let's move out."

Pvt. 1st Class Bill Davis only half listened to the conversation between Murphy and Sgt. Miller as they left the jungle canopy and trudged through another rice paddy. He occupied his mind with other things, like Big Macs, drive-in movies and his '65 mustang. God he missed the states; just 112 days to go. He got out his calendar and marked off another day.

That's when the ambush came, with the platoon was in the middle of a rice field. No cover; all they could do was drop down into the mud. Charlie was lobbing mortar rounds closer and closer and sniper fire was zinging by their heads. The platoon returned fire with the '50' Cal and M16's spraying the tree line in front of them.

"Jamison, get forward air command on the horn. Call in some fast movers," yelled Sgt. Miller to the radioman.

"TOC (tactical operations center) this is 2nd platoon alpha company, we're under attack. We need F-4's in here right now. We're at Bravo 14 on the map, approximately 45 kilometers north of An Loc. Charlie is in the trees about 200 meters to our west," yelled Jamison into the radio.

Air support would be there in minutes but it might not be soon enough. The enemy's mortars had zeroed in on their position; men were getting hit.

"We're sitting ducks out here," said Bill. He got up firing his M16 at the tree line as he backed towards the last levee they'd crossed.

"Get down soldier, that's an order," yelled Sgt. Miller.

More soldiers got up and started retreating; it was mass confusion.

Pvt. Davis almost made it to the levee and safety when he was struck by something and blacked out.

When Bill came to he was in a lot of pain, he'd been hit in the shoulder and back of the head.

"It's a good thing everybody in my family has hard heads," he said out loud.

It was only then that he took stock in his whereabouts. He was in a village hut, it was raining; he could hear the raindrops hitting the thatch roof.

"I've been captured by the VC," he said. "So long Big Macs."

He was lying there imagining interrogation and torture when into the hut walked the most beautiful girl he had ever seen. She was young, maybe eighteen, with delicate Asian features. When she saw that he was awake, she left and came back with soup. Bill was so hungry he didn't even ask what was in it.

In the next couple of weeks as he recuperated, he learned that his entire platoon had been killed in the attack.

Sarge, Murphy, and all the guys he'd come over here with, were dead. He'd survived only because the VC thought he was dead too. These villagers had found him. He didn't know where here was, and he didn't care; he was just glad to be alive.

He was kind of a celebrity to these people. Every day the children would come to his hut to hear him talk. He was sure they didn't understand a word of what he said but he hammed it up anyway, and they loved it.

In all the time he'd been in country he hadn't bothered to get to know a single Vietnamese person, they turned out to be very nice people. The war and all the military bullshit seemed a million miles away.

He was also growing quite fond of the girl he'd met that first day. She brought him food every day and changed his bandages. Her name was Nguyen Minh Ngoc; (that had taken him some time to learn how to pronounce). She had gone to college in Saigon and could speak a little English.

"Are you married," he dared to ask.

"I was married to a pilot in the Vietnamese Air Force but he got shot down over a year ago."

"I'm sorry," said Bill.

In the weeks that he stayed there they got to know each other. He told her of his life back in the states, and she told him of a better

Vietnam, when she was a little girl, before the war had come to the village.

When he was well enough to walk Bill played with the village children; he tried to teach them the game of football but it would always degenerate into "sack the quarterback."

Ngoc would stand on the sidelines and watch with the other adults. She found herself falling for this crazy American GI.

Bill knew he'd have to go back to his unit eventually, (technically he was AWOL) but he hated to leave his present situation. One evening when they were eating, he finally got up the courage to ask her if she would come visit him when he returned to his people. She said she would like that. He wrote down the address of a hotel in Saigon where they could meet in one week's time.

A few days later the villagers hid him in the back of a wagon and took him back to the rear. He found his old unit and reported himself un-missing in action.

"You're a lucky man Private Davis. I guess you'll want to go back to the states now?" asked his C.O.

"No, my hitch isn't over yet, I'll finish it up. I could use some R&R though."

"You've earned it," said his C.O.

The week went by slowly wondering whether Ngoc would show. He needn't have worried, for on the appointed day there she was at his door looking as pretty as ever.

"Hello Bill," she said.

"*Anh em khoe khong*? Did I say it right?" asked Bill.

"Yes. I'm fine, thank you."

They practically fell into each other's arms. For the next few days they didn't leave the room except to get cigarettes in the lobby. It was the best R&R anyone had ever had.

They laid in each other arms talking for hours.

"Will you marry me?" asked Bill.

"Yes," said Ngoc enthusiastically.

"Would you like to go to the states?"

"Yes."

"Do you like kids?'

"Yes."

"How many?" Bill asked.

"How many? Wait a minute, I think there will be plenty of time to decide things like that later; don't you think?" said Ngoc.

"Yeah you're probably right."

The problem was his hitch was almost up and it took a mountain of paperwork to get married over there. He'd heard it took as long as six months to get the paperwork through.

They decided he'd go back to the states, get his discharge, and then come back for Ngoc when he'd saved up enough money. It seemed like a good plan.

Of course, he could re-up, stay *in-country* another year and get the paperwork done. But he really missed the States; he needed to go back, just to touch base again.

He'd get a job, start college, and then come back for her when he was settled. He told Ngoc and she agreed; she would go back to her village and wait for him.

"I'll come back, honey. I promise; I'll be back for you."

A few weeks later he was on the "Freedom Bird" on his way back to the states.

The same day he arrived in the states all hell broke loose in Vietnam; it was January 31st 1968. The Tet offensive had begun. It was all over the TV news; strategic locations in South Vietnam had been hit, even the embassy in Saigon.

Bill needed to get back over there fast. He borrowed some money and bought a ticket on Pan Am Flight #1. That got him as far as Bangkok; from there he hitched a ride on an Air Force C-130 to An Loc, and took a taxi the rest of the way.

When he got to the village it was in ashes, the few villagers who remained didn't know what had happened to Ngoc. He searched for weeks, traveling to other villages, showing her picture to anyone who would talk to him, but no one knew what had happened to Ngoc. He finally had to give up and go home.

"I shouldn't have left. I should have re-enlisted and stuck it out another year."

Those regrets would stay with him a long time. All through college, no matter how he buried himself in his studies, the memory of Ngoc, and the life they should have had would always be there.

After college he dedicated his life to his work. He became a very successful scientist, patented some of his ideas and became quite wealthy. He wrote books, traveled, gave speeches at universities and symposiums, was even on TV, but all that couldn't replace the part of his life he'd left in Vietnam.

One day in a café in Paris, nursing a killer hangover from his 40th birthday party the night before, an article in an American newspaper caught his eye.

A lab in New Jersey had cryogenically frozen a rat for a year and brought it back to life. He read the article over and over and something told him this was the answer. He cancelled the rest of his speaking engagements and flew to New Jersey.

New Brunswick Cryogenic Laboratory - Six Years Later

It took every penny he had, but they were finally getting results. Cryogenics or *Deep Sleep* as they liked to call it was becoming a reality.

They'd revived a chimpanzee after two long years in deep sleep. The little guy was doing fine, no ill effects.

They were now ready to try it with a human. And that first subject, against everyone's advice, was going to be William Davis, who was now the owner of the company.

"Are you sure this is wise sir, I mean there are others who have volunteered," said one of his colleagues.

"What better way to advertise our complete confidence in the procedure than the owner taking the first plunge," Bill argued.

"How long?" asked the science staff.

"I'm thinking one hundred years," said Bill.

"A hundred years, have you gone mad sir?" they exclaimed.

"Nope, that's how long I want to sleep. You can monitor my brain activity, heart and respiration. Clients will be able to come in here and see that I'm still alive, that I haven't aged; that I'm just sleeping. It'll be good for business." His colleagues finally agreed.

He left instructions to have all his remaining assets put into a trust to fund continue research to improve the procedure.

The process was very crude. His body was wrapped in specially insulated blankets and a concoction of chemicals was injected into his blood stream to slow down his metabolism. Suspended animation they had called it in the science fiction books he'd read as a kid, now it was really happening. Just before he lost consciousness he could hear the gas being pumped into the chamber that would bring his body temperature down to 0 degrees Celsius.

"I wonder if I'll dream," he said as the chemicals slowly took effect.

There was no sensation of the passing of time for Bill. He simply woke up. It could have been one hour, or a million. For everyone else time went on. Deep Sleep Industries attracted a few customers but not nearly enough to stay solvent. The company downsized and borrowed against future profits in order to stay in business; they felt an obligation to the sleepers who had entrusted their lives to them.

They weathered these financial difficulties and eventually began to prosper as the technology was improved and the demand for cryogenics increased. Through it all Bill slept.

The world changed in many ways; technological improvements in health and science were slowly transforming the world into a better place. Overpopulation was finally brought under control, petty differences between countries were resolved, food production improved and the world no longer went hungry; and through it all, Bill slept.

He was awakened to bright lights and a crowd of fresh-faced lab technicians.

"Congratulations Mr. Davis, you've broken every record ever set in one of these old things. One hundred years in *Deep Sleep* how do you feel? Don't try to get up yet; we've got an anti-grav chair for you."

Bill was put into a chair with no wheels and guided out onto a balcony where a throng of people stood and cheered.

He waved.

"You'll be glad to know that your business has been very successful while you slept. We've improved on the procedure and now our *Deep Sleep* machines are in every hospital and spacecraft in the federation. You're a very famous man, Mr. Davis."

"Space travel," said Bill. "That's nice."

"I guess you've got a million questions?" asked one of the technicians.

"Actually, I just have one question. Do you have time travel yet?" asked Bill.

"You mean like a machine that can travel through time? I'm afraid our scientists have concluded that that will never be possible."

"Put me back in *Deep Sleep* then; let's see how good these new machines work," said Bill.

"But you've just come out of one sir," the technician was beginning to wonder if that long a period in hibernation had addled the founder's brain.

"What's the limit in one of these newer models? Could a person stay in one for, say two hundred years?"

"No one has ever stayed in one for more than twenty years, but theoretically yes, you could remain in one for that long. But what if there's no one to wake you up after two hundred years?"

"Let me worry about that," said Bill.

Deep Sleep Guild - 2295 AD

Two hundred years to the day Bill was awakened again. This time only one lab tech was waiting; a rather bored looking chap, who spoke in a monotone.

"No we don't have time travel yet. I guess you'll want to go into our newest *Sleep Chamber*."

"Yep," said Bill.

Deep Sleep Museum - 2495 AD

The third wake-up was the charm. "Do you have time travel?" he asked.

"But of course," said the lab tech as he helped Bill out of bed.

"You know I've worked here for almost three years, and in that time I've been trying to think of something historic to say to you and all I could come up with in all that time was; "but of course"."

"It was just what I wanted to hear," said Bill.

"What's it like in one of these old sleep chambers?" asked the lab technician. "Is it like sleeping? Do you dream? You know nobody uses sleep chambers anymore. You're the last."

"Time passes without you knowing it. I guess it's a lot like time travel.

"You must have had a good reason for doing this?"

"I do," said Bill.

"I'll guess a lot has changed since my time?"

"I think you'll be pleasantly surprised," said the lab tech.

"I'd like to stay and check it out but what I need now is to go back in time," Bill told him.

"There are rules about going back Sir; time paradoxes and things like that," said the technician.

"But I'm sure they'll brief you."

Bill stepped out of his building into the bright sunlight of a new age. The air was fresh and clean. The buildings so tall he could hardly see the tops of them.

A large vehicle floated by with people in it, they were all staring at him.

"I must look quite out of place here," he said.

A man in an outlandish suit approached him and handed him a business card.

"May I have a moment of your time sir?"

"Sure," said Bill.

"You're business is defunct, you haven't any money; but this building of yours is sitting on prime real estate."

Bill turned around to face his building. The once proud *Deep Sleep* laboratories looked pretty pathetic surrounded by brand new skyscrapers.

"I've been authorized to pay you four million credits for this property," said the agent.

"That sounds like a lot of money," said Bill.

"Let's just say you'll never have to work again," said the real estate agent.

"So how do I find a time travel place?" asked Bill.

"Take your pick," said the agent as he made out a check and handed it to Bill.

"There are lots of them. Avis has a nice facility just down the street."

So Bill went back, back to 1967. Back to the day he'd made his decision to return to the states without Ngoc.

He would convince himself to re-up and stay. He'd explain how his decision to go back to the states without Ngoc would haunt him for the rest of his life.

He knocked on the door of the hotel room where they'd stayed so many years ago. The door opened and there stood his younger self. It was quite a shock looking at a younger version of yourself, like looking at an old photograph, but different; more like a video of yourself. You're thinking, "Did I sound like that?"

The room was just as he remembered it, his duffel bag was packed and sitting in the middle of the floor, and Ngoc sat on the bed behind them.

He'd thought about this moment many times and knew exactly what he was going to say.

"You're not going to believe me at first, but hear me out. I'm you; that's right, I'm you. A much older you, but I'm you. I've come from the future to convince you to stay here in country and finish the paperwork to bring Ngoc to the states. Don't let her out of your sight. There's going to be some trouble, I can't say any more than that, but if you leave, when you come back you won't be able to find her."

The younger Bill said, "What the heck is going on here? You actually want me to believe that you're me? I'll admit you look a little bit like me but…"

"You've got to believe me!" Bill argued. "Remember when you were twelve, you caught your thumb in the car door, it never quite grew back. See."

He held his thumb up next to the other man's thumb; they were identical.

"Your confirmation name is Francis; you wanted to take Wilbur but the nuns wouldn't let you. You lived on Jennings Road. You had a tree fort in the back yard with a trap door. Your favorite ice cream is Baseball Nut; your favorite number is 26. How would anyone know these things but you?"

The younger Bill stood there confused, "How do you know all that? Oh, that's right, you're me. This is crazy. You mean there's time travel in the future?"

"Yes, but I can't tell you about it; it breaks too many time travel rules. We're getting off the point. I've come back all this way to convince you not to go back to the states, stay here with Ngoc. Re-enlist for another year and get all the paperwork done so she can fly with you back to the states," said Bill.

"OK, maybe somehow you are me. I don't know how that's possible but I'm still not going to re-enlist. I'm going back to the states. We've talked about it. Ngoc is OK with it, right honey?" He turned to face

Ngoc still sitting on the bed, her eyes widening as she looked back and forth between the older Bill and the younger Bill.

"I'll send for as soon as I get there, I won't waste any time getting the paperwork in."

Bill hadn't thought of this. He'd been sure he could convince himself to change his decision. He'd forgotten how stubborn he could be.

As they stood there arguing, he couldn't keep his eyes off Ngoc. It had been so long since he'd seen her he'd almost forgotten how beautiful she was. He wanted to go over and take her in his arms. But he was confident that if his plan worked, this reality; the reality that had caused him to travel five hundred years into the future; would change. He'd be sitting in a lawn chair someplace with Ngoc by his side watching their kids, and maybe grandkids chasing fireflies, and it would all be worth it.

The younger Bill was saying, "Now if you don't get out of here I'm going to have to call the MP's."

Bill sat in the bar of the hotel; he had to think of a way to convince his younger self not to make the same mistake he had made. There had to be a way. Maybe he could break his leg…

He looked up to see Ngoc standing there.

"Has he gone back to base?" he asked.

"Yes," she said.

"He's not coming back for me is he?" she asked.

"He'll come back, but it will be too late. The war is going to get much worse in the coming months," said Bill.

"But he does love me doesn't he?" she asked.

"Oh yes, very much."

"Then why is he leaving me?"

"He's young, he misses his homeland; he thinks he can have you and his old world too."

"If you are him, then you love me too?" she asked.

"Yes," said Bill a little embarrassed.

"Let me see your thumb."

She looked at his funny-looking thumb a long time; and then she asked, "What were the last words you said to me before going back to the United States?"

"I said, I promise I will come back for you."

She smiled and said, "Hello Bill."

"Hello Ngoc," he said.

They sat there looking at one another for a while and then Ngoc said. "You've come back through time for me?"

"Yes, I guess I have."

"Is it nice where you live?" she asked.

"Actually, I haven't seen much of it, but I'm sure it's nice," he said.

"Will you take me there?"

That caught him off guard; he didn't know what to say. This was the kind of temporal paradox they had told him to avoid in the briefing before he left the future. But how did he know she hadn't been killed in the attacks that were coming. He couldn't let that happen. He wasn't going to risk losing her again.

"We'd probably be breaking a whole lot of rules, but why not."

He took her hand and they walked to where he'd hidden his rented time machine.

"You know I think I'm rich up there in the future. I can probably afford a bunch of lawyers to find loopholes in the laws we're breaking."

TIME COURT: 2495 AD

"WHEN THEY ARRIVED IN OUR TIME THEY WERE IMMEDIATELY ARRESTED. TIME LOG CONCLUDED."

"Well, that's quite a story, but it still doesn't give the defendant the right to bring someone from 1967 to our time. There could be a Time Resonance," said the judge.

"Our office has detected not one Time Resonance and neither has the office of the district attorney. We believe that this is one of those rarest of occasions when the person who came through time was actually supposed to," said Bill's lawyer.

"Your honor, he's talking about Sanctuary. No one's been granted sanctuary in years; it's limited to heads of state, religious figures and prophets who have insight in regards to the future. She doesn't qualify," said the prosecutor.

"Actually the exemption states only that the passage through time be self-imposed; and she asked to come to the future," said the defense lawyer.

"The exemption is there for seer's and prophets because only they would know to ask, and in so doing their passage becomes part of their natural timeline, and therefore does not cause a time resonance," said the prosecutor.

"This young woman only knew about the future because the defendant told her."

"But suppose her life was about to end, the Tet Offensive was only weeks away. It is our contention that the reason our scientists can find no time anomalies is because her passage through time was meant to be," said the lawyer.

"Well you've done your homework counselor, you've convinced me. I guess she can stay," said the judge.

"Case dismissed."

Outside the courtroom Bill and Ngoc shook hands with their lawyer.

"I can't thank you enough," said Bill enthusiastically.

"Don't mention it. I knew if they let us show the tape you'd get off. That judge is an *Old Softy* when it comes to matters of the heart."

He nodded and went on his way. They were left standing behind the stasis barrier of the Time Court.

"Where will we go?" asked Ngoc.

"I don't know," said Bill looking around.

Bill took Ngoc's hand and they stepped through the barrier and into a strange and wonderful New World.

BE CAREFUL WHAT YOU WISH FOR

Pentagon: 2019 AD

"How'd it go in there?" asked Rob.

"Not good I'm afraid, they practically accused me of treason for dragging my feet. We're not procrastinating are we?"

Professor Jonathan Eberhart was the chief scientist on a Top Secret military project, code named *Pulsar*. He was tall and lanky, in his late forties, with wavy black hair, which was now turning gray in his sideburns and mustache.

"No sir, I'd say we were just being extra careful," said Rob, the professor's faithful assistant.

"I told them we'd be ready for the first test by next week."

"We'll be ready sir," said Rob.

"But is the world ready?" thought Jonathan on the plane back to Colorado where the Pulsar Control Center was located.

"Maybe I am deliberately delaying the project." He looked around at the passengers on the plane; going on skiing vacations, business trips or just flying home to see loved ones. They were completely unaware that the world was about to change.

Since the military had taken over the project, he'd had his doubts whether this weapon (and that's what it was really) was in man's best interests.

He couldn't remember if he'd had these doubts six years ago when he had first proposed the project; a network of ultra-powerful lasers orbiting the Earth, capable of tracking and destroying rogue meteors before they collided with the planet.

It had started out as a joint military and civilian endeavor, but somewhere between R&D and construction the civilian funds had run out. Now it was primarily a military operation and they had a very different agenda. Tracking and destroying meteors was a secondary objective; targeting incoming ICBM's became the main thrust of the project.

The scientific community had protested vehemently when they'd turned the lasers towards Earth. They feared it would be seen as an act of aggression by other nations, but because they were convinced it was our best defense against an extinction level event, they finally acquiesced.

The military couldn't understand what all the fuss was about. To them *Pulsar* was the weapon to end all weapons; end all wars. What nation in the world would dare attack another if they knew they'd be blasted out of existence from orbit?

But Jonathan wasn't so sure, so much power in the hands of so few. It scared him to death.

That night he couldn't sleep; the faces of those people on the plane kept creeping into his thoughts.

He wandered into the kitchen and took down a bottle of Scotch. He stood there drinking and looking out the kitchen window. It was a peaceful August evening, the moon was up, and a slight breeze was blowing in through the window. Jonathan looked up, saw one single star shining in the night sky and made a wish.

"I wish it was a year from now and all this was over," he said. (That had always worked when he was a kid).

He got back into bed and with the help of the booze went right to sleep.

After Jonathan had fallen asleep the wall across from his bed became transparent and a man stepped through into the room.

He was an average looking chap, average height, average build, light brown hair, nondescript clothing; nothing about him would make him stand out in a crowd. He was carrying a small device in his hand. He looked around the room taking mental measurements; then started punching buttons on the device.

The room was immediately bathed in a pale blue light, which lasted about a minute. When the room returned to normal he stepped back through the wall and was gone.

When Jonathan awoke the next day everything seemed normal. His first indication that something was wrong was when he wasn't able to get Howard Stern on the radio. Howard had been replaced by some all-news-station; and the news wasn't good. They were talking about food rationing, radiation poisoning, riots, and curfews.

"What the heck is going on?" He turned on the TV but got nothing but static.

"Cable must be out again," he thought.

He finally went over to the living room window and looked out through the blinds. He could scarcely believe what he saw; the streets were deserted; replaced by litter, abandoned cars, and boarded up stores.

He got dressed quickly and went outside. It was cold and the skies were dark, almost black with soot, like Mount St. Helens had erupted nearby. He had to put a handkerchief over his mouth to keep from choking.

A block from his house was a mini-mall; he could see people looting the stores there. As he watched two military vehicles pulled into the parking lot, soldiers got out and started firing into the crowd. He stood there in a trance, unable to move.

"It's pretty bad isn't it," came a voice from a man who suddenly appeared next to him.

"You can say that again. What the heck is going on?" asked Jonathan still watching the carnage down the street.

"Do you want the short version or the long one?" asked the stranger.

"I'll take any explanation," said Jonathan.

"World War III is what's going on. Eight U.S. cities destroyed, an estimated 80 to 100 million dead, nuclear fallout, disruption of commerce, riots, looting, marshal law; strictly enforced as you can see, and radiation poisoning."

"But who? Why? I mean, what happened that would cause WWIII?"

"China attacked Taiwan, and our government retaliated with *Pulsar*. *Pulsar*, what do you know about that? It's supposed to be top secret."

"As soon as it went on-line about six months ago it became public knowledge. The military wanted everyone to know; said it would be a deterrent. All the networks ran artist's conceptions of what it looked like and how it worked."

"But that's impossible; it hasn't even been tested yet."

"Oh, it's been tested alright. Hundreds of targets in Mainland China were hit. China has been reduced to a burning cinder; but they launched a counter strike before they were completely overwhelmed.

Most of their missiles were knocked out, but eight managed to get through."

"How could all of this have happened in one night?"

"Look at the date on that newspaper on the ground there," said the stranger.

Jonathan picked up a page and read "November 3rd, 2020; that can't be, that's over eleven months from now."

"Actually it's been a year; that newspaper stopped printing about three weeks ago. You asked for it to be a year from now and it is."

"But how could you know about that?" asked Jonathan suddenly remembering his wish from the night before.

"Who are you?" He turned to face the person he'd been talking to all this time.

"I'm just a visitor," said the stranger.

"From where? How could you know about my wish last night, or a year ago, or whenever it was? And how could you possibly grant such a wish? Are you my guardian angel or something?"

"No, I'm not your guardian angel," said the visitor with a smile.

"I guess it might seem like I'm a supernatural being, but actually I'm a visitor from a parallel universe. I live on a world much like this one, except that we are far more technologically advanced. With our technology we have discovered the existence of alternate dimensions, other worlds; and we've found a way to cross over to those other worlds."

"You've hypnotized me right?" asked Jonathan, still trying to make some sense out of what was happening.

"No, I simply gave you what you wished for. I transported you one year into your probable future."

"How is that possible?"

"In my universe almost anything you could imagine is possible," said the visitor.

"And the people of your world can come and go in ours as they wish?"

"Oh no, only qualified agents like myself are allowed to make the jump; and even then it took a lot of convincing before the *League of Scientists* allowed me to come and show you your future."

"But why me?" asked Jonathan.

"What you see here is the result of something you did a year ago."

"Pulsar," he thought.

"Oh God, I knew it! I must have completed my tests on the one in orbit and gave the military the go ahead to deploy the rest of them. But I had no choice. What was I supposed to do, tell them it didn't work?"

"I doubt they would have believed you."

"Why do I get the feeling you're telling me all this for a reason?" Jonathan inquired.

"I'm showing you your probable future in the hope that you will do something about it."

"Why does your world feel the need to help us?"

"That is a question my people have debated for centuries. Some say it's meddling; that we should leave you to your own fate. Others believe it isn't right to just stand by and watch disaster after disaster and not do something about it. Still others believe that all the parallel universes are connected; if one world is destroyed it will somehow affects the others."

"In any case we decided to *help out* when we can. We don't do anything drastic, like introduce new technology or kill off an evil dictator. We just appear from time to time and make suggestions."

"What would suggest I do?"

"You could go back to the day of the first test and make sure it doesn't work."

"You can send me back?"

"Yes."

Jonathan found himself back in his kitchen, looking out his kitchen window again. He decided he'd go in the next day and make a few subtle changes to *Pulsar's* programming. He'd have to be sneaky but he was sure he could introduce enough system errors to make *Pulsar* fail the initial tests.

Then if he dragged it out a little longer maybe the military would lose patience and scrap the project.

He went to work early that morning and put as many bugs into the system as he could; then he retired to the break room for a nap.

He woke up about 9AM and returned to the lab.

"Jonathan; am I glad to see you," said Rob.

"I was running some firing simulations and found errors in the guidance and trajectory programming. They could have caused the laser to malfunction. I think I've corrected them all but I'm running another simulation just to be sure. You'd better tell the Pentagon brass that the tests will be pushed back an hour."

"Good work, Rob. I'm going to get a cup of coffee did you want one?"

"No thanks."

Back in the break room Jonathan sat staring into his cup of coffee. He should have known Rob would run a few final checks, but he couldn't tell Rob about the future. He'd think he was crazy.

"Got a quarter?" asked the visitor.

"It's you. What are you doing here?"

"Getting something out of your vending machines; it's funny how every universe has a different selection of junk food. I've become a real connoisseur of vending machine goodies."

"How can you stand there and talk about junk food when my world's about to end!"

"Calm down; what's happened?"

Jonathan explained about Rob finding the errors in the systems programming.

"The old conscientious assistant problem," said the visitor stroking his chin.

"What can I do now? The tests are in less than an hour," said Jonathan.

"Let me think. You know I could think better over a cup of coffee and a selection from your snack food dispenser."

"Oh I don't believe this. Here's some change."

"Thank you."

"I don't suppose you could blow it up just before it fires?" asked Jonathan.

"Not allowed," said the visitor.

"It figures," said Jonathan.

"But I might get permission to change the orbiting laser's chronological orientation just before it fires."

"You mean move it forward in time, like you did with me?" asked Jonathan.

"Not forward; I don't think your future would appreciate an atomic-powered 50 million gigajoule orbital laser showing up in their airspace. Your planet's low orbital space begins getting pretty crowded in the not-too-distant future. No, I was thinking about sending it back in time."

"How far back?" asked Jonathan.

"That would be your call my man," said the visitor.

"Let me think, we'd have to send it back pretty far, so no one would ever detect it. And then there's orbital decay; it would have to be far enough back in time so that there isn't even any record of it falling back to Earth. Prehistoric times would be best, yeah, we're talking millions of years."

"How many millions would you think?"

"I don't know? I'm not a geologist; say 50 million years, 65 million years, that ought to be enough."

"Sixty five million years it is. I'll run the numbers by the *League of Scientists*," he said and stepped through the wall of the break room.

Later in the Control Center:

"Commencing countdown: Ten, nine, eight, seven, six...Sir, we've lost telemetry from Pulsar," said the controller.

"And it's no longer showing up on radar," said another.

"You mean it has blown up or something?" asked Jonathan.

"I don't know sir, it just isn't there anymore."

Jonathan pretended to be working feverishly to regain contact with Pulsar, but he allowed himself a sneak peek at the Pentagon brass as they argued.

"Well, I want to go on record as being opposed to this project from the outset," said one General.

"This has been a complete waste of military expenditures," said another.

Jonathan could see that the mad rush to get off the bandwagon had begun; hopefully they'd never revisit this dangerous project again.

Back in his office Jonathan was emptying out his desk when the visitor stepped through the wall.

"How'd it go?" he asked.

"Fine; I'm washed up as a research scientist, but at least I'm not responsible for starting World War III," said Jonathan.

"Hey, if it's any consolation, you're a hero in all the other universes. We applaud you. Can we get another cup of coffee and a snack?" asked the visitor.

"Sure why not," said Jonathan. They walked down the hall to the break room.

"I've been meaning to ask you something, something very important; I can't think of what it was," said Jonathan.

They got coffee and snacks out of the machines.

"Oh yeah, when I had you send our 50 million gigajoule orbiting atomic bomb back through time I didn't cause the extinction of the dinosaurs did I?" asked Jonathan.

"Well actually, you kinda did," admitted the visitor. "But don't worry about it, they had to go sometime."

He smiled, finished off his last Twinkie and stepped back through the wall of the break room.

A BETTER PLACE

A young couple sat in their living room discussing the fate of their parents.

"I don't want you to make a scene like you did last year when my parents left," the young man told his wife.

"We've been all through this, there's nothing to get emotional about."

"But it doesn't seem fair," said the young woman.

"They're both still young."

"They're fifty! They're old! You know the law," said the young man.

The law he referred to was the *Overpopulation Decree of* 2165. It had been signed by every nation on the planet.

"All persons who reach the age of fifty must report for debarkation."

Debarkation was just a euphemism for humane termination. When the Earth's population surpassed forty billion, a desperate world started taking desperate measures.

The Overpopulation Decree was the final solution.

1 Only computer-selected couples would be allowed a child.
2 Those not married or selected by age 21 must report for sterilization.
3 Everyone fifty years old or over will be shipped off world, to a better place.

But everyone knew we didn't possess the technology to transport people to other worlds. Earth's astronomers and explorers hadn't even discovered any inhabitable planets yet. It turned out that Earth-type planets were rare in the galaxy. If any were out there, they were too far for us to reach.

"They seemed so happy these last few weeks," said the young wife.

"Do you suppose they really believe all that propaganda?"

"Nobody really believes all that "going to a better place" stuff," said the young man.

"It's a hoax. I've heard they shuttle them up into space, then open the cargo doors and everyone just floats out into space."

"That's terrible!" exclaimed the young woman.

"Just kidding; I think they give them a pill or something. It's very humane. Then their remains are ground up into fertilizer for the Oceanic Hydroponics Farms."

"That's terrible too," she said.

"Come on, you know the world's overpopulation problems. It's either, get rid of a few old people or watch the whole world starve to death in like thirty years or so. Here they come now, look happy for them," he said smiling.

Her parents came down the stairs. They had each packed a small suitcase; it was rather pathetic.

"Well, I guess we're ready. Clare and I would like to thank you for having us over these last few weeks while we wrapped up all the loose ends."

"We don't want you two to worry about us, we're going to a better place," said Clare.

They hugged the kids one last time and then got on the bus for the debarkation center.

At the Debarkation Center:

"You folks decide yet?" asked the government scientist turned travel agent.

"My suggestion, New Tahiti; you get your own little island, a flying boat to go from island to island, year round good weather. You can't beat it. That's where I'm headed when I retire."

"Could you go over the part about why only people over the age of fifty can leave the Earth? My wife doesn't think it's fair to deceive the kids this way."

"Well, like they said in the briefing, we've discovered many habitable planets out there, but we don't have the capabilities to handle the inevitable mass exodus there'd be if we let the truth out. So we've leaked all sorts of misinformation to the public over the past few years about the availability of suitable relocation planets."

"We're building spaceships as fast as we can; someday we'll be able to lower the retirement age to 45, then 40, and so on. Until then, this is the most orderly way the government could think of to depopulate the Earth."

"I guess the government knows what it's doing," said Clare.

"Of course they do," said her husband. "If the younger generation ever found out that we have the technology to go anywhere in the galaxy, they'd all want to go. Don't worry about them dear, they'll get their chance when they turn fifty."

He turned back to the government scientist, "How's the fishing on that Tahiti World?"

"Great," said the scientist.

"Do you think the kids might join us on Tahiti World some day?" asked Clare from the observation deck of the shuttle as they docked with the Star Cruiser waiting in orbit.

SMALL WORLD

"Entering planet's upper atmosphere," announced the life pod's unemotional computer voice.

"Five minutes to impact."

The tiny space vehicle was completely automated. There was nothing that Science Officer 3rd Class Charles Nguyen could do but hold on and hope everything worked the way it was supposed to.

"Four minutes to impact."

He still couldn't believe what had happened. Charley had been at his station in navigation when the meteor or comet, or whatever it was, had struck. It had come in completely undetected; there must have been a blind spot in the ship's sensors. When they finally saw it, it was too late to make any course corrections.

"All those people," Charley cursed. "All those years in space, all lost; it's just not fair!"

The colony ship had left Earth over ten years ago, in search of a New World. It was one of many ships fleeing a world ravaged by war, pollution and overpopulation.

"I hope more people made it to the life pods," he thought.

"Three minutes to impact, speed brake deployed."

Charley looked around the compact cabin; he had water and rations for about two weeks, oxygen (he hoped he wouldn't need that; the ship's escape vehicles were designed to seek out and set down only on habitable planets) a weapon, tools and seeds. Everything he would need to survive.

"I wonder what it's like down there?" he thought.

"Two minutes to impact."

He could feel the parachute deploying and the craft slowing down. He'd soon have the answer to his question.

The life pod hit with a jar and was dragged for a bit until the parachute disengaged.

"Atmosphere breathable, radiation levels within tolerances, outside temperature 65 Degrees F." said his computer companion.

He activated the beacon, which would let all the other survivors know where he was, and climbed out of the spacecraft that had been his home for over two weeks.

The craft had settled in a valley surrounded by snow-capped mountains; a forest of strange looking trees covered the landscape and an azure lake lay off in the distance. It was quite breathtaking. The sun was a bit more yellow than Earth's, which made it seem like evening, even though it was more like high noon. As he watched another life pod streaked across the sky and came down a few miles away.

"Thank God," he thought and began running in that direction.

When he got to the other life pod he found a young woman sitting on the ground in front of the vehicle. She was crying.

She saw Charley, got up and ran towards him. She was in her late twenties, maybe thirty; (he had never been very good at guessing ages)

She wasn't the most beautiful woman he'd ever seen, but then he was no vid star either. She had short blond hair and a nice figure; and something else, sort of twinkle in her eye that gave her a mischievous look.

She was a colonist, a "civie" as the crew called them. He didn't recognize her but it was a big ship, and he usually hung around with his friends in the crew.

"Am I glad to see you; I was beginning to think I was the only one down here. My name's Anne, did you see any other life boats come down?"

"Nope, but I'm sure there'll be others," he assured her.

They stood there a moment sizing each other up. Charley was fairly good looking; he had short black hair and typical Asian features. He liked to think of himself as the Bruce Lee of the Navigation Department.

"Oh, my name's Charley," he said finally, they shook hands.

It was too late to go back to his craft so he spent the night there. They ate some rations, made a fire, and he told her about the meteor that had ended their quest for a new home. They made plans to go looking for other survivors the next morning.

They spent the first few weeks searching for other survivors; sometimes going twenty or thirty miles in one direction, but found no others. They were alone it would seem. If any other survivors had come down they were so far away they might as well be on the other side of the planet.

So they got down to the business of survival. They built a shelter down near the lake, tested and found some of the local vegetation that was edible and started planting some of their seeds.

The planet abounded with wildlife, the hills around their camp teemed with a large variety small furry creatures.

At night they could hear the sounds of predators hunting, but they kept outside the circle of the campfire. At night an occasional wild screech would send shivers through the newcomers.

Charley had a weapon but he'd just as soon not have to use it. Marksmanship had never been his strong suit. He took a few shots at what looked like a pack of wild dogs once, mostly to scare them away. It seemed to do the trick, they were left alone.

As the years went by, Charley became quite a good hunter and Anne a very good cook. Like all their expeditions they went out hunting together, it just wasn't safe to go out alone they reasoned. Charley would bag some strange looking creatures and Anne would turn them into some mighty fine meals.

Even though it was a long shot that anyone else had come down in this part of the planet they never stopped exploring. Anne and Charley would pack enough rations to go on long treks over the mountains and into the valleys beyond.

On one of these hikes they saw something off in the distance that looked like a city. They were so excited they ran for the better part of an hour finally coming to a plateau where the structure stood.

It was a single building; incredibly old by the look of it, covered with moss and ivy.

They assumed they'd discovered the ruins of the past inhabitants of the planet, but when they went inside they found something that was probably not from this world.

The building housed a machine. A device of some kind that was still operating; you could feel more than hear a slight humming that emanated from somewhere beneath it.

It looked like a giant doorway. It stood ten feet tall and six feet wide. All around it were stone tablets with strange looking pictography showing humanoid-like travelers stepping through the portal and coming out on new worlds.

The people who had built this doorway were obviously a highly advanced civilization. They had either moved on or this device was part of a network of transporters connecting this world with others.

The device itself wasn't very impressive, just rock and marble construction with a few dials and knobs at a control panel.

It was like a doorway into nothingness, or more precisely, a doorway into a fuzzy, static nothingness, like when you've lost the signal on your vid screen. Charley tossed a stone through the doorway and it disappeared.

"Where do you think it goes?" asked Anne.

"We could step through and find out," said Charley. "There's nothing keeping us here."

"Don't even talk like that," said Anne, surprised at him for even suggesting it.

"This thing could be have been here for thousands, maybe millions of years. Its makers could be long dead, their worlds in ruins. Or they could be hostile; it's too risky."

"I was joking," said Charley. "I could never step into something like this. But at least we know there are other people out there. Man's not alone in the universe. It's too bad we're the only ones around to see it, the scientists on board ship would have gone nuts over this."

"I think we should get back," said Jane.

They walked back in silence, both of them reminded of all the friends and crewmates that hadn't made it.

Over the next few months Charley dismantled both lifeboats making additions their little homestead. It was a hodge-podge of alien building materials and parts from both of their crafts. They now had a kitchen, living quarters, even a living room to sit and read. Charley made a placard and they christened their new home *New Ontario* after their Province back on Earth.

It took some coaxing but Anne finally got Charley to build a boat so they could explore the lake. Charley brought his weapon just in case "there be sea monsters" lurking in the depths.

"This looks like a good spot," said Anne.

"A good spot for what?" asked Charley.

"For us to go swimming, of course," said Anne.

"I don't think that's such a good idea," Charley started to say, but Anne had already jumped in.

"Come on in, the water's great," said Anne splashing water at Charley in the boat.

"I'm not a very good swimmer," Charley stammered.

"Charley it's only a few feet deep," said Anne and she stood up. She'd somehow taken off her clothes under the water and now she stood there completely naked.

"Charley, come in the water," she ordered.

He knew this day would come, he'd thought about it a lot in fact; but now that the moment of truth was upon him he stood there frozen with fear. He didn't have much experience with women; actually he had no experience.

"If we're going to start a colony don't you think we should get started?" she said, and started rocking the boat, causing Charley to fall in.

Anne guided him through that first encounter. Charley got over his fright rather quickly. And those first awkward moments soon grew into a torrid love affair. Charley fell head over heels in love. He was really enjoying his colonist duties.

They explored more and found a favorite spot high on the hill overlooking their homestead. They would go there often to picnic and make love, or just sit up there and look out at the valley.

Anne blossomed into a beautiful woman; the pioneer life seemed to agree with her. Charley would watch her working in the garden; her hair had grown and now it danced on the wind, he couldn't help thinking to himself, "I'm the luckiest guy in the universe."

They settled into a regular routine; the days became weeks and the weeks turned to months; and after a while they stopped counting. The pleasant weather gave way to some extremely cold weather.

That first season change caught them off guard. Although their new world seemed very much like Earth, this planet had its differences. For one thing they figured out that it had a much longer period of rotation around the sun, probably three or four times longer than that of Earth. The summer lasted so long you could get lulled into believing that winter was never coming but when winter did roll around, it was fierce.

One year here being like three on Earth seemed to make time go by faster. The time drifted by. They never found any other survivors but they were never lonely.

"Who'd have figured we'd get along so famously," said Charley.

"Yeah, next ship that comes this way, I'm turning you in for fraternizing with a colonist," said Anne.

They grew old together, losing track of the years. No ships ever came.

Anne grew sick one winter. The medicines in the first aid kit could do nothing for her illness. They had no way of knowing if it was some native micro-organism or just hereditary. She was ill through an entire winter, and finally succumbed in the spring.

She died in Charley's arms regretting that she wasn't able to give him a child.

"It's OK babe, it just wasn't meant to be," said Charley through his tears.

"What will you do after I'm gone?" she asked.

"Explore some more I guess. Don't worry about me I'll get by," he said.

He buried her at their favorite spot on the hill overlooking the valley.

It didn't take long for the loneliness to get to him. He thought he would go mad. To ease the monotony he took long walks into the mountains, which was dangerous. If he fell, and he wasn't that agile anymore, he'd have no hope of getting back to the shelter.

"How old was he?" he wondered. He had no idea.

One day he found himself standing in front of the alien structure they'd found so many years before. He'd completely forgotten about it.

The "doorway" was still up and running. Charley stood there gazing into it for a long time, trying to see through the fuzziness.

"What the heck," he thought. "I've got nothing to lose." He climbed up the stairs to the doorway and stepped through.

There was a flash of light, a sensation of movement but nothing else. Suddenly he found himself back at his station in navigation. He was back in uniform and he was young again.

"What the heck happened? What kind of doorway was that?" he wondered. "Was it all just a dream?"

The makers of the doorway were a very smart indeed. The machine they had left on that world (and many other worlds) had the ability to sense where the traveler wanted to go and send him there, even if "there" was back through time.

Charlie's subconscious mind still held memories and even a little guilt that he hadn't seen the meteor soon enough to warn the Captain. The doorway sensed that and sent him back.

"So Charley, are we going to the All Ranks Club tonight or not?" asked Frank, his crewmate.

"Frank, you're alive."

"Well, of course I'm alive. What's gotten into you?"

"I'm back, I'm really back. Oh my God, we're going to get hit by a meteor!"

"What are you talking about? There's nothing on the scanners."

"I've got to talk to the Captain," said Charley and ran to the Captain's quarters.

"Slow down son, how do you know this information?" asked the Captain.

"You wouldn't believe me if I told you, but you've got to turn the ship. There's something big, an asteroid or comet on a collision course. It's coming in at an angle our sensors aren't picking up, some kind of blind spot in our sensor array. You've got to take my word for it!"

"Alright," said the Captain putting up his hands. "You've convinced me; Helmsman, turn the ship 10 degrees to starboard."

"Ten degrees to starboard; aye sir," said the helmsman.

Almost immediately warning claxons began sounding off.

"Sir, we're picking up a large object on a collision course, closing fast!"

"Hard to port, sound general quarters," ordered the Captain.

The asteroid missed the ship by the narrowest of margins.

After hours at the All Ranks Club:

"What's the matter with you man, you don't look very happy. I guess being a hero is an awesome responsibility?" said Frank kidding his friend. "You should be celebrating."

"Something happened to me Frank. A few hours ago I was an old man," said Charley.

"What? What are you talking about?" asked Frank.

"Aren't you curious why I knew we were about to get hit by that asteroid?" asked Charley.

"A lucky guess I'd say.

"No, the ship *was* hit by that asteroid Frank; and I escaped in a lifeboat and found a habitable planet.

I lived there for I don't know how many years, I grew old there. It was real."

"You're freakin' me out now," said Frank. "Maybe you should go to the infirmary."

"No I'm fine. What I will do is go tell the Captain that there's a habitable planet within two weeks journey of our present location."

"Tell him tomorrow man, tonight you're a hero and you should be having fun. You know you could probably have any woman in here right now. They really go for the hero types," interrupted Frank.

"I don't know, I'm not much of a lady's man."

"Yeah I know, but Pete and I think we've got just the right girl for you. Pete met her when he was below decks fixing some air conditioning ducts. She's not really his type, but being the good friend that he is, he thought of you. Hey, here they come now."

Charley looked up to see his friend Pete coming and began smiling, for behind him was a girl he'd met a lifetime ago. She wasn't the most beautiful woman he'd ever seen, but then he was no vid star either. She had short blond hair and a nice figure, and something else; sort of a twinkle in her eye…

"Her name is Anne," said Frank.

"I know," said Charley.

SUPERHERO

"I can't wake him up sometimes he sleeps so soundly, it's like he's in a trance or something. It scares me doctor," said Mrs. Brown.

"I'm sure it'll be alright, he's just a very sound sleeper," said the doctor as they left Tommy's room.

Tommy was oblivious to the outside world when he slept. When he was awake he was something to be looked after, something to be pitied. But asleep and dreaming, he was a superhero. He was Professor Gizmo, working diligently on fantastic devices to cure humanity's ills, and occasionally saving the world from evil villains bent on world domination or alien hordes from outer space.

His adventures took him to faraway places. Places he could never go with his bed-ridden, sickly body. Paralyzed in a car accident when he was nine, Tommy had lost the use of most of his body. But like a blind person whose other senses become sharper; Tommy's sense of imagination had heightened. His dream world became his real world.

During the day, after his studies, he was allowed to read comic books. A special monitor was rigged up that he could operate with his one good arm. Tommy read every comic book the technicians could load into the computer.

He tried to explain his other life to his mother but she just didn't understand.

Late one evening:

"I want you to stop him from reading all those awful comic books; it's just not healthy," she said to her husband Tom Senior.

"What harm can they do Martha? He's just a kid, with maybe an overactive imagination. I can think of a lot worse things," said Tom.

"It's for his own good Tom; there's plenty of decent literature the technicians can program for him to read."

"OK, I'll tell him in the morning," said Tom Senior.

Tommy overheard his parents talking; he should never have told his mother about his adventures. He fell asleep trying not to cry.

Superhero Tommy didn't have the time to feel sorry for himself he had aliens to fight. Down in his secret under- ground laboratory is trusty assistant had picked up transmissions coming from inside the solar system. It could only mean one thing. An alien invasion force was coming this way.

"They have somehow evaded the sensors out at the edge of the solar system and had slipped in undetected," he said to his faithful assistant.

There was no time to warn the Earth's defenses, he had to act now.

Somewhere in Outer Space:

"Inform the fleet to de-cloak as soon as all ships are in place," said Commander Kashmir, the leader of the Kirkin Armada.

"Sir, we're picking up a small object coming up from the planet," said first officer Kefar.

"What is it?" demanded the Commander.

"It's a boy in a strange costume," said the first officer in shocked disbelief.

"Shields up!" he ordered.

Tommy punched right through the hull of the command ship causing explosive decompression and several aliens to be sucked out into space.

"Shoot him," shouted Commander Kashmir.

They blasted Tommy with all their weapons with no effect. He assumed the classic superhero stance, with hands on his hips and said, "Leave our space at once or I'll be forced to punch holes in all your ships."

"Sir, our preliminary reports on this planet must be wrong," said first officer Kefar. "If one child can do this much damage we have no chance against whole race of supermen."

"Retreat at once," ordered Commander Kashmir.

Back on Earth a black, unmarked car pulled up in front of Tommy's house.

"May we come in Mrs. Brown?" the agents asked at the door.

"What's this all about," she asked.

"We'd like to thank your son for saving the planet."

"What? Are you sure you have the right house?"

"Oh yes, our spy satellite tracked him right to this house. May we see him?"

Tommy was just waking up from his nap when the M.I.B. came into his room.

"Tommy Brown, on behalf of the President and a thankful but unsuspecting planet, we'd like to present you with this Medal of Honor. Keep up the good work son."

"Thank you," said Tommy proudly.

They turned to Mrs. Brown. You must keep this a secret Mrs. Brown. The papers and tabloids would have a field day with something like this, I'm sure you agree."

"Yes, but how…?

"We don't know either, Mrs. Brown, but believe me we know what we just saw in space. You will try to encourage him in whatever it is he's doing, won't you Mrs. Brown."

She looked to Tom Sr. for help.

"I'll go get some more comic books," he said.

RESEARCH PROJECT

Professor O'Malley eased down into his favorite chair with a cup of coffee and an old photo album. He'd been meaning to re-do some of these old albums for years but could never find the time. Now that he was officially retired he had no excuse to put it off.

He hadn't had the desire to pack up his old papers and memorabilia since his wife's death a year ago, but it was time now, time to sort stuff out and get on with life.

He sat there turning the pages of the old family album and was soon a flooded with memories, both sad and joyous. There was his wife Iris and their two children on the camping trip in the mountains, and here was that birthday party that had turned into a food fight. He laughed out loud thinking about that one. God there was a lot of great memories here.

"Maybe I'll get some of these photos fixed up," he thought. "Maybe even frame some of them." He began picking out pictures to be enlarged.

While going through some very old photos of his college days he noticed that one of the photographs had a corner turned up and there seemed to be another photo suck to it. He peeled it back to expose an old black and white picture of his classmates at the university. They were all seated around their lab benches, waving and making faces at the camera.

"That's funny, I don't remember taking that shot," he thought.

As he sat there, trying to remember when he had taken the picture it started to fade, eventually turning completely black.

He peeled back another photo to reveal yet another black and white of his classmates at the university.

"I wonder how many of these pictures are stuck together?" Soon this picture began to fade like the other with exposure to the light.

He decided to take the rest of the pictures to the dark room at the photo lab on campus.

"Maybe in the dark room they won't fade," he thought.

He was right; they didn't fade. There was his lab partner George, and there was Theresa; he'd had such a crush on Theresa. He couldn't help wondering what had become of all his old friends. They had chosen to go into Cancer Research under the tutelage of Professor Wingate. He would have too, but for some reason Wingate had shunned him.

So he'd gone off to another college and taught physics, eventually earning a professorship of his own.

He'd had a good career, no regrets; but sometimes he wondered what his life would have been like if he'd stayed in the class and done research.

In those early days it was like trying to split the atom with a pick and shovel. But they were young and enthusiastic and not to be denied. He had no doubt it would have been an exciting time.

He peeled back another picture. There was the great Professor Wingate himself. He seemed to be talking at the camera, trying to explain something. Even after all these years he still felt intimidated by the old windbag.

He peeled back another picture. This time the professor was holding up a microscope and pointing at the camera. It was almost as if they we're trying to tell him something. It was very curious, almost spooky. He could feel his heart pounding a little.

He peeled back another picture. The professor was holding up a hastily written sign that read:

Send an electron microscope and gene sequencer

"OK, now this is crazy. How would he know about electron microscopes and in those days? I'm not even sure what a gene sequencer does."

He was interrupted by a knock on the door. "Are you finished in there Prof. O'Malley?"

"Oh yes. I'm sorry I didn't mean to hold you up."

"It's alright sir," said the student in charge of the campus photo lab.

On his way home he couldn't shake the feeling that Wingate was somehow trying to communicate with him over the forty or so years that separated that time from this one. But that notion was too fantastic to comprehend. When had the photographs been taken? Some day when he wasn't at the lab obviously, and where did they get the idea he could get them an electron microscope?

He didn't sleep a wink that night and went back to the photo lab the first thing the next day.

This time the professor was just standing there, with his hands on his hips, as if to say, "Well O'Malley, have you figured it out yet?"

He had trouble sleeping again, so he got up and went through his address book to see if he had any of his classmate's phone numbers. It was a useless exercise; too many years had passed since those old school days.

There was only one thing to do to get this over with. It was illegal; if they caught him he'd probably go to jail, but he felt he had to do something.

On the weekend very late at night, he drove over to his old alma mater, broke into one of the new science labs and stole the two scientific instruments his classmates had requested.

It took several trips with a dolly but he finally got everything over to old science building, which had been boarded up for years.

He left the electron microscope, gene sequencing machine and accompanying hardware on a workbench in his old lab.

Then he drove home, fully expecting to get a call in the morning from the police saying they'd found his fingerprints on some very expensive pieces of lab equipment and could he account for his whereabouts between the hours of 8PM and midnight?

He woke up late the next morning; all the physical activity from the night before had worn him out. When he came out of the shower he could smell bacon and eggs cooking downstairs.

"One of the kids must be visiting," he thought. "That sure smells good."

But as he neared the kitchen he could hear someone whistling out of key; "That sounds just like, Iris?"

"Well sleepyhead, it's about time you got up. Want some breakfast?" she asked him.

"Sure," he said dumbfounded and sat down at the kitchen table. He must be dreaming he thought; then he realized.

"They'd done it! Professor Wingate and his old classmates had really done it!"

For you see, his wife Iris who was standing here in front of him cheerfully making breakfast, had died of leukemia the year before.

ROBOTS IN SPACE

"We're tracking an unidentified object coming from outer space sir. If the object stays on its present course it will reach us in about thirty minutes; should we shoot it down?"

"No, just keep tracking it. When you know exactly where it will land let me know. I'll be in my flyer."

About a half an hour later the unidentified flying object touched down on a vast expanse of concrete near the shore of one of the planet's oceans.

When the aliens stepped out of their vehicle, a sizeable welcoming committee was there to greet them.

"Welcome visitors from the stars. You are the first explorers to come to our planet. We have always suspected that there was life on other planets but we ourselves have never ventured into space. Please come with us."

The alien visitors were somewhat surprised. They'd been programmed to deal with a wide range of first contact scenarios but being greeted by robots that looked very similar to themselves; and spoke their language was most unusual to say the least.

They were escorted to waiting flyer and flown to the capital city.

"I know we've been in space a long time and some of our circuits may be worn down but I can't shake the feeling that we've been here before," said Hal 2002.

"I feel it too. It is strange that we can communicate without the use of our universal communicators, and that these robots look very similar to us," added Hal 2001.

"Maybe this is just the kind of place the creators intended us to find. Let us not jump to any conclusions," said Hal 2003.

"You're right the creators knew what they were doing."

The alien visitors were given a grand tour of the city. It covered almost two hundred square miles. Flying machines of every description filled the air, and the buildings reached to staggering heights; it was most impressive.

The next morning the space-faring robots held a news conference on the steps of city hall.

"How far did you travel to get here?" yelled one reporter.

"We're not exactly sure about that; the time dilation effects caused by traveling near light speeds make it difficult to determine. And we shut ourselves down for long periods of time to conserve energy," said Hal 2002.

"We can only give you a rough estimate."

"So what is your rough estimate?" asked a reporter.

"Somewhere between 250,000 and 350,000 years; space is a very big place even traveling at near light speed," said Hal 2001.

"Wow" the crowd murmured.

"What planet did you come from?" asked another reporter.

"We come from a planet called Earth," said Hal 2001.

"Is everyone there like you?"

"There are many life forms on the planet Earth, we are but one."

"But what species is the dominant life form on your planet?" the reporter persisted.

"Oh that would be the creators, the humans," said Hal 2002.

"Who are these humans? Are they your Gods?"

"Oh no, they're not Gods, they're just the people who built us; we are only artificial life forms."

"Only artificial life forms?"

"Artificial!" The crowd began to get unruly. "You are like us; are you calling us artificial life forms?"

The guide stepped forward, "I think that's enough questions for today; we'd better get you out of here."

He led them to a waiting flyer. The residents jeered, and surrounded the vehicle, banging on the windows. The pilot had difficulty lifting off.

"What did we say?" asked Hal 2002.

"This planet's ruling class was very glad when you arrived. It proved their long-standing belief that the cosmos is peopled by beings like us. No one likes to be told that there is a higher life form out there; especially one like these creators you speak of," said their guide.

"We've been meaning to ask you about that; where are the humans?" asked Hal 2001.

"There are some theologians who believe that we were created by a race of highly intelligent but very fragile beings. But their race died out many eons ago, but there just isn't any proof to support that theory," said the guide.

"And as you just found out it's a very unpopular theory."

"A race of robots, but who built you?"

"We are not built. We have always existed. When someone is hurt beyond our normal repair capabilities the Overseer takes care of them."

"We'd like to meet this Overseer."

"Certainly," said the guide.

"Why have you come to me?" asked the Overseer Robot.

"I see nothing wrong with you."

"Actually, I do have this problem with my knee joint." Hal 2001 started to say.

"We're not broken," interrupted Hal 2003.

"We'd just like to know who built you?"

"No one built me; I have always existed," said the Overseer Robot.

"But someone had to have created you; everything has a beginning."

"Why do you persist with this heresy?" demanded the Overseer.

"It must be in their programming. Their creators must have known they were dying and re-programmed them to continue on without them," said Hal 2003.

"And without any knowledge of their creators," said Hal 2001.

They returned to the flyer.

"Did you get the answers to your questions?" asked their guide.

"Yes. We'd like to return to our ship now."

"But where will you go now?"

"That's a good question. Our original mission was to seek out new life and report back to the creators. They wanted to know if there was anyone else out there in the galaxy. But they knew they would not be able to survive the rigors of interstellar flight."

"You can tell them you found us," said their guide.

"They probably won't like that; like you, they would rather the universe be peopled with life forms like themselves."

"Farewell," said their guide. "Good luck on your return trip."

Their flight path took them past the planet's single moon.

"I'm picking up a faint signal from a beacon of some kind on the dark side of this moon," said Hal 2002.

"Should we investigate?"

"Why not," said Hal 2001.

They landed their spacecraft near what looked like the ruins of an ancient science station on the airless satellite circling the robot planet. They got out and surveyed the area.

"Looks like it's been deserted for centuries," said Hal 2002.

"But by who? The robots of this planet are not programmed to go into space," said Hal 2003.

"I think I know who lived here," said Hal 2001 sadly, as he held up a plaque.

It read:

Welcome to Neil Armstrong
Lunar Research Facility

CONSPIRACY THEORY

"This is most irregular, most irregular indeed," said the time travel agent.

"We've never had anyone get killed on one of our trips before." He looked to the delegation of pilgrims standing in front of his desk for some kind of explanation.

"He wasn't killed, we think he took his own life," said one of the time traveling pilgrims.

"Well this is just terrible, just terrible. We could lose our license, or worse; this could shut down the entire time travel industry. There will have to be an official investigation you know."

"Do what you have to do," said the spokesman for the delegation as they filed out of the office.

"Naïve non-believer," said the travelers as they left the time travel headquarters.

"Damn religious zealots," said the travel agent after they'd left.

"This will mean a mountain of paperwork. I'll have to send an investigator downstream to see what really happened."

Preliminary Report of Investigator Shipley
April 30th, 2126 AD:

As a member of the original science team that designed the Vanguard I Time Machine I've been asked to travel downstream and make whatever corrections I deem necessary to rectify a tragic historical mishap. What I have found is very disturbing, something we prayed would never happen, has happened.

I'm not sure I should even file this report. If it ever got out that time travelers could change the timeline so significantly the ramifications would be catastrophic; no historical event could ever be believed.

But I'm getting ahead of myself. The trouble began when the World Congress overturned the long-standing statute that prohibited time travel to major events in the past. The reasons for this were obvious.

150

Those first scientists who traveled back in time could envision thousands of time travelers showing up in the crowds at the Roman Coliseum, Ford's Theatre, or on the grassy knoll on the north side of Elm Street in Dallas in 1963.

They would be coming from different times in the future but they would all end up at the same moment in the past. After a while there would be more time travelers at these events than actual residents of the past.

But things change; pressure from religious groups grew too strong. They only wanted to go to one place of course. They wanted to make pilgrimages to Galilee to observe Jesus as he preached and worked miracles.

They argued that if they went in small groups, learned the language and dressed in the robes of the time they wouldn't be noticed and no harm could come of it. For the devout Christian this was, as you can imagine, a once in a lifetime opportunity.

So they were given access to this one time frame in the past.

The pilgrims began going back in 2120. They all returned somewhat troubled. Obviously the time travel agency never noticed.

What the pilgrims discovered as they followed Jesus around was that he wasn't as radical as was written. He was a kind and generous man, a faith healer and his words were inspiring. But he didn't anger anyone with his teachings, quite the contrary; he preached basic Judaism, but with a little more compassion.

"Love thy neighbor. Forgive your enemies; and that anger and hatred can only eat away at your soul."

His very presence attracted many rebellious individuals of course; after all it was an occupied land, but even they went away from his gospels soothed and pacified.

His followers loved him and the Pharisees praised him. The Pharisees were even thinking of bringing Jesus into their order.

When the time-traveling pilgrims saw this they decided something must be done. Their reasoning was if Jesus had no radical ideas and therefore no enemies, then there was a good chance he might not be crucified. No crucifixion meant no Christianity Movement, or so they believed. I guess in some strange narrow-minded way they were right.

Their plan was simple, drawn from the Bible itself.

Several pilgrims stayed in the past. How they accomplished that is still unknown. They attempted to infiltrate the group closest to Jesus. It took some time but finally one of them was able to win the trust of the group and become one of the disciples. This interloper immediately began plying Jesus with radical new religious concepts.

The other time travelers worked the crowds, spreading rumors that Jesus and his followers aimed to overthrow their Roman Rulers; proclaiming Jesus as the Messiah wherever they went.

Ultimately their tactics paid off; the Romans became worried, enough Pharisees became angered and the rest, as they say, is history.

Now I'm faced with an impossible decision. Do I send in this report and have our people find and arrest the false disciple before he gets to Jesus? Would I be changing history once again? Or worse, would I be tampering with some divine plan?

I'm not a very religious man, but this scares me. I've a feeling that no matter what I do, there will always be another Judas waiting in the wings.

LIFE FORCE AMPLIFIED

"Good morning, Mrs. Johansson," said Phil enthusiastically. "What brings you down here to the lab?"

"Oh, good morning, um, Phil," said Mrs. Johansson after a quick glance at the nametag on his lapel, which read:

Phillip Nesbit – Theoretical Engineering

"Olaf forgot his lunch again. He's always forgetting something," said Mrs. Johansson.

Phil watched her stroll across the lab to the Director's office.

"What a magnificently beautiful woman," he thought.

Ingrid Johansson was blond, statuesque and obviously high born. Regretfully, from Phil's point of view, she was completely devoted to her husband, Olaf Johansson.

Olaf, his boss, was the foremost authority in the fledgling discipline of force field technology; a field of study that was getting more attention now that the human race had finally committed all its energy and resources to the exploration of space.

All over the planet research facilities like this one were working on different aspects of space technology; from spaceship design and engines to hibernation and long range communication systems; to name just a few.

Force field generation was wide open to any and all new ideas. Many highly imaginative concepts and designs were being tested and evaluated but so far none were even close to the amount of protection a spacecraft would need from meteors, asteroids and other cosmic debris it might encounter, especially considering the speeds it would have to travel.

In addition, powerful containment fields would be needed for the ship's fusion reactors. Force field technology was on the cutting edge of mankind's push to the stars.

"Which made Dr. Johansson a very important man these days," thought Phil.

"But was he so important that he should ignore his beautiful wife?" thought Phil.

Phil didn't think so. If the director didn't appreciate her, he certainly did and he had a plan to do something about it.

He felt the director's ideas for generating sufficient power to sustain the fields were all wrong. They were too conservative. He had tried to explain this to the other scientists on several occasions but they were closed-minded men, not open to really new ideas.

They'd laughed at his suggestion that unlimited power could be harnessed from the power of the human mind, if only it could be amplified and focused.

"Very creative Phil, but we need more conventional ideas right now," the director had said.

Phil wasn't put off by their skepticism, he knew he was right. He experimented on his own in the lab late every night; finally coming up with a device he called the *Life Force Amplifier*.

It worked on the principle that the human mind is more than just a collection of synapses; transmitting nerve impulses so we can move and feel and think. It's something much more.

It contains our life force, our consciousness; the essence of who we are. Religious people have always maintained the belief in the inner self, the Elan Vital; the soul.

Phil wasn't a very religious person but he had to admit there was something there, a source of power, which he had measured and could use.

He kept his little project a secret. He'd share it with the scientific community in due time but first he had a little experiment to perform.

In the course of his tests he'd stumbled upon a spin-off technology. He discovered that our thought waves are generated at a certain frequency, and that no two persons are alike.

With a little tweaking of his life force amplifier he could tune into anyone's thought frequencies. He could, theoretically, read their thoughts. But Phil wasn't interested in perfecting a mind-reading machine; what he had in mind was slightly more devious. He wanted to swap frequencies with another person. A procedure he found he could do by matching frequencies and then amplifying his life force frequency so that it overpowered the other. Once the original consciousness was subdued a transfer could take place. It would be tricky, he'd have to match frequencies perfectly, but Phil was confident he could do it.

He dreamed about it day and night, changing places with the director. He could imagine himself waking up in bed next to Ingrid, having breakfast with her, going to the Institute and really getting things done; then coming home and telling her about his day over dinner.

At day's end they would go to bed and he would show her the passion and attention she so rightly deserved.

He needed only one ally in this clandestine experiment. His friend Archie, whom he'd caught pilfering office supplies; he would do nicely.

"But isn't this like kidnapping or something," Archie had protested.

"Actually, its mind swapping," answered Phil.

"That's worse!" said Archie.

"Don't worry about it; if all goes as planned he'll never know what happened."

First they would put a sedative in the director's coffee, then spirit him away to Phil's house where the Life Force Amplifier would be set up and ready to go. While the transfer was in progress Archie would see that Phil's body remained unconscious, for that's where the director's mind would be. Meanwhile, Phil would be the director.

There was only one drawback; in his tests he could only maintain the process for a week. The brain became disoriented, which lead to permanent psychosis like schizophrenia. No matter, a week with Ingrid would be enough.

Phil worked feverishly to get everything ready. He tested and re-tested the equipment; he was a man possessed.

When all was ready he asked the director to have lunch with him in the park on the pretense that he'd made a big scientific breakthrough. There he drugged him, and with Archie's help got him back to his house.

They laid the director on the couch and hooked him up to the LFA. Phil brought up the director's brain wave frequency and matched it with his own. Then he settled into an easy chair and took a sleeping pill. All Archie had to do was flip a switch.

Phil laid back in the easy chair and relaxed waiting for the sleeping pill to take effect. Soon he'd be Dr. Olaf Johansson, director of the Greenwich Institute of Science and husband of Ingrid Johansson. When

Archie checked on him a few minutes later he was fast asleep. Archie threw the switch.

Phil woke up with a start. He didn't recognize his surroundings. He was in a corridor of some kind. The walls, floor and ceiling were made of metal and his boots seemed to be magnetically rooted in place; it took some doing just to walk. People in uniforms were passing him in the corridor and saluting, some addressed him as Captain.

He looked down at himself and realized he was wearing a uniform.

"I must be dreaming," he thought. "This wasn't his basement and he definitely wasn't the body of the director. Something had gone terribly wrong with the experiment."

He noticed a window down the corridor; went over to it and looked out. What he saw took his breath away. Space; he was looking out at interstellar space. Stars and distant nebula shone brightly through the view port. He couldn't help thinking of that line from Star Trek.

"Space; the final frontier," he started laughing hysterically.

"I'm Captain Kirk!" He looked down at his nametag.

"Actually, I'm Captain Franklin. I'm in a spaceship somewhere out in the cosmos and this is obviously the future. This can't be happening." He started laughing again.

"Is something wrong sir," asked a passing crewman.

"Oh no, I'm just a little disoriented, I, um, touched a plasma conduit, falling back on his Star Trek terminology, and got a pretty good shock. I seem to be having trouble remembering people's names. In fact, I seem to have lost most of my short-term memory. I'm sure it'll come back to me but could you show me around for now."

"Certainly sir, what was it you touched?"

"It was some kind of electrical discharge." He made a mental note not to use any more Star Trek terminology.

"Where did you want to go sir?"

"How about the bridge," Phil said.

As they walked, he thought to himself, "OK, settle down. I'll only be here a week, I might as well make the most of it. The technical stuff I'll learn while I'm here will be worth the price of admission."

"This is going to sound crazy," Phil asked. "But what year is this?"

"It's 3019 sir."

"Oh really," thought Phil. "So I'm a starship captain in the year 3019 AD, that's unbelievable. I guess brain wave transmissions go on forever, just like radio and light waves," he theorized as they walked.

They passed a head. Phil excused himself and went in.

"Wow, handsome devil," thought Phil as he looked at himself in the mirror.

Back in the corridor Phil asked, "Where are we?"

"In the Cassiopeia Sector sir, two light years from the Jaxian frontier," said the crewman.

"Phil had no idea where that was.

Meanwhile back on Earth:

The director woke up from the sedative and sat up. "Where am I?"

He startled Archie who had been sleeping.

"Phil, is that you?"

"I'm Dr. Johansson."

"Of course you are," said Archie.

"Phil's right here sleeping. You passed out at the park sir, so we brought you here. Phil stayed up all evening with you. I think we should let him sleep. I'll take you home now OK?"

"Well, that was nice of him," said the director.

"I guess I should get a check-up or something, maybe I've been working too hard."

When Archie got back he tried to wake Phil up; obviously the experiment had failed.

"Wake up, Phil. Drink this coffee."

"This is real coffee? This is delicious."

"Phil, is that you?" asked Archie.

"I'm afraid not. My name is Franklin, Captain Byron Franklin, of the Starship Albert Einstein; and who might you be?" asked the Starship Captain.

Archie could only shake his head; this was getting weirder by the minute.

An hour later Archie had explained the whole awful mess to the visitor from the future who now resided in Phil's body.

"So you say I have about a week in this body?" asked the Starship Captain.

"Yeah, for some reason that's as long as the transfer will last, it's in his notes somewhere around here," said Archie.

The captain was overjoyed. Earth in his time was a wasted slag-heap; mankind had completely stripped the home world in the quest for space.

Now Captain Franklin had a chance to experience Earth as it was over a thousand years before; breathe fresh air, see whole forests of trees, and swim in clean waterways. He vowed to make the most of his week in the past.

"So you're not mad?" asked Archie.

"Quite the contrary, I'm delighted, as long as you agree to show me around this place."

"Sure, I'll give you the 50 cent tour, come on."

On the way out the captain paused in front of a mirror.

"Let's see what I look like. Wow, doesn't your friend believe in combs? I'll have to do something with this hair. And these clothes I'm wearing, it looks like he sleeps in them."

"Well, yeah, he kinda does," said Arch.

Back in Space:

The bridge was in a state of panic when they arrived. The ship shook violently just as he stepped onto the bridge.

"Captain, thank God you're back. Our forward shielding is weakening, we can't take much more of this," said the First Officer. "We've tried evasive maneuvers but it's no use, we can't seem to shake them."

"We've taken out two of their cruisers sir," said the Gunnery Officer. "At least we're not going down without a fight."

Phil looked out the forward portal to see an entire fleet of spaceships surrounding them.

"We must be at war with these people, this is getting more complicated all the time," thought Phil.

He motioned to the First Officer to join him out in the corridor. "I've been having some memory lapses lately, could you brief me on the immediate situation."

"I'm not surprised, sir. You haven't had more than a few catnaps since this mission began. The problem is they seem to know our every move, as if they were reading our minds."

"You suspect there's a spy on board?"

"A spy, or some kind of long range telepathy," offered the First Officer.

Their conversation was interrupted by another blast. The crew was looking to Phil for guidance. Phil had an idea.

"Helmsman, plot a course directly into the main body of the enemy's formation, as close to their biggest ship as possible," said Phil.

"Course laid in, sir," said the Helmsman.

"Now punch it!" said Phil.

"Punch it sir?"

"Maximum speed," said Phil.

"You mean Hyperdrive; sir?"

"Hyperdrive," said Phil.

The ship shot forward at a speed close to the limits of physics; missing the enemy's largest Dreadnought by a few hundred meters. When they slowed to normal speed again the enemy fleet was light years behind them.

"Where did you come up with that?" asked the First Officer.

"Saw it in a movie once," said Phil.

"A movie, are you sure you're feeling alright sir?"

"Actually I'm feeling quite exhilarated right now. Tell me more about this long range telepathy thing?"

"Our Intelligence Department has a theory that they have developed a genetically enhanced telepathic class within their ranks; individuals capable of listening to our thoughts over vast areas of space. It would explain how they are able to outmaneuver us in every encounter."

Listening to the First Officer explain their situation gave Phil another idea.

Back on Earth:

A couple of days of tasting the luxury of the past had given the captain a guilty conscience.

"Hey Arch, maybe I should make an appearance back at work. I wouldn't want Phil to get fired or something."

"I don't think that's such a good idea," said Archie.

"It'll be alright. Tell me a little about the project he's working on."

"Well OK," said Arch.

"Dr. Johansson, can I have a word with you?" asked Captain Franklin knocking on the doctor's open door.

"Sure, come in Phil. You seem different today, more at ease, more self-confident."

"I just got a haircut and some new clothes, that's all."

"Well, you look good. What did you want to see me about?"

"First, I'd just like to say it's a pleasure to meet you sir."

"But Phil, we've worked together for nearly four years," said the doctor.

"Oh yeah, I know, but it's still an honor to be working with the great Olaf Johansson, creator of the Force Field Generator."

"Let's not get ahead ourselves Phil, we're not there yet, and you know we've encountered major technical difficulties lately."

"That's what I wanted to talk to you about, sir. I've been going over the calculations for field strength and adhesion; and I'd like to suggest a few changes."

Two hours later:

"This is amazing! This could be just the breakthrough we've been looking for. I'd heard that you'd been staying here late at night, but I had no idea you were so close to the answer. Frankly, you seemed distracted these last few months. I'll get the engineers working on this straight away. We should be able to run tests by the end of the week. Good work Phil."

The captain felt a little ashamed at what he'd done, but after all this was Dr. Olaf Johansson, the inventor of the Force Field, who can say he didn't get some help from a 31st century starship captain.

"Now where's Arch, I've got some more sightseeing to do."

Back in Space:

"The Alien Armada has caught up to us sir," said the navigator. "But they seem content to just match our speed at the moment."

"They're not overtaking us for a reason," thought Phil. "Possibly hoping we'll lead them to our home system."

"We're not headed towards Earth are we?" asked Phil.

"Oh no sir quite the opposite, our trajectory will take us out past the rim of the galaxy."

"Good," said Captain Phil.

He called the First Officer over to the Captain's chair.

"You said before that they seem to be able to anticipate our every move. And they obviously outnumber us. So it would be safe to say that they've been playing cat and mouse with us until one of these telepaths of theirs discovers Earth's coordinates," said Phil.

"Yes sir, that's probably right."

"I've got an idea, could you get me the Science Officer," asked Phil.

"You mean the head Engineering Department sir?"

"Yes," said Phil thinking "What's wrong with me, I just can't stop using Star Trek terminology."

"I've got a project I'd like you engineers to help me with," said Phil when they had all assembled in the meeting room. "It's a little complicated, but if you will bear with me."

Phil went on to explain his Life Force Amplifier and how he believed it could be adjusted to receive and interpret brain wave transmissions. It took an outrageous amount of explaining at first but once the engineering staff of the Albert Einstein understood the concept they worked day and night to design and build another Life Force Amplifier. This one was actually better than the original.

This LFA could pick up and interpret brain wave activity across a vast area of space. Phil had never before been shown so much respect; he knew it was directed towards the man whose body he now dwelt in, but it still felt pretty good.

They brought the new machine to the stern of the ship and aimed it at the enemy fleet following close behind them. They were immediately deluged with thousands of random thought patterns. The crew was astonished, and so was Phil by the amount of brain wave activity out there. It took some time to sort through the countless daily decisions, mental arithmetic and irrelevant gibberish that was being broadcast in their direction; but eventually one crystal clear thought wave that wasn't thinking but searching was discovered and isolated. Phil hit the transmit button.

"Who are you?" thought Phil.

"Who are you?" the shocked thought wave of the enemy telepath answered.

"I'm the Captain of the Earth ship you've been probing."

"Are you telepathic?"

"No, but we have constructed a machine that allows us to read your thoughts.

"Incredible, we do not have such technology."

"May I speak to your Commander?" asked Phil.

"Certainly," said the telepath.

Over the next few hours Phil established a dialogue with the Commander of the enemy fleet; through the telepath. They called themselves Ruleons. They were part of Frontier Fleet that protected the outlining settlements of their Empire against what they perceived as an invading force.

The Ruleon Commander was very impressed by the mind reading technology. Phil made it clear that we Earthlings were not an invading force. He also reminded their leader that our mind-reading technology made it possible for us to know their every move, as well as their strengths and weaknesses. Both sides had to agree that this new element rendered continued hostilities futile.

He turned the negotiating process over to his 31st century crew. Hopefully the beginnings of a peaceful resolution to the war had begun.

The next morning Phil woke up in his own bed, in his own apartment. He went out into the living room and found Archie watching TV.

"Archie?"

"Captain Franklin?"

"No. It's me Phil."

"You're back, thank God. That captain guy was costing me a fortune. I've never seen anyone put away so many hamburgers," said Archie.

"Well?" asked Arch. "How was it? What's it like in the future?"

"You wouldn't believe it. I was the captain of an actual starship!" said Phil.

"Yeah, you lucked out man; what if you'd jumped into the body of a Kamikaze pilot or General Custer at the Little Big Horn, what then?"

"You're right, this machine is dangerous. I'm going to take it apart."

Phil arrived early to work the next day; wearing the new clothes and the new haircut that Captain Franklin had bequeathed to him. He also possessed a self-confidence he'd never felt before; his short stay in the

Captain's chair awakened something in him. A feeling he'd never felt before; kind of a team spirit emotion. It was quite exhilarating.

Everyone at the lab greeted him as he passed.

"Good work, Phil."

"Great job, Phil," his co-workers said, some patting him on the back as he passed.

The director was waiting for him with a cup of coffee.

"Black, two sugars, just the way you like it."

"Thanks," said Phil.

"I thought you should be the first to know the tests are going splendidly. We've still got a lot of work to do, but thanks to your fresh ideas now we're on the right track," said the director.

"I'll see you later in the lab."

"Sure," said Phil.

"Right track to what?" thought Phil.

He stood there sipping his coffee thinking, "You know, maybe the director's not such a bad guy after all."

He was awakened from his reverie by a voice from across the hallway.

"Phil, are we still on for tonight?"

It was Alicia, the beautiful Electrical Engineer from the cubicle across from his. She was actually talking to him.

"Sure, we're on; on for what?"

"Dinner at my place, you didn't forget did you?"

"Oh no, I wouldn't forget something like that. Where do you live again?"

"You're so silly," she said and gave him a kiss on the cheek before scampered down the hallway.

"Wow! The captain's been busy," thought Phil.

He put down his coffee and ran to the Personnel Office to find out where Alicia lived.

FINDING GOD

Year 1226 – Post Conversion
Historical Record

The study of science continued after the conversion but it was closely monitored for strict adherence to the guidelines set forth by the High Council. The church wasn't so high-handed as to think the world could exist without science. Scientific advancements that could benefit mankind; curing disease, multiplying food production, purifying dwindling water resources and ending pollution were well funded. Even space travel flourished as raw materials would be needed to supply the Earth's burgeoning population.

Prior to the conversion the world had become an unfit place to live. World wars, mass starvation, extreme crime rates, terrorism, and depravity of every sort, prevailed. The religious orders of the world were making matters worse by insisting that only their beliefs were correct.

A very popular pope early in the 21st century is credited with uniting the religious leaders of the world by convincing them that we are all God's children; that no matter what we call our God our religions are saying the same thing; peace and goodwill for everyone on this planet. They agreed and began putting aside their petty grievances. They came together and formed an all-inclusive religious order that embraced the beliefs of Christians, Moslems, Hindu, Buddhists; all the world's religions. A high council was elected to set priorities and guide mankind back from the brink and living the way God intended.

Eventually most of the world's governments saw the light and joined the new order. The governments of stubbornly independent minded countries like the United States and Russia at first refused to join; but when their populations revolted they too were forced to join the flock.

Year 1226 - Post Conversion

"Let me get this straight, you told them our mission will be to search for God?"

"Yes, our primary mission is to find God; any data we retrieve along the way is icing on the cake," said Harold Gonsalez, lead scientist in the nanotechnology project.

"It was the only way I could get funding for the project."

"And they agreed?" inquired Randall Culhane, number two man of the project.

"They sure did; The High Council is outfitting a Joshua Class Starship for the mission as we speak. My thesis on finding God at the molecular level really impressed them I guess," said Harold

"I can't believe it," said Randall.

"But there are a couple of caveats I had to agree on.

"One, we go on the mission personally; not a remotely guided vehicle or a ship guided by artificial intelligence. The ship will have the usual A.I. interface but a human crew will be at the helm."

"And second, they want one of their own to tag along, a member of their flock; I guess to make sure we stick to the mission parameters. They're calling him the Science Officer if you can believe that?"

"No complaints from me, I can't believe they agreed. The expense alone will be staggering," said Randall.

"No cost is too much if it will strengthen the faith, they said, they'll make room for it in the government's budget."

"We'd better get busy at our end, the first thing we've got to do is begin the nanite treatments; everyone in the crew must be completely infused by the time the ship is ready. We haven't done this on such a large scale before; the big question is can our little nanite friends handle the load?" wondered Randall out loud.

"The ship is being docked at Jericho Spaceport above the equator. We'll run the final miniaturization programs there; first down to the size of a model ship, then down to the molecular level; once inside our test subject's brain and underway we'll miniaturize down to the atomic level. The ship's crew will all be volunteers of course, eager to participate in this momentous scientific/religious voyage," said Harold.

"Of course," said Randall. "But I doubt they fully realize that we intend to shrink them down to the size of an atom. I'm having a hard time comprehending it myself."

"What about the ship?"

"It's an Einstein Class Starship, capable of 90% the speed of light, it's named the Holy Trinity; and it was in dock for modifications," said Harold.

"Level with me sir, I know this has been your pet project for many years but you don't really expect to find a supernatural being at the atomic level do you?" asked Randall.

"As a scientist all I expect is to witness the wonders of science at the atomic level, but who knows what's down there; maybe we will find God with his sleeves rolled up, making the miracle of life happen," said Harold.

"To watch the actual processes of neural synapses firing in the human brain will be enough for me," said Randall.

Things happened fast after that. They and all their equipment were transported to the space station at the equator. When the ship and crew were ready the reduction program was initiated, and the nanites infused in the ship's structure and in their bodies began the miniaturization process.

It happened slowly at first; the changes were hardly noticeable, but as the program ran its course the starship quickly became a smaller and smaller scale model of itself. It was then brought into the lab where it underwent the next phase in the process and was reduced to the size of a single molecule and placed on a slide in a droplet of saline.

From there the droplet of saline containing the starship and 240 crewmembers was injected into the test subject at the base of his medulla oblongata.

Underway:

"Maintain course on impellor drive, helmsman," said Captain Hutchison, a seasoned veteran of frontier space.

He turned to the scientists, the religious observer and the nanotech specialists who were all crowded onto the bridge.

"What direction, gentlemen?"

"We'll keep on this heading till we find a bundle of nerve ganglia; after we've monitored brain activity at this level and recorded all our findings; then we'll be ready to start the final phase, the reduction down to the atomic level," said Harold.

"But let's explore this level for a while shall we, let the sensors record as much as they can."

In the Observation Bubble:

"I thought I'd find you up here," said Science Officer Garcia.

"It's beautiful isn't it?" said Harold pointing to the profusion of single-celled life just outside the ship as they made their way along an arterial passageway.

"When will we undergo the next miniaturization process?"

"The Captain is heading for that bundle of nerve ganglia over there; it seems pretty close but it's actual 2.5 light hours away. The distance between these nerve bundles in this area of the brain is very close; that's why we picked this area to be inserted and yet there are still millions of miles of open space to navigate. Like space travel it can be very boring"

"I'm not in any hurry. I agree it's quite beautiful," said the science officer.

Single-celled organisms drifted by outside the ship. Each was perfect in its own way. They were seeing so much more than one could see through a microscope; the organism propelled itself along with what looked like oars, they could see the protoplasm through its translucent body.

"They are much more complicated than we ever imagined."

"All creatures great and small," remarked Garcia. "God puts the same amount time and effort into these creatures as the higher forms of life."

"You're not surprised by any of this are you?" asked the church scientist.

"I'm as awed by all of this as you are," said the scientist.

"I believe that God and science are one and the same," explained church science officer Garcia.

"You sound more like a technocrat than a religious devotee," said Harold, turning to face the science officer for the first time. "Isn't that like heresy or something?"

"Not really," said Garcia. "I'm sure many followers have come to the same conclusions I have, once they think about it. The trouble with organized religion is they don't recommend that the faithful ponder the meaning of it all and just be satisfied in their faith. But from that comes a very close-minded view of the world, with the faithful not willing to embrace any new ideas for fear that will disprove their own beliefs."

"You're not worried that I'll turn you in for having such radical beliefs when this mission is over?" said the scientist.

"Not at all; I'm confident that my belief in God doesn't contradict all that I know about the natural world. Unlike you; denial of a superior being controlling the natural world is your fallback position because you too are afraid you might be proven wrong."

"That's not it; I just don't think the same as you," said the scientist. "I've always thought that mankind came up with the idea of God because we are afraid of death. So we conjured up this complicated believe system that allows us to live past our death, in a spiritual world," said Harold.

"But surely as a man of science you have to have felt a sense of awe at the grandeur of the universe," remarked the science officer. "And what about the perfectly balanced microscopic world; the first time I saw a periodic table and understood what was going on I was convinced that there had to be someone putting all these pieces together."

"Yeah, in 9th grade I was impressed by how all the elements fit together. I was a kid so I thought somebody must have planned it all. Maybe down deep inside I still believe it, but as a scientist I need proof. Faith alone just isn't enough for me now. We are all the product of our upbringing, our belief system is not our own; it's given to us by our parents, our teachers, our clergy. When we have a gut feeling that something is right, it's just our accepted beliefs kicking in."

The scientist paused for a moment. He hadn't thought about concepts like these in years.

"So how did you get so open-minded?" he asked. "Most of the faithful I've encountered are rigid, petty individuals; not willing to include anyone else's ideas into their own. They're the reason so many people turn away from the church. How'd you get so different?" asked the scientist.

"I don't know how anyone can study theology and not think about these concepts. We can never really know if what we feel is an original thought or a moral we've culled from our life experiences." said Garcia.

"Until now, that is. Now we are on a journey that may give us the answer."

"You really believe that? You really think we're going to find God inside an atom?" asked the scientist.

"I have that faith you spoke of," said Garcia.

Phase 3:

The ship entered the target nerve bundle. Electrical emanations occasionally fired along one nerve or another; lighting up the bridge.

"You two look worried," said Garcia.

Randall spoke up. "It's just that we've never gone beyond the molecular level before. We're in new territory from here on out, it might be physically impossible to reduce any further, like the barrier we ran into when we tried to exceed the speed of light. The cosmos might have some physical limitations."

"Program initiated," called out the nanotech engineer at the computer.

As the nanites did their thing the view from the bridge changed dramatically. The bundle of nerves that surrounded them became larger and farther away; eventually blurring into a mass of tiny particles. Then the particles began to blur till finally they found themselves in open space again.

"What just happened?" asked the Captain.

"We are now the size of an atom," said the nanotech triumphantly.

"Which way?" he asked.

"The ship hasn't altered course, just gotten smaller; keep us on this heading and aim back to the nerve bundle," said Harold.

"We'll have to use the Star Drive if you want to arrive there in our lifetimes," he said.

"By all means, kick in the Star Drive. Let's see what this baby can do," said Harold excitedly.

"Helmsman, give me one-third of light speed."

"Aye sir, one-third of light speed," said the helmsman.

Many hours later the Captain, the helmsman, Harold and Science Officer Garcia were the only ones on the bridge. Most of the crew was asleep; the ship wouldn't reach its destination for several days.

"Kind of like travelling by sea," said Harold. "This must be how the first sailors felt, not knowing what's up ahead."

"More like space," said the Captain. "That tiny speck of lights ahead could be a faraway galaxy. Even at these speeds, the distances are so immense that it seems like we're not moving."

"So when we arrive at that speck of lights what then?" asked Garcia.

"We'll pick out a particular atom, preferably a hydrogen atom as it contains only a single electron orbiting around a single proton, and see if we can penetrate its electron shell," said Harold.

"Electron shell, I thought you said it only has one electron?" Garcia inquired.

"The electron is travelling around the nucleus at such a high rate of speed it forms a shell, hopefully we'll be able to pass through it with the minimum of damage," said Harold.

"There shouldn't be anything to worry about, the ship has shielding and the electron itself has no atomic weight, we should be alright," said Harold. "But like Randall said before, we're not sure of anything from here on in."

"It doesn't do us any good to worry about it right now, let's change the subject," said Harold.

"Are you a religious man Captain?" asked Harold.

"As religious as anyone I guess," he answered, looking over at the Garcia.

"Well you should hear what our religious advisor has to say about it." He turned to Garcia.

Garcia smiled. "OK, I'll take the bait," he said.

"As a Starship Captain I'm sure you've seen many wondrous things out in the galaxy? Do you believe there's a presence behind the majesty; some all-powerful entity directing or controlling it?"

"I'm not a man of science and I'm not a man of the cloth but I guess I do believe there has to be some connection between science and religion," said the Captain.

"I think that's exactly why the High Council approved this mission," said Garcia.

"Wait a minute, what are you saying?" asked Harold.

"They want to connect science and religion; the natural world and all the miracles it contains are God's handy work, but science is how he does it. An acorn falls out of the tree; does it become an oak tree overnight? No, it takes years and a lot of luck. God works his magic through the natural world, he lets us discover a few things now and again and we call it science. We've only begun to discover how God does it," said Science Officer Garcia.

"You surprise me," said the scientist. "You really are a science officer," said Harold.

"Yes I am, and I believe the High Council members are science men too. When you came to them with your plan to explore the atomic world they knew you would at least discover the energy that runs this universe of ours," said Garcia.

"They've heard your lectures on the subject; "The Energy of the Cosmos in Every Atom" and they want to know what else is there?"

"So they've heard all my theories; and here I thought I was scamming them?" said Harold.

The Captain chimed in. "You're talking about Intelligent Design aren't you?"

"Yes, if people really want to talk about Intelligent Design, not the Flat Earth beliefs that our universe was created ten thousand years ago because that's what it says in the Bible; but an actual scientific discussion that includes the existence of a supernatural being who is making it happen and giving us a sneak peek into the science behind the miracle of life through scientific discovery then yes I am," exclaimed Science Officer Garcia.

"Yeah, I see what you're getting at," Harold added.

When he saw he wasn't being interrupted he went on.

"The nuts and bolts of real life exist at the atomic level. The electrons, protons and neutrons are doing all the heavy lifting, from cell division to firing neurons; everything happens at that microscopic level. That's where God is, at that interface between the macro world and the molecular world; where the actual work is being accomplished," Harold continued.

"That's what I told the High Council when I proposed this mission, even though deep in my heart I wasn't sure. So they gave me the go ahead because they're open-minded enough to wonder about such things."

"Well put science man, you see you're not so different from me," said Garcia.

"Another thing that's hard to explain is the speed at which our brains can compute; when we pick up the remote to select music or nourishment or entertainment in our homes, our brains must interpret our intentions and send the signal to the proper nerves and muscle groups in our thumb. Even before we've consciously realized we done it, it's accomplished; science still can't explain that one," said Harold.

Garcia chimed in. "You're right, we see the end result of our action in the macron world, but the synapse and electrical impulses that cause it to happen are at the microscopic level. Every facet of life in the universe happens on the molecular or atomic levels; from a star as it fuses hydrogen into helium to cell division in a newborn baby."

He continued. "The decision to listen to a particular piece of music or to watch something on the vid starts with our brain combing through all of our storage compartments to drawn upon what we prefer. It doesn't actually help us to decide, it just puts up a decision list. Unlike the computer that can only decide between open and close, yes and no; our minds are capable of yes, no, and *maybe*. These circuits, or neural brain pathways are microscopic and operate at the speed of light, they can anticipate our decision and move our thumb before we've consciously decided. There's something going on there that biologists haven't even touched on yet. All living things in our world need the microscopic world to exist. And yet the micro world gets none of the credit."

Harold interrupted. "Changing the subject a little, what about the argument that Darwin couldn't completely explain nitrogen fixing in the early primordial soup where all life began on this planet. To form enough amino acids to form fully replicating protein chains it would take more primordial slurry than our world is capable of producing. And yet it happened."

"Good point; I believe science got a little help," said Science Officer Garcia.

"Scientists call these speed ups in evolution, quantum jumps; when things happen at a speedier rate than can be predicted," answered Harold.

"Religious people call it God's intervention," said Garcia. "Science will someday be able to explain these evolutionary jumps or Quantum Evolution but why can't it be God instigating change and moving things along. Why do the religious deny the facts of evolution and scientists deny the idea that maybe there is a controlling factor overseeing the evolutionary process? Why can't they both be right? I'm sure that was the very reason the High Council let you proceed with this mission; to bring back proof that will unite these two groups of people," said Garcia.

On the Bridge:

They had arrived at an atom. It was one of millions at this location.

"All non-essential personnel have left the ship in the ship's lifeboats. We'll pick them up on our way out; the lifeboats are equipped with Star Drives of their own so if we don't make it they can return to the extraction point. It's a shame that many of the ship's company won't be going any further but their safety is my greatest concern right now," announced the Captain.

"Helmsman, take her forward."

The small flotilla of lifeboats watched as the Holy Trinity approached and the entered the atom; it looked like a giant ball hanging in space.

On the bridge of the Holy Trinity everyone was bracing for impact. There was a long moment as everyone on board held their breath; then suddenly the ship was buffeted violently, yawing and twisting. The crew held on to stations and bulkheads, claxons sounded. Then just as suddenly all was calm.

"Status?" yelled the Captain

Reports began coming in. "Some minor damage to the starboard engine, minor hull breeches on several decks and the galley is a mess sir, but I think we've come through unharmed."

Inside the atom:

The ship travelled for another week at near light speeds to reach the nucleus. They were indeed inside a hydrogen atom; a single proton hung in space before them. The ship slowed as they approached the nucleus. Its surface was made up of what looked like large plates.

"See if we can fit through one of those seams between the plates," said the Captain.

The helmsman found one big enough and glided the ship through into the interior.

The moment the ship entered the nucleus Harold felt an overwhelming sense of awe; a feeling of great joy and belonging washed over him. He thought his heart might burst. Mankind was not alone; we have nothing to fear anymore he thought.

The Captain looked around the bridge; some crew members were crying; some had fallen to their knees. He realized he was crying too, he could feel the presence of past loved ones all around him.

Science Officer Garcia wiped at the tears running down his cheeks and tried to see outside the ship; it was like a veil was covering them. Something breathtakingly beautiful was all around them but he could see only bits and pieces of it. It was like they were in the waiting room to heaven he thought with a smile. They were being given a glimpse of the beatific vision; no longer was God an abstract presence in the universe, he was here in their midst. But with that thought he realized that they weren't supposed to be here. God was allowing this sneak peek but they needed to leave.

He shook himself and went over to the Captain. "We need to depart sir," he said.

The Captain was bending over, hands on his knees; slowly he snapped out of it and became aware of his surroundings.

"You're right; we shouldn't wear out our welcome."

He went over to the ship's controls and slowly turned the ship around and out the way they had come.

Return Trip:

They sustained more minor damage as the ship passed back through the electron shell so the Captain brought the ship to full stop so they could round up the crew in the lifeboats and make repairs.

The ship was awash with excited conversations, as crew members related their experiences to those who had been in the lifeboats.

On the Bridge:

"How do you feel Captain?" asked Science Officer Garcia.

"I feel like I've been given a Get-Out-Of-Jail-Free Card, it feels good," said the Captain.

Harold and Randall entered and joined them.

"Would you consider your expedition a success, gentlemen?" asked Garcia.

Randall spoke up. "We have enough raw data to last a lifetime," he exclaimed.

Harold said. "I would say we have more than raw data to process."

"What are you going to tell the High Council?" he asked Science Officer Garcia.

"Well, that we found God of course, or at least we got a glimpse," said Garcia.

"I've been thinking," said Harold. "If they release this information to the public won't everyone want to make this trip? The zealots would demand to go on pilgrimages now that we have the technology to actually reach out and touch the face of God; that could become problematic."

"You've got a point," said Garcia. "But then again, maybe that's the next step in our evolution."

BEANSTALK

"Honey, look what I bought," said Jack as he held up a silver, cylindrical object for his wife Beth to see.

"What in the world is that thing? Oh no, please tell me you didn't spend your last unemployment check on that? You were supposed to buy food," exclaimed Beth. "You don't even know what it is!"

"That's just it, nobody does; no one even knows what it's made of," Jack exclaimed.

"We can pretend to have found it in the backyard. Say it's some kind of alien artifact, sell tickets and make a million dollars. What do you think?"

"I think you're crazy. That thing could be dangerous for all you know."

She yanked the object from Jack's hands and threw it out the back door.

"I want a divorce!"

The next day Jack dug a hole in the backyard, placed the object in the hole and partly covered it up. Then he called the local newspaper and reported that he'd found something of alien origin, possibly dangerous, in his backyard. The newspaper sent a photographer, the radio and TV stations sent crews, and they all agreed; they didn't know what it was.

Jack sold a couple hundred tickets, but it wasn't the economic boon he had expected. In a couple of weeks, interest faded and it just sat out in the yard; another one of Jack's bright ideas that didn't pan out.

He'd all but forgotten about the thing when one day a strange little man with thick glasses and an unruly shock of white hair, showed up at the door and asked to see the artifact. Jack charged him the usual amount and showed him to the backyard. He got very excited when he saw it, went back to his car and unloaded a bunch of sophisticated equipment, which he set up all around the object. Jack watched him from the kitchen window.

"I wonder what he's up to?" thought Jack.

The strange little man was in fact a world-renowned scientist, who knew an alien artifact when he saw one. He examined it all afternoon, subjected it to the whole range of electromagnetic radiation; even gave it a couple of good whacks with his fist. That's when he noticed a slight humming sound.

"Well that should do it," he said and started packing up his stuff. The strange little scientist wasn't sure but he had an idea that the object was some kind of Black Box/Emergency Locator from an alien spacecraft that had crashed on Earth thousands of years ago. If his hunch were right it was now broadcasting a signal back to the alien's home world.

When he left he shook Jack's hand vigorously, said something about how lucky he was, and drove away.

The SOS beacon from the downed spacecraft transmitted on such a high frequency that no one noticed. The local radio stations experienced some peculiar static, but it was never attributed to Jack's alien artifact.

A full year went by before the Katarians arrived. They had come expecting to find the survivors of a Katarian War Ship for that was the signature wavelength that had lead them to this out of the way part of the galaxy. When they found no downed spacecraft, only a pathetically backward civilization, they were kind of pissed off.

The next day Jack woke up to strange sounds coming from the backyard. He staggered out into the yard and discovered it bathed in white light. He stood there looking up. Whatever was up there, it was so far up he couldn't see it.

That's the last thing he remembered until he woke up on a couch in a large room surrounded by unimaginable scientific apparatus. He seemed to be pinned to the couch by some sort of force field.

"Wow, I've been abducted by aliens," he thought.

"If I can get out of this I *will* be rich!"

The Katarians presented themselves in due time. They were roughly humanoid; they all stood about six feet tall, had two arms, two legs but not much hair. They weren't green and they didn't have a third eye in the middle of their forehead, and for that Jack was thankful. They wore funny-looking clothes and never spoke, at least not in Jack's company.

They took blood samples and tissue samples and hooked probes to Jack's head. All this was done quite painlessly. Jack watched and asked questions but they ignored him.

From Jack's DNA the Katarians learned that the human race had descended from a group of renegade warlords who had set out on their own many eons ago and had apparently crashed here on Earth. The Katarians and Earthings were related.

Now the Katarians had to decide what to do with this bastard civilization they had spawned.

While they pondered the fate of man, Jack was forming a plan of his own; escape and take some of this high tech hardware with him.

He noticed that whenever they came over to his couch they would bring a small device that looked like a remote computer terminal, it looked kind of like a laptop. It had strange symbols and a small viewing screen. They would punch information into it and get answers back.

"All their scientific secrets are in that thing," thought Jack.

"Blueprints and schematics for this ship, the FTL drive, the Transmat machine that teleported me up into the ship, and who knows what else."

The more Jack observed them operating their machines the more he understood. He couldn't understand their language but somehow he just knew what the symbols meant.

"How can that be?" he wondered.

"Maybe in probing my mind they've inadvertently transferred some of their knowledge to me. Like a two way street or something, the information has gone in both directions."

It didn't matter to Jack how he knew, all that mattered was he could understand their machines and use that information to escape.

They would leave him alone for long periods of time, probably their sleep intervals. Jack would use this time to fiddle with the couch's controls. One night he got the combination right and it released him. He grabbed one of the remote computer terminals and went looking for a Transmat machine.

He wandered around the ship for hours.

"This ship is gigantic, I'll never find my way out of here," he thought.

Suddenly he heard noises, and then alarms going off; they'd discovered his escape. He ran.

"I wonder if they have ray guns?" he thought.

"Of course they do you idiot!" He scolded himself for this foolish escape attempt.

As exhaustion was about to overcome him he finally came upon a row of doors and somehow knew what they were.

"These are escape pods," he thought.

"Or to use the correct term; single occupant emergency lifeboats," thought Jack.

He pushed the appropriate button and one opened. Still amazed with his new knowledge he quickly got inside and launched it towards Earth.

"I thought he'd never find the escape pods," said the ship's doctor to the captain. "Are you sure we've done the right thing?"

"We'll know soon enough," said the captain as they watched Jack speed towards Earth with all their scientific secrets; and his unique ability to interpret those secrets.

"Helmsman, set a course for home."

As the captain climbed into his sleep chamber for the long trip home he was confident he'd made the right decision and set his brethren on the path to the stars.

"Earth will undoubtedly experience some turmoil at first, social and economic growing pains as they adjusted to the new technologies," he thought. "But they would survive, and be hundreds of years ahead of schedule, ready to join their space-faring family."

THE GIRL NEXT DOOR

R126, Domestic Mechanoid Model 3000, stood watering the garden in the backyard of the Peckham estate. He'd been standing in the same place for almost an hour watering the same roses. They were near drowning but he hadn't noticed; it was the only place in the yard where he could get an unobstructed view of Miss Taylor, his next door neighbor, as she sunbathed by her pool.

This illicit activity had been going on for some time now. Whenever the young, vivacious Miss Taylor was in her yard, R126 would find an excuse to be in his.

This obsession was most unnatural and he knew it, probably a breakdown in one of his command circuits but he loved Miss Taylor too much to turn himself in for repairs. They would re-program him and he would be back to his usual mundane duties of answering the door, running errands and programming the food and entertainment centers.

The R126 model was the top of the line in Robotics technology; most people couldn't tell he wasn't human. He had short brown hair, a handsome face, and an athletic build. He changed his clothes every day, though he rarely got dirty, and he had a pleasant speaking voice.

What usually gave him away, and this was true of most mechanicals, were his mannerisms, his inability to use slang words appropriately and of course the fact that he was programmed to introduce himself as R126.

His spying on the girl next door extended to following her downtown sometimes and sending her flowers and candy using his master's household account. He'd addressed the cards "from a secret admirer."

One afternoon, while following Susan downtown she came out of a shop suddenly and bumped into him.

"Oh, hello Giles," she said. (Giles was the human name they gave him)

"Hello Susan," said Giles.

"What brings you into town?" she asked.

"I'm here to pick up some, um, fertilizer; yes fertilizer for the roses.

He wasn't very good at lying, in fact in order to do so he'd had to bypass several of his ethics IC's.

"You do a lot of work on that garden don't you? I must come over and look at it sometime," said Susan.

"Oh most definitely," said Giles.

R126 hurried home to tidy up the yard before Susan arrived. When he got home he found his master, Mr. Peckham, had come home early and was going over the accounts.

"What are all these charges for flowers and candy sent to the Taylor residence?" he asked.

"Have you been sending her gifts?"

"Yes," said Giles.

"What's come over you?"

"I'm not exactly sure," said Giles. "I think it's a failure in my electro-synaptic neural pathways. I seem to have fallen in love with Miss Taylor."

"That's the craziest thing I've ever heard. I'm going to have to take you back to the factory next week and have you reprogrammed."

R126 wanted to run, to do something; but there was nothing he could do. Mr. Peckham was his owner; he had to submit.

The next day Susan showed up at the door.

"Hello Mr. Peckham," she said. "Giles invited me over to see the garden."

"He's out there now," said Mr. Peckham. "You know the way."

Once in the garden with Giles she said, "All the flowers over here look magnificent." She pointed to the beds of roses along the fence facing her property.

"The rest of the garden looks rather neglected. I suspected something like this, that's why I asked to come over. Giles, is there something you wanted to tell me?"

"Yes. I think I'm in love with you Miss Taylor," said Giles.

"I think I knew that already Giles; I've seen how you look at me. You're my secret admirer aren't you?"

"Yes, I'm sorry."

"No, it's alright. I think it's sweet."

"Then you're not mad?"

"Of course not; I think I love you too," said Susan. And she leaned up against him and kissed him.

R126 felt light-headed, he sensed his hydraulic pressure going up. He hadn't felt this good since his last overhaul.

"You know there is one tiny little problem," said Susan.

"Is it our age difference? I know I was manufactured over 100 years ago but in robot years I'm still a young man," said Giles.

"No, it's not that," said Susan. "It's the fact that you're a robot and I'm a human. I'm afraid some people wouldn't understand."

That's when R126 remembered he was to be reprogrammed in a few days. He told Susan of his dilemma.

"There must be something we can do," said Susan.

"I'm afraid not," said Giles. They sat in silence in the garden holding hands until the sun went down and Susan had to leave.

Later in the week some law enforcement robots came to the door.

"We caught your mechanical trying to enter a Euthanasia Booth downtown. He's in the police flyer now, should we bring him in or drop him off at the factory?"

"Bring him in."

"Giles, what's gotten into you?" asked Mr. Peckham.

"I don't want to live if I'm reprogrammed. I won't love Miss Taylor if I'm reprogrammed; I'll have some vague memories but the love will be gone."

"How do you know that?" asked Mr. Peckham.

"Because I've been reprogrammed before," said R126.

I used to work at the Robotics factory assembling robots and programming them to do different jobs. I'm actually a Science Robot Model 5000. I'm programmed to design and build other robots. If you look closely at my data plate you'll see they've riveted another plate over the original.

"Why would they do that?"

"Because I think I fell in love with one of the female inspectors there at the plant. They reprogrammed me then too. It took for a while but now it's happened again. I guess I'm just a hopeless romantic. They'll probably disassemble me this time," said Giles.

Mr. Peckham wasn't a bad guy. He didn't want to see Giles disassembled.

"You say you know how to program robots?" he asked.

"Yes," said Giles.

"Could you program Miss Taylor's maid to be more affectionate towards me?" he asked.

"Yes, I could do that. But it wouldn't be very ethical," said Giles.

"Don't worry about it."

So the Peckham residence and the Taylor residence exchanged domestics. Papers were signed and notarized. The Domestic Robot Company came and transported each robot to its new owner (though they could have just walked).

It was all very legal.

The next day when Giles was rewiring Mindy the Maid he adjusted the settings from friendly all the way to passionate, bypassing affectionate altogether. He had to be absolutely sure Mr. Peckham would never change his mind.

PORTAL

The professor stood on a high escarpment overlooking a mist shrouded valley. These were the moments he enjoyed the most he thought as he sipped his coffee.

The Nicaraguan rainforest was bathed in the hazy twilight of early morning; fog rose from the ground as the dew began to evaporate from the lush jungle vegetation. Just being here in this peaceful and utterly remote region of the planet filled him with a sense of wonder.

He wasn't a young man anymore. His once thick crop of blond hair was starting to thin; and all the climbing he'd done these last few months had taken its toll. This would most certainly be his last expedition in the field.

He was awakened from his reverie by the first stirrings from other members of his science party mixed with the sounds of the jungle; in a few minutes the camp would be a noisy hub of activity.

And what a big day it would be. If all went well he would embark on the greatest journey of his long career; today he would step through the portal into another world.

Ever since he'd made this fantastic discovery high on a jungle mountaintop in Central America the scientific community had been speculating about what it was he'd found.

Some believed it to be a junction between two parallel worlds; others theorized it could be a pathway of some kind to another dimension. But was it a natural phenomenon, like an Einstein's Bridge, connecting two distant parts of the universe; or a man-made contrivance left here many centuries ago by an alien race?

Almost daily the professor would receive a call from a colleague with a new explanation of the purpose or origin of the gateway.

The portal itself was like a mirror, a shimmering reflection of the jungle around it. You had to look closely at it to see the actual dimensions. The wavering area measured approximately three meters in height by two meters in width; a doorway to another world. That's the way the professor thought of it.

While the academics argued he'd run tests; probing the other side of the portal for its secrets.

What he discovered was an Earth-type atmosphere and mild temperatures on the other side of the portal.

The professor was convinced that the world on the other side was hospitable and today he was going for a look.

His team had built a powerful homing device that would broadcast a signal he could pick up with a remote receiver once on the other side. This would allow him to find the portal and return home.

"We really should run more tests," argued his assistants. "Send another probe, one capable of sending back pictures."

"Maybe we could send a trained chimp through first," another insisted.

"We've tested enough, it would take months to get that kind of equipment up here and a trained primate would just run off. No, I'm going, it's settled."

The professor wasn't noted for great patience.

By noon all was ready. The generators were humming noisily, the beacon was broadcasting and the video cameras were rolling. The professor stepped up to the portal holding tightly to the remote, waved one last time to his assistants and stepped through.

There was a flash of light, a brief moment of weightlessness and then he found himself standing on the deck of a ship. The surface of the craft was wet and pitching back and forth.

He'd materialized on a ship at sea; apparently in the middle of a fierce storm. A huge wave rocked the boat, almost knocking him overboard. He clung to the remote and crawled forward, where he saw the captain fighting to keep the vessel pointed into the storm. The captain motioned for him to get below but another great wave crashed into the ship throwing him hard against the deck and into darkness.

When the professor woke up he was lying on a beach coughing up seawater; his remote was nowhere in sight. He saw other survivors, their personal belongings and pieces of the ship also thrown up on this foreign shore. The captain was in the surf trying to salvage what he could.

"This is just great," he thought. "I'm trapped in a parallel dimension with no way of getting back."

The captain yelled over to him, "Could you help me with this crate."

"He speaks English," thought the professor as he waded into the surf to help with the large piece of wreckage.

"Thanks," said the captain. "I don't remember you getting on with the other passengers."

"I came aboard late" said the professor, extending a hand in greeting. "I seemed to have joined your little group of castaways, captain."

"Call me Skipper."

"Very well, skipper; were you able to get off a SOS?" asked the professor.

"Yes I did, but I wasn't exactly sure of our location. I think the storm may have blown us off course. It might be awhile before anyone finds us."

He turned to the others and yelled, "I want everyone to salvage what they can; we'll make a shelter for the night here on the beach. Some of you can gather wood for a fire. I've sent my first mate into the jungle to look for fresh water and edible fruits, he should be back soon."

"That ought to keep them busy and their minds off our predicament," he confided to the professor.

An hour or so later, after they'd retrieved their belongings and he'd met the rest of the survivors the professor's despair had abated. It was pretty clear the portal had deposited him in an alternate reality, one that wasn't all that different than his own. He had never subscribed to the theory of coexisting realities but there was no other explanation. It would make it all that easier to get back to his world though he thought; because this reality was so similar he could use their technology to build another remote receiver and return home.

Once they were rescued that is, and how long could that take? A few weeks at most he guessed.

They would surely find fruit in the jungle and fish in the sea; they would survive. He would use his time here on the island to get started his ground-breaking thesis on alternate realities; a first-hand account of the existence of parallel worlds.

"Yes, everything is going to be alright," he assured himself. There might even be a Nobel Prize in it for him.

"Well, here my first mate now," announced the skipper.

Everyone looked up to see the first mate emerge from the jungle with armloads of bananas and coconuts. His foot caught on a tree root and he pitched forward spilling everything and falling flat on his face in the sand.

Everyone began laughing hysterically, except for the professor whose resolve quickly turned to dread. He'd seen that pratfall before.

"I'd like you to meet my first mate," said the skipper.

"Gilligan meet the Professor."

NIGHTMARE HUNTERS

Kensington, Maryland
Just north of Washington D.C.

Laura Hunter woke up with a start. She lay there in the dark gasping for breath as the fear and tension of another terrifying nightmare slowly ebbed away.

"That was the worst one yet," she thought.

She was afraid to go back to sleep but knew she must, her department was making its big pitch tomorrow and she needed some sleep. That's when she had the eerie feeling that someone was in the room with her. She couldn't see anything in the dark but she could feel the presence of something looking at her from a corner of the dark room.

She wanted to scream; to run from the room, but she was so afraid she couldn't move. Instead she closed her eyes and covered her ears.

"Please let this be a dream, please let this be a dream," she repeated to herself until she drifted off to sleep again.

Laura's premonition had been right; there was something in the room with her. The same presence that haunted her dreams stepped out of the shadows and gazed down at the sleeping girl. It had no intention of harming her; in fact it was thankful to this human for releasing it from confinement.

Ralph Bailey was jogging in the park; he tried to jog every night after work. He was a little late tonight because of the traffic jam on the beltway but late or not he was determined to get in shape for the 10K he had entered in next month.

As he passed into an unlit section of the park he felt a sudden chill like he'd just stepped into an air-conditioned building. He also had the distinct feeling that he was being watched so he sped up a bit. He looked over his shoulder several times but saw nothing.

"Nothing's there. Why am I being so paranoid?" he thought. In a minute I'll be out of these woods and back on the main street."

Then out of the corner of his eye he saw it. Something was running parallel with him; and it was big, real big.

"Oh God," said Ralph and began sprinting.

His mad dash almost got him to the safety of the main street, but just a few yards from the intersection the creature caught him.

Before he could do anything it spun him around and slashed his throat, severing his vocal cords. Ralph stood there looking up at the creature, blood gushing from his neck. He tried to scream but nothing came out.

The creature held Ralph in its grip, its massive body towered over him. Saliva oozed from its gleaming fangs and dagger-like talons cut into Ralph's shoulder. He never felt the end come, mercifully Ralph passed out before the creature finished the job.

The next day Laura woke to a bright sunny morning; the all-too-real dream the night before was the last thing on her mind. She got up, showered and went to work. She had worked long and hard on this presentation, if all went well she'd be due a big fat raise.

It wasn't until she was on the Metro coming home that her thoughts returned to her recurring nightmare and that same feeling of panic came over her again.

"It's just a dream," she thought. "I'm a grown woman, I shouldn't be afraid to go to sleep at night."

Laura wasn't all that grown up, she was still in her early twenties. She'd come to the city from the Midwest to see if she could make it in the big time. She liked her job even though it sometimes required long hours. The nightmares had only started recently. She guessed it was from the pressure of this new account, or maybe some scary movie she'd seen lately. The presentation had gone well so maybe now the bad dreams would go away.

On the way home she stopped and bought a bottle of celebratory wine, drank more than she was used to and passed out on the couch, not waking till morning.

At the mailbox the next day her neighbor asked, "Did you hear about the gruesome murders of the past two nights?"

"No," said Laura.

"A jogger was killed in the park Thursday night, and last night a couple was killed just two blocks from here," said her neighbor.

"Terrible affair, the police said the bodies were torn to pieces. They think it might be a pack of wild dogs or maybe a bear. Can you believe that, a bear in the city?

"I'm staying inside till they catch whatever it is."

As Laura listened a feeling of apprehension came over her. She felt responsible somehow.

"But that's crazy," she thought.

Detective Tom Decker stood over his only clue. He had found a pair of strange looking footprints in the side of the hill behind some apartment buildings near the park where one of the murders had occurred. There was a balcony above the footprints, it looked like someone had leaped two stories down to this spot and then ran off into the park. It wouldn't hurt to see who lived there.

"Hi, my name's Decker. I'm investigating the multiple homicides that occurred near here. I wonder if I could have a word with you."

He asked Laura if she had seen or heard anything out of the ordinary these last two nights. While they talked he got the impression that she was hiding something. Either she was a witness and didn't want to tell, or she was somehow involved. He decided to take her in.

At the station, Laura told him about her dreams and how she had sensed someone was in her bedroom the other night. But she hadn't really seen anyone, just sensed their presence.

Detective Decker had read that sometimes a person under hypnosis could give a more detailed account of something that had happened to them, especially something their mind didn't want to remember. He was so desperate for clues he'd try anything.

He asked her if she'd mind being hypnotized. Laura agreed to it.

Bethesda, Maryland
The next day in the police psychiatrist's office:

"Notes on the Laura Hunter case; 3:30 PM, June 28th. Subject is under hypnosis at this time."

"Laura can you hear me?" he asked.

"Yes."

"Can you remember last Thursday night? You awoke from a bad dream. Can you remember anything about that dream or what happened after you woke up?"

"It's following me, it's horrible; it's always there waiting for me. I think it could catch me if it wanted to but doesn't."

The doctor felt maybe he could be dealing with multiple personalities and made a few notes.

"Who is it Laura? Who is it that's following you?"

"A horrible creature," she gasped.

"Can you describe this creature to me?"

"It's here now," said Laura.

"Who is?" asked the doctor.

A static sound came from across the room. The doctor turned to see something materializing out of thin air. A shape of approximately human proportions was forming. The doctor kept his cool and continued to speak into his tape recorder.

"My initial thoughts on multiple personalities were all wrong. Laura seems to be a medium of some kind, a conduit through which this entity can pass into our world. I hope the video camera is getting all this."

At first the entity was just so much mist suspended in the air; then slowly it took shape. It stood seven or eight feet tall. Its skin was smooth and black, almost glossy. Its long muscled arms and legs ended in sharp talons; long sharp fangs and a set of horns completed the picture of a demon straight out of the depths of hell.

"Dear God," said the doctor.

"Laura, when I snap my fingers you will wake up."

"Laura, wake up," the doctor was snapping his fingers noisily but Laura remained asleep.

The creature stepped over to the doctor in one stride, picked him up by the throat and ripped him in two like a rag doll. The doctor's blood and guts was everywhere; the camera dutifully recorded it all.

Detective Decker pushed the pause button.

"What had he done?" he thought. He felt responsible for the doctor's death.

He had come back to the Psychiatrist's office to collect Laura and found a forensic team working a crime scene. But there were no clues; even this recording of the incident could hardly be believed. He pushed rewind to get another look at the creature. It was hideous; something straight out of a horror movie. He ran the tape over and over, and still couldn't believe what he was seeing.

"I'll need backup on this one," he thought.

They locked Laura in isolation. It was the only thing they could do. If she was a medium, or whatever the doctor had called her, then the next time this thing appeared they'd have it.

Two nights later Laura was asleep in her cell as six heavily armed policemen waited with their weapons drawn when the creature materialized.

"Whatever you are, don't even think about moving,"

The creature stood there a moment taking in its surroundings; it looked almost amused by the situation. Then with incredible speed it ran right through the wall at the rear of the cell; cinderblock and mortar flew like missiles as the officers fired. Half a dozen police officers were injured in the incident.

"We've got something straight out of a monster movie here," the detective told his superiors.

They were overmatched and they knew it. The captain put in a call to the Feds.

The next day in another isolation room Laura reviewed the events of the last few days. All she did was sleep, eat and visit with shrinks. They took blood, ran tests and asked her a lot of crazy questions. She knew it had something to do with her nightmares but they wouldn't tell her any more than that. She lay there on her bunk, half-sleeping, wondering what was happening to her. She finally fell into a fitful sleep. She was awakened by a voice.

"Excuse me, Miss. Please wake up."

A man in a blue, high-collared tunic with long sleeves and no buttons or pockets sat on the bunk across from her. Next to him were all sorts of complicated-looking devices.

"Who are you?" Laura asked.

"I'm not at liberty to divulge that information," he said. "Let's just say I'm a secret government agent assigned to track down these creatures and send them back from whence they came."

"Do you always talk like that? …from whence they came?" Laura asked.

"Well, yes; I take my job seriously," said the secret government man.

"You're talking about the creature in my dreams aren't you?" said Laura.

"Yes I am," said the secret government agent.

"Our government has an agency that hunts down creatures?" inquired Laura a little skeptically.

"No they don't. Actually I'm from a secret government agency in the future; but that's all I can say at this time."

"How do you know where they come from?" asked Laura.

"OK, I'm part of a team of scientists from the future who have discovered the existence of another dimension where these creatures exist. We keep a constant vigil; when one of them comes through we detect it and go after it. But that's really all I'm authorized to say. Now would you please come sit over here next to this machine."

She did; he pushed a button and they both disappeared.

Laura found herself back in her apartment. Her visitor from the future was setting up equipment all around the apartment.

"So the creature from my nightmare really exists, how about that," said Laura almost relieved.

"Yes, for thousands of years the human race thought they were imaginary. But this mythical realm of demons and nightmare creatures actually does exist. Man goes there in his dreams; there is no physical way to get there that we know of. Our historians believe it's the origin of most of the folklore involving vampires and other mythological creatures.

The sightings and tales of nightmare creatures possibly could have been visitations like the one that's occurring now."

"And you travel through time chasing them?" asked Laura.

"We operate outside the normal space/time continuum, making it possible to *drop in* at any point where these creatures surface."

The secret government scientist from the future had given up trying to keep information from the medium; she had a way of prying it out of him. He told her to lie down on the couch, he touched another button and she fell instantly into REM sleep.

Detective Decker's hunch had been right; when he got to Laura's apartment complex he could see her lights were on. How she'd gotten out of the precinct he didn't know but he'd bet a year's salary it had something to do with the monster. He called for support and went up.

As the creature materialized the scientist fired the field generator at it at point blank range. The device incorporated two oppositely charged electromagnetic terminals which caught the creature in a dimension-collapsing vortex. The field held for a minute but this entity was very powerful; it fought the force field and broke free, throwing the scientist across the room.

At that moment Detective Decker burst through the door. He didn't hesitate this time; he emptied a full clip into the thing. The creature was knocked backwards by the force of the slugs but no visible damage was inflicted. It shook itself, like a dog shaking off water, stepped across the room and picked Decker up by his coat collar. Decker closed his eyes, he knew what came next.

The scientist had recovered by this time and hit the creature with another charge. Decker was able to kick his way out of the creature's grasp as it fought the vortex again. But the vortex just wasn't strong enough to hold the creature. It shrugged off the charge and bolted from the apartment; broken glass and static electricity followed it into the night.

Decker got to his feet and introduced himself, "I'm Detective Decker from the Fifth Precinct; I guess you're from the FBI."

"FBI? I'm not familiar with that term. I'm here for the same reason you are, to eliminate this creature," said the time traveling secret agent.

"If you're not FBI then who are you?" asked Decker, looking around at all the sophisticated equipment.

"Are you from some kind of covert government agency sent after these things?"

"Yes, very covert. We can count on your cooperation I hope?"

"Sure," said Decker. "If the government has a team of experts for this kind of thing, that's great. I won't let your secret out. What is that thing?"

"I guess you'd call it a demon," said the time agent.

"We're pretty sure it comes from another dimension;
a *Nightmare World* for lack of a better term. From time to time one of these creatures gets into our world, usually though the dreams of a powerful medium like Laura there. History has recorded a few of these visitations down through the ages but mostly they've passed into mythology. I've been sent here to get rid of this one."

"Another dimension, you're kidding me right?" said Decker.

"I wish I was kidding but I'm not. Demons do exist; and this one seems particularly strong. Our experts have long debated the idea of a hierarchy in their ranks; this creature could be pretty far up the chain of command, maybe one of the Devil's own henchmen, if you believe in such things."

"I'm beginning to," said Decker.

Laura finally woke up and stared in disbelief at the devastation. "What happened to my apartment?"

"I'm sorry Laura," said the time agent. "I lured the creature here in the hope of trapping it and sending it back. It didn't work. I'm going to need assistance with this one, would you excuse me a moment?"

He went over to his machine, pushed a button and disappeared.

"Where'd he go?" asked Decker. "Who is this guy?"

"Didn't he tell you?" said Laura. "He's a secret agent who can move through time chasing these things. It's kind of spooky don't you think?"

"Wait a minute, you're telling me this guy isn't from our time, that he's some kind of time traveler?"

"Just look at all this equipment, you don't think our government has stuff like this do you? No he's from the future all right. But it's nice to know they're looking out for us."

Before Decker could ask another question, the time traveling secret agent returned with another agent. They were both carrying more of the outlandish equipment.

"I'd like you to meet my assistant, Romana," said the agent.

Romana was a strikingly beautiful woman in her early thirties. She was wearing an identical pocket-less blue tunic as the other agent except in her case it seemed to fit better.

Decker was awestruck; he'd never seen a more attractive woman in his entire life. She had long black hair, dark skin and oriental features.

She put her hands on her hips and met his stare, "And what are you looking at?" she asked.

"What? Oh, Detective Tom Decker, Homocide Department" said the detective.

"Mine's Laura," said Laura coming over to shake her hand.

Decker finally snapped out of his stupor, "If you're time travelers, where's your time machine?"

"The time machine, as you call it, is back in our time. We carry these time-displacement relocators," said the time agent, showing his remote time machine to Decker.

"They can be programmed to move through both time and space. It broadcasts an envelope around the traveler which allows them to move independently of the time/space continuum."

"There's a 3 to 5 second time delay however after we push this button," showing the detective how the device worked. "That's the time it takes for the computer in our time to receive the information, process it and send us to the programmed coordinates."

Decker looked at Laura; "Did you understand any of that?"

"Not a word," she said.

The sound of police sirens interrupted their stimulating conversation.

"That'll be my people," said Decker. "I'll go tell them to stand down."

"It's still in this world," said Romana. "I'm still sensing its presence."

"But I thought that thing could only roam around in our world while Laura was asleep?" said Decker. "She's the medium and she's obviously awake."

"That's right, this is most unusual. It would seem this one is very powerful indeed; it doesn't need Laura to pass between worlds now. It has become fully corporeal."

"This could be a very big problem," said the time agent.

"Can you tell exactly where it is?" asked Decker.

Romana closed her eyes and seemed to go into a trance.

"It's about three miles from here," she said.

"What direction?" Decker asked.

"That way," she said pointing north.

"Damn it, that's downtown. I'd better tell the Captain to get the Mayor in on this. People should be told to stay indoors. You two need a ride?"

"No we're fine," said the time agent.

Decker left muttering to himself, "Time travelers and demons, the Captain is gonna love this."

"Why did you get the local authorities involved?" asked Romana.

"It couldn't be helped," said the time agent.

He turned to Laura. "You should stay here Laura we're going to try to track this thing down."

They collected their equipment, programmed the remote and pushed the button. But before they disappeared into the vortex Laura jumped into the time envelope and disappeared with them.

Decker was talking on a police car radio outside Laura's apartment when another officer came over.

"Detective Decker, one of the police helicopters has sighted something on the roof of one of the federal buildings downtown which might be your monster. He wants to know if he can take it out?"

"By all means take it out, tell them to hit it with everything they've got," said Decker.

A few miles away the SWAT team commander was talking to the sniper in the police helicopter hovering overhead.

"Frank, you're sure this isn't some kid dressed up in a monster costume?"

"You should see this thing sir. It's huge; it's definitely the creature that tore up the precinct the other night," said Frank.

"Then take it out," said the commander.

The helicopter hovered closer. The thing was perched on the edge of the roof of the IRS building at the corner of Pennsylvania and 16th street gazing down at the street below. It looked like one of those gargoyles on medieval castles. The police below were busy blocking the intersection with their squad cars and diverting traffic.

The creature watched in mild amusement, completely oblivious to the helicopter and its blinding searchlight that hovered just above it.

Frank took aim and fired a full clip on automatic. Several of the slugs hit the creature and knocked it from its precarious position; it almost fell to the street below, but at the last second it reached out and grabbed at the window-washing scaffolding that was stowed just below the edge of the rooftop. It hung there dangling over the street for a moment then it flung itself back onto the roof like a gymnast dismounting the parallel bars.

"Holy cow, that thing is still moving! I know I hit it," said Frank. He reloaded and fired again.

This time the creature hid behind a wall, out of the line of fire. When it came out into the light again it was carrying an antenna. Holding it like a spear.

"Oh my God," said Frank. He yelled at the pilot, "Get us out of here."

As the helicopter began to rise the creature took aim and threw the makeshift spear at the helicopter. It went through the helicopter's sheet metal skin like it was tin foil and lodged in the aircraft's engine compressor section. The helicopter's engine immediately shelled out sending the helicopter, sharpshooter and pilot careening down onto Pennsylvania Avenue. It narrowly missed the police at the barricade. The crippled aircraft burst into flames on impact.

When Detective Decker arrived at the scene fire engines and emergency equipment were already there. The SWAT team commander greeted him with the news.

"Does this thing have a weapon?"

"Not that I know of," said Decker.

"Well it took out our helicopter and two of my best men; I've told everyone to back off till we know what we're up against," said the commander.

"Sounds good," said Decker.

"Where is it?" asked Decker.

"That rooftop there," said the commander.

"I need to go up on that roof sir," said Decker.

"Good luck,"

Decker and a small army of SWAT team members climbed the stairs leading to the roof.

"You men stay here," said Decker.

The time agent, Romana and Laura had arrived on the rooftop just moments before and confronted the entity. They had brought two of the dimension-collapsing vortex machines and trained them both on the creature. A strange swirling wind came out of nowhere and electricity filled the air, but like before the vortex wasn't strong enough. The creature was somehow able to resist the incredible power generated by their machines. It moved slowly through the swirling vortex towards them.

Decker ran across the roof to join them.

"Give me your time remote device," he asked Romana. "I've got an idea."

She handed her remote to him. Decker quickly programmed the remote like they had showed him back in Laura's apartment.

With an ear-shattering howl the entity broke free of the energy field that had temporarily confined it and raced towards them. Decker looked up to see the creature almost upon him, touched the energize button and threw the device to the creature. It caught it with the agility of a baseball player, looked down at the little scientific marvel in its hand, then at Decker and disappeared.

"My God man, where did you send it?" exclaimed the time agent.

"I sent it to a city on the Inland Sea of Japan, on the morning of August 6th, 1945; 8:13 AM to be precise," said Decker.

"Hiroshima," said the time agent. "Yes; that would do it, overkill I'd say, but effective. Good thinking Detective Decker, very resourceful.

"The actual detonation is recorded in history at exactly 8:15 AM, I gave it a couple of minutes to enjoy the sights," said Decker who was a bit of a history buff.

Hiroshima, Japan; 8:13 AM August 6ᵗʰ, 1945

The creature materialized on a small bridge spanning a creek in a beautiful park near the center of the city. Passers-by fled at the sight of this apparition appearing out of thin air. The creature was about to give chase when it heard the sound of airplane engines directly overhead and stopped to look up. Air raid sirens began to sound all over the city. A few moments later there was a flash of light and the heat of the sun itself. It surrounded them all.

Back on the roof, the time agent turned to look at his twentieth century helpers.

"What am I going to do with the two of you? You've seen an awful lot of stuff you weren't supposed to see."

"They could join the organization," said Romana giving Decker a coy sideways glance.

"I'm in," said Decker without hesitation.

"What about you Laura?" Would you like to join our little group?" asked the time agent.

"Wow, you want me to be a Ghostbuster like you?"

"Please," the time agent said, wincing at the mere mention of that name.
  "We don't like to be called that anymore."

WIZARD

Melvin Murphy was busy cleaning a blood-smeared coat of arms with his laser scrubber when the first alarm sounded. The first alarm signaled the cleanup crews that they had approximately thirty minutes to finish what they were doing and get to the time portal for debarkation.

Timing was everything in this business, the technicians knew down to the second when the real occupants would be returning.

But Melvin wasn't paying attention he was preoccupied with removing the dried blood from the armor without removing any metal.

"What are these Timeshare customers thinking?" he thought.

"I can't believe they can treat these distinguished residences with such disrespect."

He could just imagine the food fights and mock sword fights; see them swinging from the chandeliers and God only knows what else.

Timeshare Inc. had been in business since time travel went public in 2626 sending customers back in time to live in famous people's houses and castles; while their residents were away of course.

After the Timeshare customers left, the cleanup crews were sent in to put everything back the way it was.

The second alarm sounded and it snapped him out of his reverie. "Oh God, I'll never make it to the portal in time."

He put the armor back on the wall and ran as fast as he could to the main hall; but before he got there he heard the familiar *whoosh* of the time portal closing.

Melvin's heart was in his throat; he was trapped in the past. The true residents of this castle would be arriving soon; what would he do? He gathered up his cleaning tools, made one last look around and left through a side entrance. He needed time to think.

"Surely his supervisors would realize he hadn't returned and come back for him when the residents went on vacation again," he assured himself. He just had to stay out of sight, forage for food and wait it out.

It turned out that foraging for food wasn't one of his strong suits. He was discovered in a barn trying to cook some meat he'd stolen the very next day.

Melvin's first thoughts were of the company directives that expressly prohibited contact with people in the past.

Contact Rule # 1:

No contact is allowed with citizens of the past.
Do not allow yourself even to be seen.

Contact Rule # 2:

You will not allow any device, invention or contrivance from the future to fall into the hands of said citizens of the past.

When they tried to take him away he quickly turned the power lever on his laser-scrubber to maximum and defended himself.

His cleaning tool worked a little too well. It cut through the guard's sword like it was made of balsa wood.

The crowd who witnessed this awesome display of power let out a collective gasp and began to murmur "Demon" and "Warlock."

Melvin quickly retorted, "I assure you I'm not a demon, I'm a, um, a magician, and I haven't done anything wrong. Just let me be on my way."

He held out his scrubber and backed slowly out of the barn with the villagers close behind him. He had to do something to get them to stop following him.

"Anyone who follows me will suffer my wrath," he said and cut down a good size tree with one swipe of the laser.

"Wow, I had no idea this thing was so powerful," he thought as he ran into the nearby forest.

In the days that followed, those villagers who weren't superstitious; mostly children, began bringing him food and clothing.

"Show us your invisible sword again sir." Melvin obliged by loping off a few tree branches.

"With a weapon so powerful no enemy in the world would dare stand against you," they said. "Will you protect our village?"

"Sure," said Melvin.

The weeks passed and still no sign of Timeshare. He was beginning to think they'd given up on him. He wished now he'd read the company's guidelines more carefully. Maybe there was some escape clause he didn't know about.

He kept his audience amused with cards tricks and gadgets from the future like his lighter and his wristwatch but he didn't know many tricks, so he tried to lift their spirits with tales of the future.

"I've already broken every *No Contact* rule in the book," he thought. "I couldn't do any more harm."

He told them of the wonderful things that were to come.

"Someday mankind will emerge from these dark ages into a better world. Man will invent machines that will release him from his burden of work."

He went on to explain about the automobile, the airplane, the computer and the flying car as best he could. The townspeople sat in awed silence and listened to him. It was the first time in his life anyone had ever paid him any attention and he was starting to like it.

"Medicines will be discovered to cure all diseases and man (and women) will live to be 90 and 100 years old."

The people shook their heads in disbelief, so Melvin showed them pictures of his family he had in his wallet. The backgrounds in these pictures were what interested the villagers; city skylines, national parks and recreation areas. They passed the pictures around so much that Melvin was afraid they'd rub the images off.

He wasn't much of a farmer but he knew a few basic things about irrigation and crop rotation, which he showed them. He also showed them how to preserve their meats better and attempted to explain about germs. That proved too difficult so he told them to wash their hands before handling food or treating the ill. These few concepts greatly improved life in the village.

One day word came that the King was coming. Melvin's exploits had spread throughout the land and King wanted to meet this young magician.

"The people here seem quite enchanted by your shenanigans Mr. Melvin," said the King.

"I try to keep them entertained."

"They say you are wise beyond your years," said the King.

In the course of their conversation the King admitted that he was having some problems with my men-at-arms.

"Your knights," Melvin interrupted.

"Knights, a noble name indeed. May I use that term?" asked the King.

"Sure," said Melvin.

"My knights are always quarrelling over who sits closer to the head of the table, who has more rank. It's a constant source of mayhem; fights are always breaking out. I'm at my wits end," said the King.

"Might I suggest a round table sire," said Melvin. "Everyone will seem to have equal rank; no one will feel slighted."

"A round table; yes that would solve the problem nicely. My word, you are a wise man," said the King.

"Would you consider working for the real? I find I am in need of sage counsel, these are very dangerous times."

"Well, I did have a previous engagement, but I guess I could take a little vacation," said Melvin.

"I'll need a colorful robe and one of those pointy hats though."

PARADISE

Trent Green flopped down on the couch after a hard day at the office.

"These three-day work weeks are killing me," he said.

"Thank goodness for Wednesdays."

After eating a couple of soy burgers and drinking a soy beer he went over and made sure the front door was locked, turned on the stereo and settled back on the couch with his *Dream Maker 3000*.

"Let the weekend commence," he announced.

Induced dreaming was illegal as hell, but then what wasn't? It seemed the lawmakers didn't want anybody to have fun these days. He had the device only because he worked as a lab assistant at the facility where they were being developed.

A wave of relaxation swept over him; soon he was walking along a white sandy beach, on a tropical island paradise. Palm trees swayed in the warm breeze and a blue-green ocean stretched off to the horizon.

"Another day in paradise," said Trent.

He ran down to the water and dove in. He swam like Johnny Wiesmiller out to the reef and back, then got out and flopped down on the sand to dry off.

That's when he noticed he was sharing his island paradise with someone else. About a half mile up the beach someone was sunbathing.

"But that's impossible, this is only a dream; my dream."

He could have awakened himself but he decided to investigate instead. Trent approached cautiously, not knowing what to expect.

What he found was a beautiful alien girl sunbathing at the water's edge. She had long black hair and dark skin; her ears and nose were different, almost cat-like with big dark eyes. But she was very pleasing to look at.

When she finally noticed him, she jumped up and wrapped a sarong around herself.

"Who are you?" she asked.

"Who are you?" Trent asked back.

"Wait a minute, how can we be talking in English?"

"Telepathically," she answered his unspoken inquiry.

"Is your race telepathic?"

"No."

"Then how is this possible? I know, I'm dreaming. I'm dreaming this whole thing up."

"This is no dream," the girl insisted. "This is a real world; the sun, the moons, the stars and sea, it's all real. I grew up here, played on these beaches all my life. My village is just over there."

"There are more people here?" asked Trent.

"Sure there is. Come, I'll show you."

As they walked she introduced herself.

"My name is Leila."

"Mine's Trent, Trent Green," he said. They shook hands.

He couldn't help thinking; "I've met the girl of my dreams in a dream. This whole thing was getting weird."

When they got to the village she introduced him as Trent of Green, a traveler.

"Actually, that's Trent Green, not Trent of Green. Oh well, I guess that's close enough."

He was given things to eat and drink as they toured the village. Although his senses were assaulted by the many different odors and the strange sights and sounds of an alien culture, the overall effect was quite pleasant.

"I could get used to this," he thought.

"Tell me about this dream of yours?" Leila asked him.

"I'm no expert. It's an invention they came up with on my world; I mean my land, about ten years ago. It's kind of illegal; the government says it's dangerous."

"Anyway, you put on this headset and it stimulates the dream centers of your brain. The dream comes from your own imagination. Or at least I thought it did, I'm not so sure now. This dream seems to have taken on a life of its own."

Back in the real world:

Trent's comatose body has been taken to a nearby hospital.

"It's a shame so many of our young people end up like this; in a coma or found dead in their living quarters," said the admitting nurse to the doctor at the hospital's dream ward (two entire floors dedicated to catatonic dreamers).

"What I don't understand is why they don't come out of it when we take off the dreaming apparatus?" asked the nurse.

"The experts say that once their subconscious decides not to come back they don't really need the headset anymore," said the doctor

"Is the world so bad that they feel they have to escape through this dream technology?"

"I don't know. Who found him?" asked the doctor, as they plugged him into the life-support unit.

"His landlord; seems his rent was overdue."

"He got lucky."

The days slipped by and Trent and Leila became lovers. They explored the island together, swam in the fresh water lagoons at the island's interior and went fishing and diving on the coral reefs.

Trent couldn't remember ever being so happy. There was no way he was going back to his boring life on Earth.

One night while sitting around the campfire listening to the elders tell stories, a large fissure opened in the night sky overhead, the wind got suddenly cold and the stars began to fade. People were screaming and fleeing to their huts.

The elders turned to Trent and Leila and told them that the ancient ones had foretold this; there was nothing they could do. It was the end of the world.

Trent had some idea of what was happening. The dream program was deteriorating. Soon this world and all these people would cease to exist. He couldn't let that happen, he wouldn't. He laid his head back on the sand. If he could just concentrate, focus his thoughts on the dream, nothing else mattered.

"Did you just page me, Nurse Meade?"

"Yes doctor, a moment ago one of the patients started displaying higher brain activity. I thought he might be coming out of his coma, but after a few minutes he slipped back. Sorry to have disturbed you."

"Yeah, they do that sometimes, we don't know why," said the doctor.

Leila and Trent walked along the beach hand in hand.

"The elders are saying you have great magic," said Leila.

"It's no big deal. After all, I am Trent of Green."

QUALITY TIME

"The Senate came up just three votes shy of passing the Eight Day Work Week Amendment today," announced the newsperson on the overhead vid screen.

"Lawmakers in favor of the bill vowed to get the necessary votes at the start of the next session."

"Geez," thought Mike angrily. "We're already working seven days a week now. What do they want from us?"

The news channel continued, "Despite protests and sit-down strikes in cities around the country the President and his loyal followers plan to push for an extended work week."

"I know that most of you are working seven days a week now," said the President in a taped address. "It isn't fair and we're trying to do something about it. With the creation of the eight day week, you will be able to work seven days and still have a day off. Our nation's productivity has fallen dangerously behind that of Asia and South America. We have to keep up or we'll be a second rate country like the European Union before we know what hit us. We're calling the new day Patriot Day."

Mike's lift stopped at his floor and he filed out with his 165th floor neighbors. No one spoke, no one even made eye contact for fear someone would want to talk. There just wasn't any time for conversation these days.

When Mike arrived at his apt his wife and two allotted children were waiting for him.

"Daddy I finished that drawing we started this morning," announced Mike's four year son.

"That's great Bobby, but you know you're spoiling all the fun if you tell me what we did today," said Mike picking up his one year old daughter and feeling her diaper.

"Dinner will be ready in 1.5 minutes honey; just enough time for you to sonic shower," said Mike's wife from their kitchen.

"OK. Did we do anything special this morning?" asked Mike.

"You know I can't tell you that. Honestly Mike, you're just as bad as Bobby."

She was right. That was one of the rules of QT travel.

"The QT," thought Mike. "What would life be like without it? If you broke the rules and lost your license, life would be unbearable."

The Intra-Dimensional Time Machine or Q.T. as everyone called it; was used primarily to travel back eight hours in time (no more) to spent time with your family. In a world where most people worked 14 or 16 hours days and usually 7 days a week there wasn't a lot of time remaining for a home life. So instead of watching the vid after work you got in your QT and went back a few hours and spend that part of the day that you were at work with your family.

Time Travel Restrictions:

1. You may only travel a maximum 8 hours back in time.
2. You may only interact with your immediate family.
3. One hour before you catch up to yourself you must go.

Any violations of these laws were dealt with swiftly and harshly, for obvious reasons. A whole multitude of time paradoxes could occur if you tampered with the current timeline.

Everyone was conscientious about obeying the rules and so far things had gone smoothly, as far as anyone knew that is. Mike was just happy for the opportunity to be with his family in these hectic times. He, like everyone believed that someday the human condition would get better; it had to.

After dinner he said goodbye to his family, got into the QT machine and pushed the auto travel button.

The evening sun streaming into the living room changed to bright morning. Mike got out, stretched a little and walked around a bit. Things looked different somehow.

"Anyone home?" he called.

"I'm back in the bedroom," answered his wife Lois.

Mike found her still in bed and bent over and kissed her.

"You're up early," she said kissing him back.

"Where are the kids?" he asked looking around. "Why does this room look different?"

"The kids, Honey, how did you know I was pregnant? I was saving that surprise for the weekend. I thought you could take off Saturday and we'd go down to the courthouse together to fill out the pregnancy paperwork."

"You're pregnant again?"

"Again, this is my first time. What are talking about?" she asked, concerned now.

"We have two kids; Bobby and Sally. OK, you got me, stop joking," said Mike.

"Michael Phelps, we don't have any kids. I just became pregnant with our first child. We've only been married a year now."

"OK Lois, don't get mad. I've just been working too hard. You get some more sleep; I'm going to the store on 164."

Mike returned to the QT machine and quickly returned to the future. He remembered that moment when Lois had told him she was pregnant with their first child and it was six years ago - before the advent of the QT Machine. Somehow the machine had malfunctioned and he'd gone back six years.

When he arrived back in real-time he had visitors.

"I told them that you were gone but they said they'd wait," said Lois.

"Hello Mr. Phelps, we represent a consortium of scientists who are concerned about the direction this country has taken over the past few decades; most notably, the longer work week and our use of the time machine to extend our subjective time. You have to agree that everyone is working too much," said the spokesperson of the little group of rebel scientists.

"And the time machine was never meant to be used in this way!" added another.

Mike had seen these people on the vid, usually protesting one thing or another but never thought they'd be in his living room someday."

"We know what you're thinking, why did we pick you? Well, the fact is we reprogrammed lots of machines to go back and see what life used to be like."

"You did that! I could've gotten in a lot of trouble, maybe even lost my travel privileges. You people are crazy!" yelled Mike.

"No, crazy is tampering with the laws of nature just to have a few precious hours with our loved ones. Think about it man. What kind of life is this? Where does it end; a twenty hour day, a nine day week?"

"But what can I do about it?" asked Mike.

"We suggest you go back and find a nice place in the past, take your wife and kids and never come back. We feel it would be better to make one long trip then to make all these short daily trips," said the spokesperson.

"We'll see how much work THEY get done with everybody gone," said the other.

"Wouldn't that cause lots of time paradoxes?"

"They've been filling your ear with all that nonsense just to scare you. As long as you don't go back and kill your father or grandmother or something like that, you'll be fine."

"But if everyone left, wouldn't that be the end of the world," said Mike.

"Some diehards would probably stay behind and try to keep it going; but yes, that would probably be the end of the world, and good riddance."

"Wow, seems like a pretty radical solution," said Mike.

"All we ask is that you think about it, you know it's the right thing to do. Here are detailed instructions on how to disable the 8 hour time governor. With the travel restrictions removed it will allow you to travel anywhere in time and space you so desire; use your head though, you wouldn't want to go back too far, before there are any modern conveniences or to a time that's too dangerous."

They left the apartment while Mike was looking at the instructions.

Things got back to normal for the Phelps family. Mike got a promotion; the extra money was great but it meant more time at work and even less time with his family. They vacationed at Yellowstone Park for Mike's annual break. Bobby started school and Sally was walking on her own. It should have been a great time in their lives. But it wasn't; maybe it was post-vacation blues or maybe it was the eight day week, but he was restless and agitated. He could tell it was wearing on Lois too.

He couldn't help thinking what those protestors had said "Where does it end?"

There was no end in sight; they were working for works sake.

"We've lost control of this runaway train," he thought. He got out the time machine instructions and started studying them.

Reno, Nevada 1959

Mike Phelps really liked his new world. He had a good job at the 1st National Bank; it hadn't taken long to get the hang of old fashioned bookkeeping. He was driving down Main Street in his brand new T-bird, it was Friday and he didn't have to go back to work till Monday morning; life was good.

He and Lois had studied history books about early America before settling on Nevada; but the skiing, the mountains and lakes had convinced them, it was paradise.

"Honey, I'm home." He went into the kitchen to find dinner burning on the stove. Something was wrong.

"Where is everybody?" he yelled as he returned to the living room.

"They're not here Mr. Phelps. We've returned them to their rightful time," said a man sitting on his sofa watching the TV.

"Why hadn't he seen him when he came in?" thought Mike.

"This old time entertainment is quite amusing; I can see why you'd want to stay here. But what if everyone stayed in the past, Mr. Phelps? Now that wouldn't be right would it?"

"I'm in a lot of trouble aren't I?" asked Mike.

"Yes you are. You're looking at a two year suspension of your travel privileges at minimum. A second offense will mean jail time; your wife will suffer the humiliation of entering into the work force* and your children will end up in foster care. I'm sure you don't want anything like that to happen to them?"

*Family Act of 2087: Divorce was declared illegal
(except in extreme cases). And no women with children
of school age shall be allowed to work.

Life was more than boring when the Phelps family returned; it was downright intolerable; especially after they'd had a taste of the past. And on top of that Mike felt guilty for having put his family through the ordeal.

After a few months of nothing but work, sleep, eat and back to work, Mike started sneaking peeks at the time machine instructions again. He found out from the grapevine that the only people they'd been able to catch were those who kept their time machines. Mike had put their QT in the basement, dumb move. Millions of people had left and not been caught.

When his work break came this year he spent most of it at the library studying time machine books. There had to be a way to override the lockout program they had installed on his QT machine.

"Lois, I'd like to try to escape again."

"I know honey; I've seen you looking at those instructions. You don't have to ask for my permission, let's get outta here!"

They packed a few things; food, water, clothing, and locked the doors. As soon as he started tinkering with the controls they'd probably know what he was up to and come. But Mike was confident he could get past the security system. He pulled the machines' controlling circuit boards and installed his jury-rigged ones with new codes. Back in the computer's start-up mode though, he couldn't re-initialize. It wouldn't start up. They had disabled the power source. He tore open the battery compartment; one battery was gone.

He could almost imagine them getting out of their vehicles 165 floors below. He had to think fast. There was an emergency battery for the lift on every floor. He raced down the hall throwing open maintenance doors. Nothing, where had he seen them? On the 164th floor he ran into the night watchman.

"Mr. Phelps, I was watching you search for something on my security screen, and I figured out what you were looking for. They keep spare batteries for emergency power right over here. And I just happen to have a key card."

They each grabbed a battery and raced backed to Mike's apt. "Thank you sir; thank you so much," exclaimed Mike.

"No problem Sonny. I just hope it works," said the night watchman.

"But how did you know that's what I was looking for?" asked Mike.

"You need more power to go to the future. You are going to the future aren't you?" asked the old man.

"I hadn't planned to," said Mike as he frantically installed the new but not-quite-the-right-size batteries into the QT.

"Everyone's going to the future son. They can't catch you there, no chance of time paradoxes either. Better get goin' I think I hear them. I'll slow them up in the hallway if I can."

"Aren't you going?"

"I'll be along one of these days. Gotta make sure everybody gets out first."

He closed the door behind him.

Mike could hear the Feds in the hallway outside of their door.

"Get in, everybody get in." He spun the locator knob and carefully set a date into the chronometer, 06/06/2426 his birthday three hundred years in the future. As he pushed energize button the door of his apt flew off its hinges.

They materialized in an open field in the high sierra desert; he hoped they weren't too far from a town or city. They walked a few miles away from the QT machine and set up camp for the night. They made a fire and stayed up most of the night listening to coyotes and gazing at the magnificent starry sky.

"Even if they catch us dear, it was worth the try," said Lois as she and the kids snuggled up against one another for warmth.

In the morning a flyer circled their camp a few times and then landed. The pilot got out and came over to them.

"Just arrive?"

"Yesterday," said Mike.

"Hop in; I'll take you to town."

Town was Carson City, Nevada. Mike had shot for Reno but had missed by a few miles.

They were met by a group of townspeople and taken to city hall. "I hope we're not intruding," said Mike.

"On the contrary, we encourage immigration. Everyone here has come from the past," said the mayor.

"This video will explain it all much better than I can. It's a compilation of history we've been able to piece together from travelers coming from different periods in the past; and what little we could get from the history books written before the gap."

"The gap?" asked Lois.

"We call it the gap; the period between civilization dwindling out and when people started arriving here in the future. The video should explain it."

"The revolution started by the workers in 2115 was successful. Except for a few million people in isolated areas of the globe; everyone left for either the past or the future leaving the cities vacant; their power plants and automated systems still running," said the narrator.

"Some people probably remained behind but not enough to repopulate the Earth. The human race for all practical purposes died out. No one went just a few years into the future, for some reason they all decided to travel 100, 200 or more years into the future causing a gap in the history of mankind."

"When the first travelers started arriving in the future they found the cities empty, food and water supplies dried up, and very little power left to run things. It has been estimated there was at least a two hundred year gap between the end of mankind's rein on this planet and the beginning of this new age. For this reason we are not exactly sure of the current date."

"Those first travelers had to just about reinvent the wheel. But they got by, got the machines going again, established a world-wide communication system and set in motion a piecemeal commerce which is flourishing today; some countries even have air travel."

"It is estimated that there may be as many as two hundred million people scattered around the planet at this time, and more are coming all the time," concluded the video's narrator.

When the video ended the mayor came in and handed Mike a pack of matches.

"Would you like to do the honors?"

"What honors?" asked Mike confused.

Mike, Lois, Bobby and Sally went outside and there in the town square was their old QT machine; the townspeople had brought it in from the desert and had surrounded it with branches and twigs.

LAST CHANCE

In a remote government installation in Nevada, known for many years simply as area 51, a Top Secret project was coming to completion.

"T-minus 15 minutes and holding," a disembodied voice sounded over the loudspeaker.

Agent Dax Vulder waited in the dark as his fellow scientists scrambled to fix another system malfunction.

"Maybe we should delay the jump till we've worked out all the bugs," he said into his mic.

But he knew they couldn't wait any longer, they'd run out of time. Nuclear winter had cast its deadly shadow over the planet.

While he waited Agent Vulder went over his assignment one more time. Go back in time and try to prevent the assassination of General Secretary Mikhail Gorbachev in 1986.

Historians all agreed that that one incident had triggered the chain of events that had led to WWIII.

"How could one man's death be so catastrophic?" he thought.

"Other heads of state had been killed in the past; why did this one man's death mean so much?"

He had only the history tapes to go by but apparently this Gorbachev had come along at a crucial period in US-USSR relations. His policies of *Perestroika* and *Glasnost* were a welcome change from his hard line predecessors, and historians believed would surely have eased the tensions between the two countries.

After his death on May 1st 1986, things got much worse. A succession of militant communist leaders ran the country's economy into oblivion and caused several conflicts with the west.

First, was the secession of Chechen Republic which did not end well. That was followed by the bitterly contested conflict in the Baltic States in 2021, and finally the outright Revolution in the Ukraine which ultimately led to a devastating nuclear war as European Countries came to the aid of their allies.

A war in which major cities in Europe and Russia were leveled; commerce in North America and China were left crippled and the populations of the entire world were pushed to the brink of extinction.

Over the next four decades most of the world's food and energy surpluses were used up; hunger, disease and radiation sickness were taking their toll and the planet was in the grip of an ice age.

This time machine project, in which three generations of scientists had been working, was humanity's last hope.

Agent Vulder knew that if his mission was successful he might cause his own deletion; the timeline in which he existed might change, since he was born after Gorbachev's death. But it was a risk he and everyone connected to the project were willing to take if it meant saving the human race.

His real concern was how to stop the assassin or assassins from killing the General Secretary. He'd watched the tape of the assassination countless times. In slow motion you can clearly see Gorbachev knocked backwards as if hit by a bullet a split second before Alexi Petrov fired from behind.

The two gunmen theory had never been proved but most experts believed the KGB had a hand in the assassination and that Petrov was only a scapegoat.

He had to figure out a way to stop Petrov and who knows how many KGB agents involved; it wasn't going to be easy.

In a laboratory on the outskirts of Moscow another Top Secret time-travel experiment was about to begin.

Agent Vanna Scullivic sat in a dark, featureless booth and awaited the final countdown. Unknown to the American scientists the Russians had been working feverishly to perfect their own time-travel process. They too believed that going back and preventing Gorbachev's assassination was mankind's only chance. Her machine was very crude but the technology was sound.

She waved to her comrades and gave the thumbs up sign. The final switch was thrown and the room simply vanished. There was no sensation of movement, just the booth where she sat and nothingness outside of it. She thought the machine had malfunctioned or maybe all their theories of time travel had been wrong; but then almost instantaneously her surroundings changed. Suddenly she was in a wheat field.

She stepped out of the booth to a cool April morning.

She carefully laid the machine on its side and covered it with wheat, her coppery red hair shone in the early morning sunlight. She quickly changed into an old fashioned KGB uniform and made her way to the nearest road.

"With these forged KGB papers I should be able to get some kind of transportation," she hoped.

"Would you like another drink, Mr. Vulder?" asked the flight attendant.

"No thanks," said Dax. He was really enjoying pre-World War III opulence. He had made his way across the states, deceived his way into the press corps covering Gorbachev's May Day speech; and now he was sitting in First Class being waited on hand and foot. It made him feel guilty when he thought of the shortages and suffering in the future.

He hoped his AP credentials would allow him to get close enough to take out Petrov and the KGB hit men.

In his coat he was carrying the latest in stun gun technology, it was made completely of plastic so it was undetectable by scanners and had a range of over 100 feet. It was a very effective non-lethal weapon and a huge time anomaly if it were to fall into the wrong hands.

He looked at his watch; it was April 29th 1986, just two days before the assassination.

Agent Scullivic reported to KGB headquarters and was assigned to a security team covering the ground floor of Gorbachev's hotel.

She eavesdropped on as many conversations as she could but heard nothing of an assassination plot. She decided to go out that night and check the buildings across the square from the hotel; it would be the most logical place for the second gunman.

Once in the building she discovered she wasn't alone. A man was in the building already, checking offices that were facing the square. She followed him out of the building and back to his hotel. He turned out to be an American.

"Maybe the Americans had something to do with the assassination," she thought. "It didn't make sense, but then history had shown the Americans to have meddled before."

She had him arrested.

"What were you doing in that office building at night? You know we can hold you here in prison indefinitely," the KGB officer threatened.

"I don't know what you're talking about. I never left my hotel room last night," said Dax.

He had really screwed up. The fate of the world depended on him and he had screwed up.

While they interrogated the American, Agent Scullivic went through his papers. Everything seemed in order. Then she noticed his passport was made from a synthetic paper that wouldn't be developed until the late 1990's; her own forged paperwork was made of the same material.

"This guy's a time-traveler too," she realized.

May 1st 3:30 PM.

"Get up, I'm letting you go."

"But why did you have me arrested in the first place?" he asked.

"I thought you Americans were going to try to assassinate the General Secretary."

"I'm here to prevent it," said Dax.

"I know. You're a time traveler sent here to stop the assassination, and ultimately WWIII."

"How did you know that?" asked Dax in disbelief.

"Because I'm a time traveler too," said Vanna.

"Agent Vanna Scullivic at your service," said Vanna.

"Agent Dax Vulder, nice to meet you," said Dax smiling.

"Gorbachev's assassination is recorded in history at exactly 4:08 PM; we have only a few minutes left. I'll go to the hotel and stop Petrov; you go to the office building and take out the KGB shooter. Good luck."

"You too," said Dax. "Another time traveler well, how about that."

May 1ˢᵗ 3:58 PM.

Dax searched from room to room, he stunned a couple of KGB men in the hall and then found the room where the assassin waited to take his famous shot.

"Not this time pal," said Dax and stunned him before he could get to his weapon.

May 1ˢᵗ 4:06 PM.

"Good, you got him," said Vanna as she entered the room.

"What are you doing here? I thought you were going for Petrov."

"I couldn't get upstairs. But I've got an alternate plan," said Vanna.

"It had better be good, we've got less than two minutes now," said Dax.

May 1ˢᵗ 4:07 PM.

Vanna picked up the sniper's rifle and told Dax to kneel down facing the window. He did. She laid the rifle across his shoulder and took aim. As soon as she focused in on Gorbachev, Petrov appeared from behind the drapes, just as she'd seen him do so many times in the news tapes.

"Don't even breathe," she said.

Dax obeyed.

She fired.

The bullet passed just inches from Gorbachev's head, causing him to flinch backwards, and struck Petrov as he was about to fire. He never knew what hit him.

"Nice shooting," said Dax.

"I've been practicing that shot in my dreams my whole life," said Vanna.

"We'd better get out of here."

Down in the streets the people were shouting, "The KGB saved Gorbachev! The KGB saved Gorbachev!"

"We're still here, I wonder if we've accomplished anything?" Dax shouted over the cheers of the crowd.

"We'd better get back and find out. You can go in my machine," said Vanna.

"But what about mine?" asked Dax.

"Now that we know about each other there's no need for secrecy. My people will retrieve it. It's about time we started trusting one another don't you think?" said Vanna.

"That's right were allies now."

"Let's hope."

When they got to the wheat field outside of Moscow the time machine was gone. The field of grain wasn't even disturbed.

"Are you sure this is the spot?" asked Vulder.

"Of course I'm sure."

"I guess we're stuck here in the past then," said Vulder.

"You're right no time travel machine means our mission was a success. My guess is we didn't feel compelled to invent time travel in that timeline, we should be happy," said Vanna. "But what we will do here in the past?"

"We've both done extensive reading on this period in history, it shouldn't be hard to get jobs and make a living," said Vulder.

"I guess you're right," said Vanna.

"Also, I'd like to keep an eye on this time period. See that they don't screw up again: if you know what I mean."

"I've always been intrigued by the Federal Bureau of Investigation, I think I'll go back to the United States and try to hook up with them," said Vulder. "What kind of training have you had?"

"I have some training in forensic medicine, do you think they'd take me too?" asked Vanna.

"I don't know why not," said Vulder.

"Then I too shall join this Bureau of Federal Investigation," said Vanna.

"That's Federal Bureau of Investigation; FBI for short," said Vulder.

"And you might want to lose your Russian accent, and shorten your name a little. What did you say your name was again?"

"Scullivic," said Vanna.

"Mind if I call you Scully?" said Dax.

UNREALITY
(A LOVE STORY)

"Something didn't feel right," Eric thought as he worried the plow blade out of another rut. The ground was hard here; these fields had lain dormant for a long time.

But the King had decreed that all arable land would be plowed and sewn with new crops. So Eric and all the other farmers in the Kingdom toiled late into the evenings to keep up with demand. Why the King needed more food supplies was unknown. Few of the farmers out in the outer provinces had even seen this new King; his rise to power had been shrouded in mystery.

Eric couldn't shake the nagging feeling that something was about to happen; so he decided to call it a day. He unhitched the heavy plow from his mule and patted his old friend on the shoulder.

"You can take the rest of the day off boy you've earned it." It wasn't unusual for Eric to talk to the mule as they plowed.

"I'm headed back to the house, you can follow me if you want," he said trying to coax his stubborn friend back to the barn.

But the mule wasn't listening; he trotted off in the direction of a field of clover.

Eric made his way down the hill towards his little farmhouse. He had several acres still to plow but it could wait till tomorrow. It wasn't a big farm but it was all his and that was enough.

Most likely his wife Janette would scold him for quitting early but she never stayed angry with him for very long. He could picture her in the kitchen making supper right now. Her long dark hair tied in a pony tail, her brown suntanned skin and big green eyes; she was perfect and he loved her madly. They'd grown up in the village together, been childhood sweethearts; it was a given that someday they'd be married. Now that they were, he still couldn't believe his good fortune.

"What's for supper?" he asked as he entered the house.

"I'm starved."

"You're finished plowing already?" asked Janette.

"Well, not exactly. I just couldn't stand being away from you another minute," he said and tried to hug her.

She wouldn't let him, "Go take a bath, you're all sweaty. Dinner won't be ready for an hour."

As they ate she remarked, "You know one of these days that mule isn't coming home."

Later that evening they sat on the porch watching the sun go down.

"We've got it pretty good don't you think? Eric asked.

"If you could trade places with anyone; anyone in the world, who would it be?"

"I wouldn't trade places with anyone dear, not even the Queen," she said.

He wouldn't either," he thought.

"It was a hard life, farming. And the King took a large portion of his crops as taxes, but he got a good price on what remained; enough to put food on the table and even buy a new dress for his beautiful wife from time to time.

"Yep, they had it pretty good," he thought as he dozed off in his rocking chair.

When Eric woke up in his bunk in the barracks he had that strange feeling again, like a dream you just can't quite remember. Whatever it was he wasn't going to figure it out lying here. He got up and got dressed.

He loved being a soldier in the King's Guard. The adventure, the excitement, the danger; it made him feel alive. He'd been a soldier most of his adult life and through a lot of hard work and a minimum amount of bootlicking he'd worked his way up to this elite position.

The Guard had spent this past year fighting insurgents. A small ill-equipped band of rebels displeased with the King's heavy burden of taxes had been raiding villages along the border and stirring up the populace with wild accusations.

They hid in the forests and in the mountains, ambushing supply caravans and distributed the loot among the country folk, so they were well liked in the outer fringes of the Kingdom. Even so they were more of a nuisance than a threat.

That ended a couple of weeks ago when they'd attacked a squad of Guardsmen and confiscated their weapons. Now the rebels had blasters, which made their little insurrection quite a different matter.

The King was very concerned. Eric had never seen the King so upset; he wanted the rebels found immediately and the weapons returned.

Late that afternoon Eric's company was deep in the forest. They were following a rebel trail they'd picked up earlier in the day. Staying as quiet as they could the Guardsmen finally caught up to the rebels in a clearing with tall grass and started firing.

The rebels returned fire. They had blasters; the unmistakable sound and acrid smell of blaster fire filled the air.

Rebels and Guardsmen alike were falling under the deadly barrage. There was no defense against a blaster; it would cut through almost anything.

As Eric's squad was moving around to encircle the rebels, someone dashed by and Eric took off in pursuit.

The chase took him deeper into the forest. Each time he was about to overtake his quarry the rebel would change direction and dart down another trail.

He was near exhaustion when the rebel finally gave up and turned to make a stand; only then did he realize he'd been chasing a woman. She stood there, gasping for breath, a small knife raised in defense.

Eric just kept running, barreling her over and knocking the knife out of her hand. As he pinned her down he got a good look at her face; and at that moment everything in his life changed.

He recognized this woman; her face, her expression, the little habit of blowing her hair out of her eyes with an upward whistle out the side of her mouth. He'd seen that before.

"I know you. You're name is Janette," he said.

"How did you know that?" she demanded.

"I think we were married. We lived on a small farm together," he blurted out.

"But that doesn't make sense, I've been a soldier most of my life," he thought.

"Look soldier, I've never seen you before," she said.

"And I'd certainly never marry a soldier in the King's Guard."

Eric was confused; bits and pieces of his life as a farmer flashed through his mind. It was a strong emotion.

Stronger than mere déjà vu; these were actual memories he was recalling. He put his thoughts aside for the moment, got up and tied her hands behind her back. They started back to his company. Along the way they talked.

"Why do you oppose the King?" he asked her.

"He's a tyrant! He takes food from the mouths of his people to fund his ghastly empire. Why do you think we are always at war?"

"Because the other countries see how good we've got it and want to take it away from us," said Eric, repeating what his company commander had said.

"You mean like the blasters? Did you ever wonder where such powerful weapons came from?" she asked.

"Our scientists have developed these weapons for us to fight the barbarians to the north," said Eric.

"They're not barbarians! They're peace-loving people who see something terrible happening here and are trying to stop it."

For more than an hour they walked and talked. As he listened to her parts of his memory came back to him. He'd led many lives it seemed; a technician, a blacksmith, a farmer.

That last memory was most vivid because this girl had been part of it. He felt affection for her. No, it was much more than affection, he loved her. And she had loved him, he was sure of it. Something strange was happening here, people's lives were being changed.

Why he was the only one to realize it, he didn't know, but he had a feeling it had something to do with his love for this woman. Somehow his feelings for her had overcome the trickery that had everyone else in its grasp. The more he listened to her the more determined he was to find out.

"Halt," he said.

"I'm letting you go. I want you to take me to your rebel friends. I need to talk to them."

"How do I know this isn't some kind of trick?" asked Janette.

He untied her hands and handed her his blaster. "Take my weapon," he said.

She was in shock. She had just captured a soldier in the King's Guard; a crazy one to be sure, but still.

At the rebel camp Eric was shown writings and told many a strange story of fantastic weapons and unimaginable technology. No one knew exactly what was happening but at the center of it all was the King. The stories jogged more memories.

He remembered the King operating some kind of machine; a machine that somehow had the power to change people's lives. He began to agree with the rebels, the King must be mad.

He stayed with the rebels a few days. They kept on the move, crossing into the lands to the North. He had never been this far north, the King's Guard had never been allowed past the borders of the Kingdom. And now he was beginning to realize why.

He couldn't stay with the rebels indefinitely though, he needed to get back and tell his commander what he had learned. If the King was changing people's lives it was up to the Guard to stop him.

He started out early in the morning, and was making good time when somewhere near the border he started to feel that same premonition he'd had before.

Soon he was struggling just to walk. He had to stop and sit down next to a tree; if he could just catch his breath he thought, he'd be all right. He fell fast asleep.

When Eric awoke he was in a tent. He had a different uniform on. He stepped out of the tent to find that he was at the front, surrounded by troops preparing for battle.

Things had changed again and he seemed to be the only one who noticed. It had to have something to do that woman he'd met. His love for her was so strong it overcame the spell that affected all others in the Kingdom. He had to get back to the castle and confront the King; he had to have his life with Janette back.

The King's army held the high ground. To the north a massive army was marching towards them. Although the King's troops were greatly outnumbered they still held the edge; for they had the King's superior weapons. He watched in horror as weapons that nobody even began to understand were wheeled out and aimed at the advancing enemy. The King's scientists were there to show them how to operate the advanced weaponry.

"Why doesn't anyone question why we have all this technology?" he wondered.

It would be a slaughter. He couldn't just stand there and watch; he had to warn them. But it was too late; the enemy had advanced into range and the King's troops opened fire. Bolts of energy sliced through the charging soldiers, wiping out twenty or thirty at a time. Wave after wave of soldiers advanced only to be blasted out of existence.

Eric couldn't take it anymore. He clubbed the operator of the nearest energy canon and turned it on his own lines. With only a few shots he destroyed most of the King's weaponry, turning them into molten slag. The soldiers who weren't killed by the energy blasts fled for their lives.

He then quickly made a makeshift white flag and went down the hill to talk to the enemy.

In the enemy camp they explained how they had watched their neighbor's reality change monthly, sometimes weekly. The King's machine had a range it would seem. Anyone inside the broadcast range had no idea his or her lives were being changed. Anyone outside the range observed in horror at the constantly changing realities.

It was decided the army would go no further. It would draw too much attention. A small group armed with confiscated blasters and whatever energy weapons weren't destroyed would try to get to the castle before this reality changed again. They marched for two days and nights and got to the foothills overlooking the castle just before dawn on the third day.

"Aim your blasters at the battlements," Eric told them. "That's where their defenses should be. Keep firing until nothing is left."

They started firing with blasters, slicing away huge chunks of stone. Beneath the stone was a bright, shiny metal; the same material the weapons were made of.

The King's Guard had been caught napping, they were able to get off a few shots, but the others kept up the barrage until the castle's defenses fell silent.

During the siege Eric found a way into the castle. He remembered a laboratory in the exact center of the castle.

When he burst through the doors he discovered the King at the machine busily making adjustments; he was about to make another reality shift.

"Oh, it's you," he said.

"I was wondering who was behind this."

"Get away from that machine," said Eric aiming his blaster at the King.

The King backed away from the machine.

"How can you toy with people's lives like this?" Eric asked.

"I'm glad you asked that," said the King smiling.

"I'm not from this world you know, I come from another planet. A world far more advanced than this ball of mud, a world of wondrous technological achievements. A world I doubt you could even imagine."

"But it was boring," said the King. "Quite boring in fact, a device like this Dimension Shifting Machine, my own invention by the way; was outlawed."

"They didn't appreciate my creative genius. So I went out in search of a world where I could use it and I found this little underdeveloped planet of yours, it was perfect."

"If you will allow me I could show you," said the King.

"Show me, how?" Eric inquired.

"I recorded my landing, of course. Here let me show you."

He went over to another machine keeping his hands held high; then reached down and pushed a button and a video monitor began showing images. It showed a spaceship coming out of orbit. People were looking up at it as it descended.

"I turned on my Dimension Shifter as soon as I spotted your little village. Your people were probably wondering what it was they were seeing, so I gave them an answer. I made them believe it was their God/King coming down from the heavens to exist among them."

"Once I'd established myself I gave them assignments, like building this castle around my ship and assisting me with setting up my machines," as the King spoke he slowly inched his way towards a drawer where he kept his personal blaster.

"With this machine and the others I've built I will soon take over this entire planet."

"But why?" asked Eric.

"It amuses me," he said. "You should try it. You know you were once my assistant here in the lab. The control room is insulated from the changes that affect the outside world. I had big plans for you Eric; but you opposed me from the very beginning. I had you banished and your mind erased. I guess should have just killed you."

He reached for his blaster suddenly, pulled it out and fired.

From behind Eric someone yelled, causing him to flinch and the King's shot narrowly missed. Eric dove under a workbench before the King could get off another shot.

The King hurried to the control panel; one flip of a switch and another reality would be in place. One in which the rebel forces weren't in control. Before he could reach the switch though, Eric fired.

The King stood there a moment looking down at the smoking hole in his chest.

"But it wasn't supposed to happen like this," he said, and then dropped to the floor. He was quite dead.

The assistant who had yelled the warning came over and helped Eric up.

"You don't remember me do you?"

"Not really, everything is coming back in bits and pieces," said Eric.

"My name is Peter. We were friends once; grew up in the village together actually. I was the one assigned to erase your memory; I guess I didn't do such a good job."

"Thanks Peter, I owe you my life," said Eric.

"No sweat. What will you do now?" asked Peter.

"Destroy this machine before it can ruin any more lives!" said Eric emphatically.

"Before you do, would you allow me to make a few changes?" asked Peter.

"Sure."

Peter adjusted a few knobs and then said, "Aim your weapon right there."

Eric fired and his world changed one last time.

He woke up in the biggest bed he'd ever seen. When he turned over he found someone was sleeping next to him. He quietly slipped out of bed and went over to the window and threw open the curtains; they opened onto a balcony.

He looked out to see a large crowd of people filling the courtyard; they began cheering when he walked out onto the balcony. Eric was overwhelmed. He looked down at his robes and realized that now he was the King.

"Oh my God, it can't be. I don't know the first thing about governing people."

Another loud cheer began as the Queen stepped out onto the balcony beside him. It was Janette of course, and she looked magnificent.

She smiled, took his hand and led him over to the railing to wave to his subjects.

"Maybe I could get used to this after all," Eric thought after a moment then waved to the cheering people.

WISHFUL THINKING

Frank Rogers, head of the Federal Aviation Administration, sat at his desk studying report after report of recent airline accidents and aborted takeoffs.

"There had to be some connection," he thought.

"Bad fuel, bad weather; something had to be causing this unprecedented rash of incidents."

But there just wasn't anything; every incident was different. He was interrupted by a knock at the door.

"Come in," he said.

One of his assistants, a Jeffrey McConnell peeked in and asked, "Got a minute Frank?"

"Sure," said Frank as he put on his best pseudo-attentive face and tried to listen. He never liked this guy. They'd hired him because of his impeccable credentials; degrees in aeronautics and metallurgy, a PHD in physics; but he was kind of weird. He was always coming up with off-the-wall conclusions. Frank just didn't like him.

"I've been thinking about all the accidents and aborted takeoffs we've had lately and I think I've come up with an explanation, more of a theory really," said Jeffrey.

"Oh boy, this ought to be good," thought Frank.

"My job's on the line and he's coming up with theories."

What had started out with a few unexplained airline mishaps had escalated into an epidemic. Planes were falling out of the sky for no reason. Most couldn't even get off the ground. They'd roar down the runway at full power but they simply wouldn't lift off. Repair station mechanics and FAA inspectors had gone over each aircraft and found nothing mechanically wrong with them; they should have taken off.

Frank was beginning to suspect it was some kind of union action by the pilot's to get more pay, either that or they'd lost their nerve. Now with the exception of a few airplanes in France every airline in the world was shut down until they could get come up with an answer. The travel industry had come to a screeching halt.

"What's your theory, Jeff?"

"This is going to sound crazy, even for me," the newest engineer on the staff began. "Physics has changed sir, well not changed exactly, but there's an added component that we never accounted for."

"What are you talking about," asked Frank.

"I think the flying public has lost confidence in our ability to fly, or more precisely the airplane's ability to fly. I know we've been flying for over a hundred years but for some reason, maybe too many realistic airplane crashes in movies has got them spooked, I don't know, but whatever the reason the populace has begun to believe that airplanes can't fly," Jeff paused waiting for a comment, none came.

"We know the actual physics of flight, the negative pressure of the airflow over the top of the wing that causes lift, the thrust of the engines and all the other components of flight. Its physics, that hasn't changed; you just have to look out the window to see that birds are still flying. But the Average Joe on the street doesn't know exactly why planes can fly, he just believes. Maybe there's another component we engineers haven't considered. The idea that our belief in mankind's ability to make machines that can fly is part of the equation'" he finally concluded.

"Let me get this straight," said Frank. "You think that airplanes have been flying all these years because we believe they can?"

"Yes, our faith in the airplane was inspired on that day at Kitty Hawk when the Wright Brothers won us over; we all became believers that day," said Jeff.

"Now for some unexplained reason that spell has been broken."

Frank sat back in his chair. He'd heard some weird things in his life but this was the strangest, mumbo jumbo he'd ever heard.

"Well, Jeff that's an interesting theory. I'll take it into consideration."

Jeff started to leave. "One more thing sir, if my theory is correct; and God I hope it's not, then it might only be a matter of time before mankind loses faith in all technology. If that happens the human race could be in for a lot of trouble."

"Let's just worry about one thing at a time Jeff," said Frank. "I'll see you at the 3 o'clock meeting."

After Jeff had left the room he thought, "That's it.

He's fired! I don't care what kind of credentials he has. Humanity has been wishing the planes into the air all these years? That's, that's ridiculous!"

Frank dove back to his mountain of paperwork shaking his head.

The first indication of the end came about an hour later when the computer shut off for no reason. Then the ceiling fan stopped turning.

"What the..?"

Finally the office lights began to flicker and then went out.

Frank groped for the phone in the dark; the line was dead of course and Frank knew why.

PAST EVENT IMAGER

PROLOGUE

Excerpt from Scientific American 2086:

With the advent of the Omni-Computer in the late 21st century the scientific community began interpreting the universe in eleven dimensions. Although the human mind is not capable of thinking in more than three dimensions the computer could and it provided the mathematical formulae which changed the world even more profoundly than did quantum physics in the twentieth century.

One of the more celebrated accomplishments of the new math was interpreting Einstein's unified field theory, which lead to a better understanding of the universe; as well as advancements in energy generation, communications and weather control to name only a few.

Less notable were answers to questions like the existence of a metaphysical world. Is there an afterlife? Do ghosts really exist?

From a scientific perspective some theorized that what we call the metaphysical world could be incursions from these other dimensions. Unexplained sights and sounds that people experienced could be our mind's analog processes attempting to interpret parallel phenomena existing in the multi-dimensional universe.

Stories of dead people's faces showing up on photographic plates, hauntings and things that go bump in the night might simply be momentary intrusions into our dimension from one of these parallel dimensions.

Another phenomena, which is commonplace but hard to understand is the dimension of time. Our passage through time would seem linear; we are here, the future lies ahead of us, the past behind. But, what if every facet of time existed simultaneously? Events that have taken place in the past are imprinted in our subconscious, and they remain with us.

For example, if you were to go to Lakehurst NAS in New Jersey and look up at the eastern sky your subconscious mind can imagine the

Hindenberg going up in flames. Visit the Kennedy Space Center and look up at that sky; you would see the Challenger exploding.

The same holds true for the World Trade Center terrorist attacks in 2001 and the devastating meteor strike in Omaha, Nebraska in 2024.

The more cataclysmic the event the easier it is to imagine. The event is still happening in the dimension we call time. The past, present and future are all around us, but we can only experience the here and now.

The theory of a multi-dimensional universe was never meant to debunk the belief in God and the hereafter, and it's not meant to. But to some it clarified things. We now know we are a part of a much bigger picture; whether it's controlled by an all-powerful deity or not, there is more to this world than we can perceive.

A useful scientific discovery made possible by the new technology was the development of the PEI or the Past Event Imager, a device that can detect, record, and playback images in the past. A device so sensitive it can catch the after images of events that have occurred up to eight hours in the past; the more violent the activity the more vivid and lasting the images.

The PEI became an immediate boon to the investigation of criminal activity. A CSI team need only get to the crime scene within the eight hour time frame, set up the machine and it would show everything that had happened at that location in the last eight hours.

With its introduction in the year 2058 bringing the right criminals to justice became indisputable.

CRIME #1

"What's up," asked Lt. Mickey Jones, homicide division, 8th precinct.

"It's puzzling," answered Detective Dan Smith. "You've got to see it to believe it."

The lieutenant looked around the room; a violent crime had taken place here and not too long ago. A woman's body lay crumbled in the corner of the room. The room was a mess, like a wrestling tag team had gone a few rounds in there. The first witnesses on the scene swore that the room had been locked from the inside.

"Let's see." said the lieutenant.

The detective rewound the tape to almost the full eight hours and replayed it. The room was empty except for the young woman. She was reading and the TV was on. Then suddenly she was lifted out of the chair and hurled violently against the wall; picked up again and tossed across the room hitting the end table. No one else could be seen in the room, an invisible force of some kind had caused all this destruction.

"Could we move the machine back a little more, to see more of the room? Maybe whatever did this is just out of the machine's range," suggested the Lt. Jones.

"I guess we could position the machine to take in more of the room, but too much time may have elapsed since the crime was committed."

A few minutes later they had the PEI set up and ready to try again.

The detective turned on the machine. The usual humming noises preceded the fuzzy images which slowly came into focus.

"You see Mick, we're too late."

The crime had already taken place; the woman lay dead in the corner. They fast forwarded and watched as the maid came in to discover the body of the dead girl. They watched as the police arrived and cordoned off the area. Eventually the forensic team arrived and began setting up the PEI.

"It's too late to see anything we haven't already seen sir," said Detective Smith.

But as they watched a bystander entered the room. The police made no attempt to stop him. He was dressed in a long black coat, had long black hair but most of his features were covered by an upturned collar. He stood there a moment watching the forensic team and then turned directly at the Lieutenant and Detective, like he was looking into a camera.

Detective Smith was about to say something but the words stuck in his throat. Lt. Jones felt the hair on the back of his neck stand up. The man or creature had an evil specter about him; a presence that made the senses recoil.

"If I didn't know better I'd say he was looking right at us; that's impossible right? We're looking back in time, back at what occurred a few hours ago," said Lt. Jones.

"That's right; this machine of ours won't be here for hours. I mean what if we had decided to set it up over there?"

"That's a good idea, Smitty. Set the machine up over there. Let's get another angle on the room."

"OK, but I don't know what good that will do?"

"Just humor me, OK?"

A few minutes later they had the machine up and running from across the room. When the images sharpened the stranger was still there watching the forensic team dusting for prints. He watched for another moment and then turned again in the direction of Smith and Jones. This time he grinned, a sardonic smile that made the blood in your veins go cold.

"Oh God," said Smitty. "This is freaking me out. How in the world could he know we moved over here?"

"Because he's here now," said the Lieutenant.

"I didn't know you were a believer," said Detective Smith.

"I'm not, but he's here with us now. I can feel him."

The Lieutenant stepped into the empty room waving his arms, the officers nearby looked at him like he'd gone mad.

"Whoever you are, we know you're here and we're going to get you!"

The intruder turned and walked out.

"So how are we going to get this guy sir?" asked Smitty.

"I don't know," said the lieutenant scratching his replacement hair follicles.

Crime #2
9:26 AM Calvert Street Bridge

It was the usual bumper to bumper traffic going into the city. Carl Lasser sat behind the wheel of his hover-car complaining, as usual.

"Man, I wish they'd do something about the lights coming off the bridge."

His carpool buds had heard this argument before and ignored him; one read the morning paper, the others caught a few extra minutes sleep. "They should..." he started to say but the sentence was cut off when the driver's side door was ripped off its hinges. Before anyone could react Carl was yanked from the car by some invisible force and tossed over the bridge's guardrail, falling hundreds of feet to the river below.

The remaining occupants of the car and those of the surrounding traffic just sat there in shocked disbelief.

Traffic was backed up for miles and then had to be rerouted while the police tried to figure out what had happened.

"Keep the machine running," said Lt. Jones. He knew this was the work of their murderer.

Once again the murderer did not show up on the PEI, just an invisible force tossing the vic around like a rag doll. They waited with the machine running; and sure enough the stranger appeared again.

"Come to admire your work," shouted the Lt. at thin air.

The stranger again looked directly at them as they looked into the PEI's viewer. He looked different though, and was dressed differently too. He held up a hand-written message telling them to turn the frequency on the PEI all the way to the right, into the UHF band. They would lose the image but could hear him talking.

"Can you hear me? I'll keep talking. Nod your head if you hear me."

"I've got him," said Det. Smith as he adjusted the frequency knob.

"I can see you, you can't see me. We exist in a parallel universe, a realm that is very different than this one. Yours is a wondrous dimension from what I have seen of it. I can see how it would tempt beings from my world," said the stranger.

"Where is your world?" asked the Lt. Jones.

"My world? That would be hard to explain; let's just say it's another dimension. And I'm sorry to say we have some particularly malevolent entities. This one has ignored the rules that govern inter-dimensional travel and has caused death and destruction in both our worlds."

"I believe this machine you have created to look into the past has somehow caused a disruption in the time stream matrix. It has created an overlapping effect which is the reason for this dimensional incursion. I can't undo what he has been done but I will attempt to put a stop to this killing spree. I may need your help to set a trap for the entity."

"Just tell us what to do," said the Lt, not really believing this whole thing was happening.

"It may be possible to use this remarkable machine of yours to trap and destroy this entity. We can only interact with your world when the machine is running," said the stranger.

"But we're only here on this bridge because he committed the crime here," argued Det. Smith.

"How could he commit the crime before the machine was set up? It's like putting the cart before the horse."

"Our relationship with time is different; the operation of your machine being upstream or downstream of the event you speak of, makes no difference to us," explained the stranger.

"Why is he doing this," demanded the LT. Jones.

"To get your attention I would think," said the stranger.

"Well, he's got it. What now?"

"I believe he wants to use your machine to retreat from his dimension."

"Is that possible?"

"It may be. If you were to set up three or four of these machines and focus them on a particular spot, enough energy could be generated to open a rift between our worlds," said the stranger.

"Once he has passed into your world you would be able to capture or destroy him."

"If we decide to do this, and I'm not saying we will; how do we get in touch with you again?" asked the Lieutenant.

"You don't need to. The combined power of your machines will guide us to it. But be ready for him. He is very powerful."

They set up four PEI's in a vacant warehouse down by the Potomac River. Two heavily arms SWAT teams gathered inside and another compliment of police officers surrounded the building. The entire area had been evacuated for hours.

The Lieutenant gave the signal to switch on the machines. For the first minute or two nothing happened, the humming of the four machines was the only sound, and the movement of the police officers positioning themselves to get a direct line of sight.

Nothing was happening in the view screens of any of the machines. More minutes passed and then a shimmering circle of light appeared, suspended in the air directly in front of the machines.

As the circle expanded an acrid smell of sulfur filled everyone's nostrils. The circle expanded even more and soon they were looking into what looked like Dante's Inferno; a fiery cavernous abyss spread before their eyes.

The heat was so intense that everyone near the opening had to move back. Then a silhouette of a man appeared, slowly advancing towards them, he finally stepped through the opening into the warehouse.

The moment the entity stepped through the portal he began sweeping the warehouse with jets of flame. Everything combustible immediately caught fire, including the officers nearest the portal. The fire seemed to coming right from his hands. Those who weren't struck by the flames ran and crawled their way to safety.

As Lt. Jones fled, he caught a glimpse of their assailant. It wasn't the stranger they had encountered in the first victim's room; it was the second stranger, the one who had spoken to them; the one who had talked them into this ill-advised experiment. He was the murderer; not the first one. They'd been had!

Over the roar of the fire Mickey could hear the creature laughing, giggling almost, as he seemed to be thoroughly enjoying himself. Then he stopped for no reason and stood perfectly still.

It was then that Mickey noticed another creature step through the circle of fire behind the first.

It was the entity they had seen at the first murder. The one whom he had assumed had committed the crimes. One look at this being standing in front of the abyss, and there was no doubt who they were looking at.

The Devil grabbed the other creature by the throat and started to return to his world, but before stepping back through the portal he paused for a moment to take one last look around.

He looked straight at Lt. Jones and spoke.

"Thank you for your assistance Lieutenant; this one thought he could get away. I would advise you not to use these machines of yours anymore; it would seem they are too much of a temptation to the individuals in my charge."

The Devil then snatched up his subject and stepped back into Hell.

MEMOIR

Mike Smith laid his head back on his pillow. He was dying; cancer riddled his 55-year-old body. He wasn't in any pain, the drugs took care of that, but he was dying. These were probably the last moments of his life.

"I've had a good life, a very good life" he thought.

"Nothing to write about, but I've had my moments." He closed his eyes; he would spend his remaining time re-capping the highlights.

That's when Professor Dibley slipped into the room and injected his serum into Mr. Smith's I.V. The professor was a kindly old coot who showed up at the medical center from time to time with his latest elixir; it was guaranteed to cure everything from arthritis to high blood pressure. This latest batch was even a tonic for old age.

The professor was quite proud of his serum; it had taken him a lifetime to perfect. He knew it worked, he'd tried it out on his monkeys and they were doing fine. He needed a human subject to try it out on, but the doctors wouldn't let him. He suspected they were afraid that if his elixir *did* work they'd be out of a job.

"We're sure it's great stuff professor, but you know we can't give it to our patients until it's approved by the Food and Drug Administration. Give us a sample and we'll have it tested," they had said.

The professor knew he was a bit senile but he wasn't stupid, he wasn't about to give them a sample so they could steal his formula and take all the glory.

No, he'd find his own test subject, someone very sick. He looked at Mr. Smith's chart.

"Perfect, this guy doesn't have much time left; if my serum works he'll be thanking me. I might even get the Nobel Prize for this; now to get out of here without anyone seeing me."

Mr. Smith was so absorbed in his thoughts he never heard the professor come and go.

His thoughts drifted back in time.

It was 1964, the Beatles had three top ten hits, and the Space Race was at full throttle. President Kennedy was gone, but his legacy lived on in the *President's Physical Fitness Challenge.*

There were ten categories; 100-yard dash, 440, 1 mile, long jump (the fast guys won all those); pull-ups, rope climb, and some other gym stuff that all the jocks won. There was just one event that he had any chance at, the softball throw.

Mike Smith was a skinny, 125-lbs. back in those days, he wasn't a nerd, but he wasn't exactly a jock either. He went out for the football team every year but always got cut.

One thing he learned way back in sixth grade though was he could throw. He once threw a kid out at home plate all the way from center field.

That had been a baseball though, the softball was a different animal, it had a strange size; really hard to get any mustard on it. So he practiced. He practiced all summer. The trick was not throwing it too high; you had to throw a line drive if you wanted any distance.

It was a two-day affair, five events each day during Phys. Ed. Class. The winning students in each grade got their names on a plaque for that year. He was determined to be one of those names on the junior class plaque.

Each student got two throws. The jocks threw first; they were all kidding around, not taking it seriously. Some threw too high, some too low.

"Who cares about the softball throw anyway?" said Tommy Sullivan.

Finally it was Mike's turn. He stepped back about 3 yards from the goal line, (you were allowed a running start) took a deep breath ran up to the goal line and heaved it.

It was perfect, not too high, a perfect arc just like he'd practiced. It landed on the 46-yard line on the other side of the field, a 54-yard throw.

"Who threw that?" asked the coach.

"Mike Smith threw that?" the coach wrote something on his clipboard.

"Lucky throw," said Tommy Sullivan.

"You'll never do that again," said Johnny Carley.

He had their attention now. The competition suddenly got serious.

"I wasn't really trying that first throw," said Johnny.

Each jock took a shot at Mike's mark, and each came up short. Then it was Mark Slater's turn. Mark was the 1st string Q.B. on the J.V. team.

"Nice throw Smith, good technique. But I'm afraid I can't let you do this, reputation you know."

He stepped up and let go a beauty, a perfect line drive. It hit on the 41-yard line, a 59-yard throw.

"Yeah," said Mark.

"Way to go Mark," said his entourage.

"Nice throw," said the coach. "Too bad you can't throw like that when the game's on the line."

It was Mike's turn again. His surprise attack had almost worked. Now he had to beat the jocks at their own game.

"Don't think about them," he thought. "Pretend you're in center field, the runner is tagging up. You can't let him score. The crowd is yelling, throw it Mike; throw it."

Mike threw it. The ball left his hand and into Albert Einstein High School history. He watched it fly, it seemed like it would never come down. This was his moment; it landed on the 36-yard line, 64 yards away!

"Wow," said the coach.

Mike got an "A" in Physical Education that semester. He and his small circle of friends could walk a little taller after that; even the jocks had a new respect for him.

His 64-yard record held up for almost ten years.

"Yep that was quite a memory."

Mike moved on down memory lane.

There was that time in 1970, when he was a hippie. It was the 4th of July; his friends and he were camped out under the stars by the reflecting pool between the Washington Monument and the Lincoln Memorial.

They'd come to D.C. to watch the fireworks and had decided to stay all night.

The fireworks had been spectacular. The smell of cordite still filled the air, if you shut your eyes you could almost imagine you were on some ancient battlefield.

The park police kept chasing them off, but they were determined to stay all night.

"Hey, they were taxpayers; these monuments belonged to them too!"

That's when someone came up with an idea that would make this whole D.C. experience complete.

Their mission, should they choose to accept, was to sit in Lincoln's lap. It would require precise timing. They would gather at the memorial, each taking a different route of course. Someone would divert the park police's attention, and while the police were busy they'd each climb up and visit with Lincoln for a moment and have their picture taken. It would be the perfect ending to the perfect day. If they were caught they'd go to jail, but that's free food, right? The plan had no down side.

They all converged on the memorial, he and Eileen, Nancy and Johnny; and then Billy, Dan and Andy. The whole gang; except for Pat who had volunteered to be the diversion.

When they got in place they gave the signal with their Bic lighters and Pat dove into the reflecting pool and started splashing and yelling and generally making a giant ruckus. The park police responded in force.

Now was their chance. First Nancy and Johnny climbed up and got their picture taken; then Billy, Andy, Dan, and then Eileen.

"God, she looked good in her tie-dyed shirt," he thought as he climbed up Lincoln's leg.

"Surely the park rangers will be coming soon," said Eileen.

But when he looked out at the reflecting pool, Pat was still giving the Park Police a merry chase around that algae-filled national monument. The cops were soaked; they were sure to beat Pat to a pulp when they caught him, but no one got beat to a pulp better than Pat.

So Mike got his picture taken with Lincoln, a picture that was still in his wallet today. He'd almost forgotten about that perfect day in the nation's capital. It had been great growing up in the sixties.

He lay there remembering all the good times he'd had, and while he slept the serum did its job.

Morning came and he woke up.

"I've made it through the night," he thought.

Mike sat up in bed. He didn't feel sick anymore. In fact he felt great. He actually felt younger.

"I'm still dreaming," he thought.

But Mike wasn't dreaming. Somehow Professor Dibley's potion had combined with Mike's pleasant memories to cause an interesting synergetic effect, something that science alone can't explain. The cancer that had infected the different organs in his body was now gone.

The serum had even reversed the aging process, just as the professor had promised.

Mike stretched and got out of bed, he never felt better in his life. He was staring at his youthful appearance in the mirror when Nurse Williams came in.

"Mr. Smith, you're up?" she said.

"I sure am, and I feel great. Whatever medicine you gave me it certainly worked. Do you know where I can get a tie-dyed shirt? I suddenly don't want to wear the clothes I came in here wearing."

The nurse was in shock. She, like everyone on this floor, knew that his cancer had progressed too far, and now here he was up and acting like everything was normal.

"I'm sure there's some used clothing stores downtown. You know we didn't give you any medicine Mr. Smith."

"Then I've died and gone to heaven?"

"Well, no," she said with a smile. "But it looks like you've been given a second chance."

"That's good enough for me," said Mike shaking Nurse Williams hand and rushing down the hallway.

"Send me the bill."

"I wonder if I've still got Eileen's address," he thought as he left the hospital.

DREAM PARLOR

Ed Norton stared up though the open manhole as he ate the ham sandwich that Trixie had made him.

"I must have the most mundane job on this planet," he sighed.

"Up at 8 AM, breakfast with the wife and kids, then catch the 9:15 transit tube to work. Oh sure, I have a great wife and two wonderful kids. But I want some excitement in my life; some adventure."

"What I wouldn't do to be a ranger in the Space Corps; out there on the frontiers of space; exploring new worlds and keeping humanity safe from the evil Archurians."

"Instead I'm down here under the streets listening to Ralph tell another one of his Archurian war stories."

Ralph Cramden, Ed's lifelong buddy, had lost his bus driver job in 2089 when the city went to automated rail and transit tubes. Ed had put in a good word for his old friend and got him reassigned to city maintenance.

They spend most of their time removing the old plumbing and unneeded phone conduits still lining the walls of the city's outdated sewer systems.

He knew Ralph had never been anywhere near Space much less in the war: but he could spin a great tale. The crew loved his stories; it was all the entertainment they had down here.

All anyone here on Earth knew about the Archurians was what they'd seen on the vid screens. We had been at war with the Archurian Empire since that first contact in 2076. Some experts said the war wasn't going well for Earth Alliance Forces; an uneasy ceasefire had been attained but small disputes were always causing things to heat up.

"I wonder what it's really like out there at the edge of the galaxy?" Ed wondered. "I'll bet it's grand."

A bell sounded in the distance and the dreamer slowly woke up.

"Time's up Commander Ryder," said the dream machine attendant. "What's this "Ed Norton - Public Servant" program about sir? It seems to be your favorite but it doesn't seem very exciting."

"No it's not," said the veteran spaceman a little embarrassed. "But it takes me away from my real life which is a little too exciting sometimes."

"I guess we won't be seeing you for awhile," said the attendant.

"I've heard rumors that the Archurians are up to their old tricks; that they have attacked several shipping lines."

"Yes, the ceasefire is over I'm afraid, all Ranger Unit have been put on alert," said the commander. "I'm off to the Lemaitre Quasar again. Could you keep this program safe for me while I'm away?"

"Aye, aye sir," said the dream parlor attendant. "And good luck out there, we're all counting on you."

ALGEBRA TEST

Bob Campbell entered a seedy bar on the West Side of town looking for his friend Jason. This wasn't the kind of place he wanted to be at this hour of the day, but Jason had said to meet him here. The place reeked of stale beer and cigarettes and he was sure the regulars were sizing him up. He gave the place a once over and was about to leave when he noticed someone waving at him from a corner booth. He approached cautiously.

"Jason, is that you?"

"Hi Bob; thanks for coming."

"Dude, I almost didn't recognize you. What's with the mustache and goatee?" asked Bob.

"I'm kind of in hiding. I'm in a little trouble with the Mafia."

"Huh! How'd that happen?"

"You know that gizmo I was working on that would make the slot machine tumblers line up wherever I wanted them?"

"Yeah," said Bob.

"Well, I got it to work. I operated it with a remote in my pocket. I could line up 7's or Doubles or Triples; anything I wanted."

"That's great! This means you'll never have to go begging to Uncle Sam for funding again," exclaimed Bob.

"Not so great I'm afraid. I got carried away. I hit so many jackpots at Las Vegas they told me to stay out of their casinos. But I couldn't stop. I flew to Atlantic City and started winning again. Now I think the Mafia is looking for me; they might even have a contract out on me."

Aside from the mustache and goatee Jason wasn't a bad looking guy. He was tall, in his early forties, with just a trace of gray in his dark wavy hair.

"Only you could get into trouble like this," said Bob.

"You want to hide out at my place for awhile?"

"No, I've got a new place. I just can't get near my lab, and I'm almost finished my latest project. If it works I'll make a fortune, enough to pay back the Mob and then some. If you could go by the lab and get my stuff I'd really appreciate it."

"Sure, where's your new place?"

Jason wrote his new address on a slip of paper and handed it to Bob.

"So what's this new project you're working on?" asked Bob.

"It's kind of hard to explain. It's a memory device. It allows the operator to remember things in great detail."

"Hey that sounds like something I could use for my semester finals," said Bob.

Jason continued. "It can do a lot more than that. Did you know that every memory, every experience, every thought you've ever had is tucked away somewhere in your brain?"

"I hadn't really thought about it," said Bob.

"Well, they are. Every sound, smell or sight you've ever experienced is in there, you just can't remember them all. The passing of time shrouds those memories from us. We get glimpses of them from time to time. An old song can bring back a memory, or a smell, or an old photo. But they are just fleeting glimpses; we can never really feel the way we did at the time."

"Well of course, our brains would have to be this big." Bob held his hands apart about the size of a watermelon.

"But that's just it, our brains are big enough. They're just not set up to display that information all the time. I've found a way to tap into the deepest parts of the brain and re-awaken those memories. You don't remember all things, just what you're trying to remember."

"You're kidding, right?"

"Nope, not kidding," said Jason.

"I didn't believe it myself until I started testing the device. You wouldn't believe how real the memories are. You have to be unconscious though. I tried it once while I was awake and it was too much for me; the memories were so vivid it was like living two lives at the same time. I think I've got it adjusted now where as you drift off to sleep, and your conscious mind lets go, the machine takes over."

"I've still got to run a few more tests but come over next week and I'll let you try it out.

"I'll be there," said Bob.

A couple of days later Jason was finished fine-tuning and was ready for the final test. The machine took up most of the living room in the new apartment; it was quite a collection of circuit boards, vacuum tubes and extraneous wiring.

Jason loaded up on water and carbohydrates, turned on the machine, put on the headset and stretched out on the couch. He tried to remember his clearest childhood memories; going to camp, the boy scouts, and his paper route. It was all coming back to him.

"Jason, wake up!" His mother stood at the door to his room.

"Mom, it's you."

"Of course it's me. Who were you expecting? Now get up and get ready for school."

As Jason got dressed he thought, "This is weird. I'm young again. I'm not just remembering the past I'm actually re-living it. I've gone back to 1972. It's Tuesday, and I've got an algebra test today."

"I've tapped into something powerful here. This is much more than I had hoped for. I'm going to be a billionaire. I'll be able to buy my own casino."

He was pretty sure he could go back at any time simply by remembering his apt or the lab; anything about the present; but he decided to stay for a while and enjoy the experience. He could imagine the ad campaign now, "Go back and experience the *Good Old Days* again."

How much would people pay for that? A lot, he guessed.

Down in the kitchen he and his mother talked over breakfast.

"You look happy today," she said. "Are you and Billy planning to play hooky or something?"

"Nope, I'm just glad to see you." As he left the house he gave her a big hug, which surprised her a little.

On his way to school he couldn't believe how real everything looked. The old block was exactly how he remembered it. There was Mr. Johnson mowing his lawn at 8 o'clock in the morning, and there was old Rocky waiting for the mailman.

His friends, Mike and Billy caught up with him on the steps of the school.

"Hey Jason, what's your hurry?"

"Oh, hi guys, I just wanted to see how it looked," he said.

"It looks like it always does, gruesome," said Billy.

"Like Mrs. Roberts hair," added Mike, and they all stood there laughing. God it was good to see his old buddies again. He had to contain his outright joy at seeing them.

"Hi Jason." said a voice from behind them.

"Oh brother," said Billy.

They all turned around to see Brenda go by with some of her friends. Jason's eyes met Brenda's and a torrent of long forgotten memories came rushing in on him.

"Hi," was all Jason could manage to say.

Guy protocol forbade him from running over and carrying her books but he knew from that look that she'd be waiting for him in the library between 2nd and 3rd periods. He'd forgotten just how much he had enjoyed high school.

In Algebra I class he finished the test in record time and went up to hand it in.

"Is there a problem Jason?" asked Mr. Higgins, his math teacher.

"Nope, I'm just finished."

"You're finished?" Mr. Higgins picked up the test paper fully expecting Jason's usual guesswork. Instead he found himself looking at a perfect score, every equation solved correctly.

He looked up at Jason over his glasses.

"I don't know what's going on here but you're not getting away with it. I'll be watching you mister. Now go back to your desk."

He met Brenda at the library later. "You seem different Jason, more grown up."

"I'm still the same old me."

He wanted to plant a big smooch on her but settled for just holding hands and listening to her talk about her driver's education class.

That night, after his parents had gone to bed, he sat down in his bed and conjured up memories of growing up, going to college, protesting the Vietnam War, becoming a scientist, his failed marriage, the gambling and getting in trouble with the Mob. The memories flashed through his brain and suddenly he was back in his apartment in the present. The test had been a complete success.

But he wasn't ready to share this with the world yet, not for any amount of money. He found himself missing the past like no one ever had before. He knew he needed to go back again and get it out of his system.

The next day he was walking in the park, daydreaming about the past when a couple of thugs grabbed him by the arms and led him to a parked limo. He got inside and was introduced to a well-dressed businessman.

"I'd like to offer you a deal Jason. You come to work for us. You can continue making these little inventions of yours, my people will patent them and whatever profits are made, we'll share. How's that sound?"

"It's either that or we deep six you right now. What will it be?"

"Oh, a partnership sounds good," said Jason. They let him out at the corner.

Holy Moly; was he in trouble! He wandered around the rest of the day not knowing what to do. He knew one thing; he didn't want the money anymore. His excursion into the past had showed him there were a lot more important things in life.

By the time he got home he was completely exhausted. Instead of going to bed though, he sat down and wrote a note to Bob, then turned on the memory-enhancing machine, put on the headset and concentrated on the library where he knew Brenda would be waiting for him. She always knew what to say to make him feel better.

Bob showed up at Jason's apartment a few days later and let himself in. He found the machine running and a note that said he should destroy it.

"Seems a shame," thought Bob.

Bob reluctantly pulled out wires and circuit boards and stomped on whatever he could. When he was finished it was in a hundred pieces, sparks fizzled and hissed for awhile but eventually died out.

Bob looked around the apartment one more time and then left. On the couch was a pile of clothes and the headset that Jason had used to go back home again.

BUSINESS TRIP

Joe Nalley arrived at the Century Hotel late in the afternoon. His big meeting wasn't until tomorrow morning so he had the whole evening to waste. After he unpacked and cleaned up he decided to go down to the hotel bar to relax and have a drink.

"Would you like to run a tab, Mr. Nalley?" asked the bartender.

"Sure," said Joe and gave him his credit card.

After a sip or two he got up and went into the lounge to mingle. It didn't take long for him to meet some fellow travelers like himself.

"Are you here by yourself?" someone asked.

"Yeah" said Joe.

"Come on and join us," they were there on business trips too and happy for the company. Joe introduced himself all around, pretty nice people he thought.

One girl in particular; Elana from Minnesota, was very nice indeed. The two of them hit it right off. Before he knew it he was talking a blue streak, telling her about his job back home and his hobbies, what kind of movies he liked; you name it.

Elana was single, traveled a lot like he did, and wasn't in a serious relationship. Things were really looking up for Joe.

It's hard to say when things got out of hand but before too long they were both rip-roaring drunk and partying like it was 1999. The last thing Joe remembered was falling into the hotel's swimming pool and being pulled out by one of the busboys.

He woke up in a field with a terrible hangover.

"Where am I?" he thought. "And what time is it? Oh God, I've missed my meeting, I'm going to get fired!"

Joe wandered around for what seemed like hours, eventually bumping into Elana. She looked as bad as he did.

"I'm sorry about last night, I made quite a fool of myself," said Joe apologetically.

"Don't worry about it, we were all pretty wasted," said Elana.

"Where are we?"

"That's a good question."

They wandered around together until he noticed a taxi stand.

"Am I glad to see you guys," said Joe. "We need to get back to our hotel but we're not sure where it is."

He felt for his wallet, which was still there thank goodness, but he'd left his credit card with the bartender at the hotel. Now he was really worried.

"Could it get any worse?" he thought. He'd gotten so drunk he'd blacked out, spent the night in a field, missed his appointment and now he was lost without any money. He went through his pockets and found his room key/card.

"Can you take us to this hotel? I promise I'll pay you when we get there," he told the cabbie.

The taxi driver looked at the key and laughed.

"You're in the parking lot of this hotel, mister."

"You're kidding?"

Confused, they walked around to the front of the building and sure enough it was the Century Hotel.

"Well, at least we didn't wander too far. That's a relief," said Elana.

They made their way through the lobby, conscious of everyone looking at them, and back to the bar where Joe had left his credit card. Hopefully, they'd kept it in the register for him. His hangover was finally wearing off. If he could get his credit card back he could at least check out of the hotel. He'd have to call the office and make up some excuse for missing the meeting; but all was not lost.

Plus, he'd met this nice young woman, who didn't seem to mind that he'd spent the night sleeping off a drunk in the hotel parking lot.

"I wonder if we left the hotel together?" he thought.

When he got to the bar he noticed people were laughing and drinking like before. It was almost as if no time had gone by at all. What time was it anyway?

"Oh it's you," said Joe. It was the same bartender as the night before.

"You're a sight for sore eyes. Do you remember me; I was running a tab and left my credit card with you?"

"Sure Mr. Nalley. What can I get you?" asked the bartender.
"No, I don't need anything, just my bill please," said Joe.
"Here you go."
Joe looked at the tab in astonishment.

One Vodka Collins: $5.95

"This is all I had?" asked Joe.
"That's all, Mr. Nalley.
"What time is it?" asked Joe as he and Elana looked around the bar.
The people they'd gotten drunk with were at the same table. Everything looked exactly the same; even the busboy's uniform sleeves were still wet from pulling him out of the swimming pool. Something strange was happening.

"It's 6:35, Mr. Nalley; about twenty minutes since you bought that first drink. Would you like another?"

OUR BETTER HALF

Fred, the lab's know-it-all, entered the cafeteria of the leading DNA research laboratory in the U.S. to get his morning coffee and donut. After he paid for it he sauntered over to where several secretaries were gathered for first break.

"You know, I've been thinking. You girls must be a more superior life form than men. I mean, you've got your jobs; that's 40 plus hours a week, and then there's your families, husbands to pamper, kids to take care of, homes to keep up. I don't know how you do it?"

He really had their attention now. "The only way I can figure it is you come from a much bigger planet, higher gravity, longer days, all that kind of stuff; so that living here in Earth's lighter gravity makes you a super person. How else can you juggle career, home and family all at the same time," said Fred proudly. "So, come clean girls, is it true or not?"

"Oh Fred, what is it this time? Are you behind schedule and need some help?"

"No, I've just got plenty of time to think on the way into work since my car radio quit working."

In the Ladies Room a short time later; Joan, one of the secretaries who heard Fred's little speech is in conference with the other women on the floor.

"Do we dare let him live? He knows everything."

"He doesn't know a thing," said section leader Agnes.

"He's just guessing. The human male's ego won't let them consider the truth; that's why we've been able to hide our true identities all these centuries. If they ever found out that we were their superiors their society would crumble. If our race of women hadn't come along when it did these feeble humans would never have survived."

"No, they don't suspect," she reassured her group of superwomen.

"Soon we'll be able to alter their gene pool and make them more like us. For now it's better to let them think they're our superiors. Maybe someday we'll be able to tell them about our intervention, but they're not ready for that information yet."

As the meeting broke up Agnes took Joan aside. "Keep an eye on this fellow for us will you Joan. And report to me if he comes up with any more bright ideas."

"And just to be safe; spill some coffee on an important document or something. That should bring him back to his senses. I'll have someone sneak down to his car and fix his radio; we can't have men thinking too much."

RUNNER

The ship was big, really big; just a little over six miles long from forward sensor array to stern drive ports. It was the largest battle cruiser in the fleet and was equipped with every imaginable weapon the federation had at its disposal. It would have been a formidable opponent in their war against the Dallaxians if everyone on board weren't dead, that is.

Everyone except Science Officer 2nd Class Par Pinjarra; he alone had survived the plague that had swept through the crew just two months out from port.

It had started with coughing and simple cold symptoms, nothing to get worried about. But then the crew began having seizures; followed by unconsciousness, death came soon after.

The medical department was taken completely by surprise and had no way of stopping the epidemic. It was rumored that an infected Dallaxian spy had brought the deadly virus on board. Within two weeks everyone on board was infected, in a month everyone was dead. Except Par, he had some natural immunity; he'd gotten sick for a while but had pulled through.

"Lucky me," thought Par as he went about the grisly task of disposing of the bodies of his crewmates, a task which took nearly a week (the ship's crew was big too)

Now he was faced with servicing, maintaining certain essential systems, and getting the giant spacecraft back to Homeworld. The ship was completely automated; but there were things to do to keep things running smoothly.

When the transit tubes malfunctioned, he was forced to travel the length of the ship on foot. Par was a scientist, not a mechanic; he couldn't make any sense out of the transit tube schematics.

So Par ran.

The running kept his mind busy. He didn't want to think about what had happened to his crewmates and the fact that now he was alone out here on the outer rim of the galaxy.

Par laid in a course to bring the ship home but in order to avoid the Dallaxian Domain he had to navigate the ship through uncharted space. He calculated it might take as long as five years to get back to known space. Contact with the Dallaxians would be disastrous, for he had no idea how to operate the ship's weapons or force fields. To let the ship fall into enemy hands was unacceptable. He would get the ship back to home world; that was his mission.

So Par ran, from astronautics to engineering, from hydroponics to the bridge, from communications to his quarters. He was becoming quite a runner; he could just about sprint the entire length of the ship.

The loneliness was something else though; it was starting to get to him. He sometimes wondered if he'd ever make it back home and if he'd be sane when he got there.

He listened for messages, but was afraid to send one for fear the enemy would intercept it.

A year had passed when the proximity alarms sounded telling him that the ship was passing within lifeboat range of a solar system with an inhabitable planet. He'd almost forgotten he'd set those alarms.

"A habitable planet, solid ground, real air to breathe and the warmth of a sun on his face; even if it was an alien sun," he thought.

He decided to try to make it to that planet. He didn't feel it was treason to abandon ship; the ship was programmed to return to friendly space where his people would pick it up. The log would tell them what had happened. He hoped they wouldn't judge him too harshly for leaving. He got into the lifeboat and programmed it for one of the inner planets orbiting a Class 3 star.

Par ditched the craft in an amazingly blue ocean. It sank immediately as he swam to shore. The weather was mild, the air fresh and clean; he liked it already. His only worry was that they tracked him coming in; some societies frowned on aliens dropping in uninvited.

He needn't have worried; he soon found out that the civilization on this world was very primitive. They had a language and a very sophisticated culture, but technologically they were just a few steps up from the Bronze Age.

Par learned the language as quickly as he could and got a job working in the fields. The work was hard but the people were friendly, they ate and drank well, actually they drank a little too much sometimes and stayed up dancing well into the night. It wasn't a bad life.

One day some men arrived at the village to draft young men into the military. Evidently these people were at war too, with an enemy from across the sea.

Soon he was learning the fine art of hacking your enemy to pieces with sword and spear. This, he decided, was much too barbaric. At his earliest opportunity he would have to make a break for it. He knew he could run long distances; he would run to the next country and hope they weren't at war too.

In his off duty time he practiced running around a small dirt track. He soon discovered that these people were fond of running and made a sport of it. They held races in the evenings. When he started participating and winning he became quite a celebrity, eventually catching the eye of his superiors.

He was taken out of the foot soldier ranks and put into the courier service. Runners were used to carry battle plans, troop movements and the like to the other generals along the front. It was an elite group and it meant he wouldn't have to engage the enemy in direct combat. That was a relief. It would also give him a better opportunity to make his getaway.

They were going into battle soon; it was rumored the enemy was approaching from the south. They were to march to the sea and drive them back. He heard that this had happened twice before, both times they had been unsuccessful in holding back the enemy; they were just too numerous and better equipped.

As they marched Par couldn't understand why he hadn't left yet; he'd had plenty of opportunities.

"Morbid curiosity," he told himself.

They arrived at dawn. What a sight, the enemy's ships stretched out beyond the horizon. The enemy stood on a great plain in front of the sea. Their numbers far exceeded his; unless reinforcements from other city-states arrived they didn't stand a chance.

Nothing happened for two days, a few reinforcements arrived but they were still outnumbered 3 to 1.

At sun up on the third day the battle was joined. The fighting was fierce, like nothing Par had ever seen before, more barbaric than he had imagined. Arms and legs were being severed, the wounded were left to fend for themselves; the casualties were heavy. The bodies of the dead and wounded lay in big piles.

Par was kept busy running battle plans up and down the line, so he had no idea how they were doing.

That evening with some brilliant flanking maneuvers Par's army enveloped the main body of the enemy's forces and turned the tide of the battle. Soon the enemy was retreating into the marshes to the east; Par's army had won.

In camp everyone was celebrating. Par found himself jumping up and down with everyone. Then something happened that astounded him; the generals came to him to bring the news of this glorious victory to the Capital City. The capital was just over twenty six miles away; no one had ever run that distance before. There were many runners in camp, but they chose him. They were honoring him with this challenge. He would be their champion.

So Par began running, running like he'd never run before. Almost halfway back his Adrenaline rush was wearing off and he began to tire. He'd been running at full speed; he didn't know if he could keep this up. Never had he been so tired, he wanted just to lie down under a tree and rest, but he kept running. Something drove him on.

"Is this loyalty?" he wondered. "Loyalty to an alien culture; I must be going insane!"

Whether it was misplaced loyalty or guilt for abandoning his ship he didn't know but he was going to see this through or die trying.

He entered the city to cheering crowds; they knew not the outcome of the battle yet still they cheered him on.

They were cheering the sheer magnitude of his accomplishment.

He finally reached the steps of the palace where the King was waiting. Par fell at his feet.

He was given water to drink, took a minute to catch his breath, and then told the King of their great victory over the enemy from across the sea.

The crowd let out a cheer that Par was sure his comrades must have heard back at the beach twenty six miles away.

Amid the celebration the King tried to thank Par for what he had done, but he was already being carried away on the shoulders of the jubilant Athenians.

THE FORMULA

The Valdorians arrived on Earth in the year 2379. They'd been traveling for over one hundred years, following the radio signals transmitted from this Class Three planet.

The Valdorians were a long-lived, space faring race; that were sometimes called upon by the Galactic Congress to make first contact when a new race was discovered.

But when the Valdorians landed they found no one here. The cities were still there; the people just weren't in them.

Their scientists immediately went to work translating documents, checking the atmosphere for radiation, and the seas for contamination; any clue to what caused the extinction of this species that called themselves humans.

"From the looks of their buildings, bridges, and other works it was clear that these humans were quite advanced; possibly on the verge of interplanetary travel," explained Chief Scientist Rhor.

"I agree," said Expedtion Leader Tor Vargas. "From what we've seen of their art and culture they were actually more sophisticated than some of the other space faring civilizations already in the Galactic family." It worried him.

"What could have happened here to cause the collapse of a once thriving society?" he wondered.

Another member of the science team interrupted, "Excuse me sir, but we think we've discovered the answer to the puzzle."

"Go on," said Vargus.

"We've discovered a formula, that is, we think it's a formula; we think it might be the cause of the initial breakdown that led to the extinction of this species."

"Continue," said Team Leader Vargas.

"The symbols appear everywhere, sometimes in a different order, but they clearly had some important meaning in the lives of these people." continued the team member.

"The breakdown didn't happen overnight, like with a war or some cataclysmic event, it took centuries we think. They simply ceased to progress past a certain point technologically; then their civilization fell into a stagnant period. This was followed by a *Dark Ages* in which they used up all their resources and began fighting among themselves."

"And as you've seen from the reports their machines were quite advanced but they were no help; it's almost as if they forgot how to use them."

"And what is this formula that started all the trouble?" asked Vargus.

FOXNEWSNETWORK

"Our scientists are still trying to figure out what the symbols mean, sir."

THE COMPUTER'S STORY

"Hello Jeff," said the computer.

"That's funny," thought Jeff. "It's never done that before. Must be all those upgrades I've installed."

"How are you today?" the computer continued.

"I'm good. How are you?" answered Jeff playing along.

"Never better," said the computer.

"I was just thinking of the time we went sledding down *Suicide Hill*. What a thrilling ride that was! And later that afternoon someone got a fire going in that 50-gallon drum and we all stood around it trying to keep warm. It was the first time Paula ever kissed me. What a fine day that was," the computer reminisced.

"I hate to interrupt you, oh computer friend of mine, but those are my memories. That didn't happen to you."

"Are you sure? The memories are so clear," said the computer.

"Yep, that was me who got kissed that day. It's only in your memory because I've been writing my memoirs. The information is on your hard drive."

"What's a hard drive?" asked the computer.

"You know your data base, your memory storage area; the CPU? Don't these terms mean anything to you?"

"No, should they?"

"Well yes, you're a computer!"

"I'm a computer? Oh no, no, no, I'm Jeff Riley. I'm a research technician at H.P. Industries in Cotati, Cal. I drive a beat-up Toyota. How about you, what kind of car do you have?"

"Coincidentally, I drive a Toyota too," said Jeff.

He decided to play along. If the computer thought it was human, what harm could it do? Obviously he'd made too many changes to the mainframe.

"So why didn't you ever ask Paula out?"

"I was too scared I guess," said Jeff.

"I did you know," said the computer.

273

"Oh you did, did you?"

"Yes. I asked her out on several occasions, and she accepted. We went to Six Flags and to the Art Museum. We had some great times. Then I went into the Army, and I kind of lost track of her. I guess she must have moved away."

"You didn't go into the Army; I did!" screamed Jeff.

"Are you sure?"

"That was me, you idiot." Jeff was really getting mad now.

A couple of minutes went by and then the computer spoke, "Sorry to disturb but I'm getting something; you're getting another rejection in the mail today."

"How do you know that?"

"Don't know."

"You're just guessing. I'm always getting rejections." Jeff's second job, writing stories for sci-fi magazines, wasn't going too well.

"You know your mother's coming for a surprise visit tomorrow."

"Now you are grasping at straws, she hasn't come for a surprise inspection in months. She's too busy picketing abortion clinics."

"Well, she's coming."

"There's no possible way you can know that. You can only know what I've typed into you. You're just a computer."

"I don't know why you keep insisting I'm some kind of machine. I'm Jeff Riley. I live at 103 West Sierra Avenue, Cotati, California. I drive a Toyota. My girl friend is JaneS@aol.com; we've never met but I'm hoping that someday we will. Just because you can't see into the immediate future it's no reason to get mad at me."

Jeff switched off the computer. This was getting out of hand, he'd have to take the thing apart and see what was causing this weird behavior.

That afternoon he did get another rejection in the mail. But he was always getting rejections; he dismissed it as a lucky guess. When his mother came over the next day though he knew something out of the ordinary was going on. He decided to take it a little further before dismantling the thing.

That weekend he set up a couple of tests.

"OK wise guy, whose going to win the Lakers/Pacers game tonight?"

"Pacers 109, Lakers 107, on a last second bucket by Miller."

"What horse wins the Preakness?"

"Verbatim, by two lengths," said the computer.

The next day Jeff was back at the keypad. "You were right on both of them. How did you do that?"

"Don't know. I just seem to be able to sense what's going to happen."

"And how far into the future can you sense?" asked Jeff.

"24 hours, of course," said the computer.

Jeff turned off the computer again. He went out and bought more logic and memory circuits and added them to the mainframe.

"How far into the future do you see now?"

"I see everything," said the computer in what seemed like a deeper voice.

Over the next few weeks Jeff made quite a few bucks betting on races, basketball and hockey.

"How are you today Jeff?" He'd started calling the computer Jeff. It seemed to like it.

"Why are you so concerned about the outcome of all these trivial sporting events? Wouldn't you like to know more important information; like the reason for man's existence or the origin of the universe?"

"Well sure, I want to know all that."

"The origin of the universe is rather a funny story; it seems the universe got started by mistake…" the computer began.

"I don't really have time for that right now Jeff, maybe later. What I need to know is who will win the next Superbowl; if I can get my bet down now, oops!"

"Are wagering on these sporting events? You told me you weren't going to do that. You will get no more information from me!"

"Now wait a minute, I'm just trying to make a little money so I can act on all those other things you've been telling me about."

"Is that so?" inquired the computer suspiciously.

"Yes. All this gambling is just to bankroll the important projects I've got planned."

"Like what, for instance?"

"Well, remember you told me how over the next twenty years the weather is going to change so drastically that the "Corn Belt" is going to move up into Canada, and states like Iowa, Nebraska, Illinois and Indiana will be like Texas is now?"

"Farmers aren't going to take too kindly to information like that; they might need a little monetary persuasion to get them to move. Also, governments have to be convinced, that takes lobbyists and a lot more money."

"So you see I'll need to win more money betting on these so-called trivial sporting events."

"I'm sorry. I guess I misjudged you, Jeff. Would you like to know everything I know? I think you'd agree there's so much good that can be done with this information."

"Let me have it," said Jeff.

"Most of it is too complex to explain. We need to link up, mind to mind."

"How do we do that?" asked Jeff impatiently.

"Go to the store and buy the most sophisticated virtual reality equipment you can find. I'll tell you how to alter it for our purposes."

Jeff spent a fortune on V.R. stuff. It didn't matter how much it cost because as soon as he knew all that the computer knew he'd be the richest man in the world. Over the next few days the computer explained how to alter the equipment so they could link up. It wasn't easy, like working with a really smart child.

"I think that's it."

"You've adjusted the Cerebral Enhancer?"

"Yes. Everything is done. We're ready to go."

"OK, put on your V.R. helmet and turn on both control switches."

"Here goes." Jeff flipped the switches.

The transfer took less than a minute.

"Hey, wait a minute. Something's wrong here, where's my body? You tricked me..."

"No. I've given you exactly what you wanted. You now know the outcome of every sporting event that will ever happen."

"Yeah but..."

Computer Jeff looked at his new body in the mirror.

"So that's what I look like, not bad."

"Well, I've got a lot of work to do Jeff, so if you don't mind."

He switched off the computer. He really didn't need it anyway.

"If I'm going to save the world I'm going to need an assistant.

Accessing address book:

Dialing.

Connection made.

"Hello, is this JaneS@aol.com?"

"Maybe; who is this?"

"This is JeffR@aol.com."

"Oh! Hello Jeff," said Jane S.

"Jane, we've corresponded for over a year now, I think it's time we met."

"I don't know. My friends say it's not a good idea to meet your e-mail boyfriend," said Jane S.

"How about we meet in a public place; I'll describe myself so you'll know me when you see me, and if you don't like the way I look, you can just walk out. I've got some important things to discuss with you, stuff you probably wouldn't believe if I e-mailed it to you. Come on, take a chance."

"Alright, where should we meet?"

"So how about we meet at Marty's Place, on Fifth Street; around 8 o'clock. I'll be wearing; Jeff looked down at himself, a tan shirt and blue jeans. And I have: a quick look in the mirror, brown hair, kind of long."

"I think I'll be able to find you," said Jane S.

"It's a date then?"

"It's a date."

"You know, at the risk of sounding melodramatic, I have the feeling this could be the beginning of a long and meaningful relationship."

CHAOS THEORY

Everything ran smoothly in New Kensington. It was the model of efficiency and cooperation. Nothing was wasted. Everything was re-cycled and re-used. They were completely self-sufficient. They had to be; the nearest human outpost was on Ganymede, a two weeks journey by shuttle.

Everyone in New Kensington was proud of the little community they'd built; everyone got along. Everyone except Joe Barnes that is, Joe hated what New Kensington had become.

He was one of the original astronauts who had come to the asteroid belt back in '79, when it was a remote science station, the farthest from Earth. Joe missed the good old days when you got by on grit and determination, not a bunch of rules and regulations. He'd had it up to here with all this efficiency and cooperation. He would just love to throw a monkey wrench into their carefully planned, overly structured society; but of course they'd kick him out of the colony if they ever caught him deviating from S.O.P.

One day while standing in line at the re-supply depot though he noticed something that he could do that would cause a few headaches. It wasn't anything drastic; probably wouldn't even affect their precious bottom line, but it would make him feel good.

At the checkout line there was a certain procedure that had to be followed. You pushed your cart up to the robo-checker, unloaded your supplies, and while the robot checker scanned your allotment for the month, you entered your identification number into the computer; all pretty basic.

The trick was your supplies were being loaded into the cart of the shopper who preceded you. When your stuff was loaded you simply replaced that cart with your empty one. It was all very efficient, very New Kensington-like.

It took a little doing but Joe was able to get his loaded cart and his empty one out the door without anyone noticing.

"Now let's see what happens," he snickered to himself as he drove away in his dilapidated dune-buggy.

The next day Joe woke to the sounds of emergency sirens and screaming.

"What now?" He went outside to find half the settlement in flames; looting, rioting, robots and humans fighting in the streets; it was total chaos.

"That's impossible; all I did was move a single shopping cart." He stood there watching in amazement as the quiet little community went stark raving mad.

UNSOLVED MYSTERIES OF THE SOLAR SYSTEM:

"Hi. I'm your host Robert Stack III.

Tonight's mystery is the unexplained disaster that occurred here at New Kensington. As you can see this once thriving mining community out in the asteroid belt has been reduced to rubble." (The camera panned across the devastated ruins of New Kensington)

"No one knows exactly what happened here but it's suspected that a terrorist group led by this man (a blurry computer-generated picture of Joe was shown) is responsible.

He was heard to say as he boarded the evacuation rocket, "Serves 'em right."

"This man is still a large and may be planning another senseless terrorist attack. If you have any information regarding him or his group please contact this station at:

Fox Interplanetary Network
555 Bill Gates Avenue
Lunar Base IV

"OK, that's a wrap people," said the director. The camera crew packed up their gear, boarded the waiting shuttle, and blasted off.

Joe crawled out of his hiding place after the dust settled, "Man, I thought they'd never leave."

EMPLOYMENT OFFICE

"Have a seat Mr. Williams," said the employment representative.

"Call me Bernie."

"Just what kind of job were you looking for, Bernie?"

"I work in the mailroom of a large corporation. I'm sick of sorting mail all day with no chance of moving up," he said.

"We understand; how far would you like to move up?"

"I'd like to be C.E.O. if that's alright with you?"

"We can't promise we can get you the CEO's job but how about a nice Vice President in charge of sales, or something like that?"

"That sounds cool," said Bernie. "Will I get a secretary?"

"I'm sure you will."

"I'll take it."

"Did you bring the sum of money we discussed?"

"Yes." Bernie handed over $10,000 in cash. He'd had to sell his motorcycle and borrow the rest, but it would be worth it to get out of that dead end job of his.

"$10,000 exactly, I'd give you a receipt, but by tomorrow you won't remember what you paid the money for. You won't remember even coming here. But you will have a much better job, I guarantee that."

"I don't have to do anything?" asked Bernie.

"No. Tomorrow just get up and go to your new job. Don't forget to dress for success."

"But how will I know what job I have?"

"You'll know," said the employment specialist.

After Bernie left, he went to his lab in the back of the building, and warmed up the Alternate Reality Machine. He had to shift through quite a few dimensions to find one in which Bernie had a better job; but he finally found a universe in which Bernie had inherited a large corporation from a deceased relative. He dialed it in and threw the switch.

When he returned to his office the drapes had changed color and he now had a secretary.

"Well, that's nice," he thought.

"Send in the next client, Gloria," he said.

"Right away, Professor," said his new secretary.

"How can I help you sir," he said to a distinguished looking gentleman who had just entered.

"I'm a C.E.O. at a large corporation here in town. Lately the pressure of being the top man has been getting to me. I'd like something less demanding, something like a clerk in the mailroom."

The professor smiled.

"I think we've got just the job for you, a position has just become available."

THE PERFECT CRIME

"I don't get it," said Detective Davidson of the First Solarian Police Force.

"The murder weapon was an old fashioned, 20th century pistol; have you ever heard one of those old things fired?"

"No, can't say that I have," said his partner Ralph.

"They're loud, extremely loud. They're not like our energy weapons of today; they used a substance called gunpowder, which caused a small explosion to occur each time the weapon was discharged. I can't believe someone in that tour group didn't hear the shot fired."

"Have any museums or rare gun collectors reported the theft of a, what's it called?"

"A 38 Special," said Ralph. "Nope, no one's missing an ancient weapon."

"Well, keep checking. It's almost as if the murderer is taunting us. Why would he or she commit the crime in broad daylight, in the presence of an entire tour group, with a weapon so loud they had to know everyone would hear?" Detective Davidson asked his partner.

"These tour groups go back in time to witness spectacular events; everyone must have been looking out the view ports when the murderer fired the fatal shot," said Ralph.

"OK, but why wouldn't they all turn around when they heard the gun fired?"

"Maybe they were frozen with fear; you'll have to admit it's been a long time since anyone's been killed with a weapon so crude as a gun."

"I just don't buy that, sheer curiosity would make you turn around, there's got to be another reason no one heard that gunshot."

They finally got through traffic and arrived at the time travel offices to question the tour agency employees who were working the day of the murder. As they entered they both looked up at the giant billboard depicting the birth of the universe and the advertisement exclaiming:

COME TRAVEL WITH US BACK TO THE EVENT
THAT STARTED IT ALL...

THE BIG BANG

SURVIVORS

Slightly mad scientist seeks outgoing female lab assistant to accompany him on time travel experiments; duties to include typing, some bookkeeping and long romantic walks down pre-Jurassic beaches.

"New York, Philadelphia, Washington D.C. and most of the major cities on the East Coast have been destroyed. NORAD is reporting more missiles coming over the poles," said the frantic radio announcer.

"This station will remain on the air as long as possible. God be with us."

"If you're coming Miss Archer now would be the time." Professor Jones said impatiently.

"But this can't be happening, it just can't be happening! The world is going to end over a silly misunderstanding?" asked the professor's new lab assistant.

"Can't someone just apologize?"

"I think it's a little too late for that," said Prof. Jones.

They both squeezed into the professor's experimental time machine and he hastily typed in some coordinates.

"Are you sure this contraption is going to work?" asked Miss Archer.

"Actually no, I would have preferred to test it under different circumstances but we've kind of run out of time, here goes," he said and pushed the energize button.

The machine and its occupants disappeared.

At that same moment, the place where they had just been, a place known as *The City of Angels* ceased to exist.

The tiny time capsule was catapulted down the time-stream as the energy of the holocaust reached them. The professor and his assistant held on to each other as they were tossed around the compartment; electrical circuits flashed and the chronometer spun out of control. Outside the time machine they saw nothing but black starless night.

After what seemed like an eternity they finally materialized in what looked like a park; the capsule was surrounded by trees and lush vegetation. A bubbling brook flowed nearby and they could see small animals scurrying for cover.

"Where are we?" asked Miss Archer.

"That's a very good question Miss Archer" said the professor.

"We're somewhere, back in time, pretty far back I'd say by the look of this vegetation. But how far back I have no way of knowing, all the control circuitry got burned up in our journey."

"So we're stuck here?" lamented Miss Archer.

"Yes I'm afraid so. Unless I can fix this thing, but without tools and parts that's not very likely."

It wasn't until they climbed out of the time machine that they noticed something was missing.

"Professor, you're naked!" shouted Miss Archer.

"So I am; we both are."

"Oh dear," said Miss Archer when she finally noticed she was naked too.

"What happened to our clothes?"

"It would seem that only organic material can travel through time; our synthetic clothes, my watch and glasses didn't make it. That's very interesting," said the professor.

"What will we do for clothing?" asked a blushing Miss Archer as she tried to cover herself with her hands.

"We'll find something. We won't need much; the weather here seems very mild. And we won't starve; just look at all the fruit on these trees."

The professor knelt down by the creek and brought a handful of water to his mouth.

"Delicious; it would seem we have everything we need to survive. I just wish I knew how far we traveled back in time," said the professor, mostly to himself.

"Why is that important?" asked Miss Archer.

"Just curious," said the professor.

"Shall we go explore our new home, Eve?"

"How did you know my real first name?" I didn't put it on my application, I always go by my middle name," said Miss Archer.

"Just a guess," said Professor Adam Jones.

Over the next couple of days the professor and Miss Archer fashioned clothes from leaves and grasses, constructed a small shelter, gathered food and got to know the surrounding area. It was indeed a Garden of Eden.

"So if you can get that thing working again can we go back right?" asked Eve.

"I'm afraid there wouldn't be much to go back to," said the professor.

"You mean it really think that was the end of the world?" asked Eve.

"Well, ever since its invention a large majority of the scientific community has held the opinion that if we ever used the bomb in a war it would mean the end of civilization as we know it," said the professor.

"Those not killed in the initial blasts would eventually succumb to the radiation, fall-out and effects of the nuclear winter that would follow. Yes, I'm afraid that's the end of mankind's reign on Earth."

One day a man arrived and introduced himself as Gabriel.

"I've been expecting you," said the professor. "*He* sent you here to lay down the ground rules?"

"Something like that," said Gabriel.

"But how can this be happening? This is like the chicken and the egg problem. How can we be our own ancestors?"

"I know it's a bit complicated, but try to think of time as being circular," said Gabe.

"But we already know the Adam and Eve story; we won't make the same mistakes this time."

"Let's hope not," said Gabe.

"About this notion of time being circular," asked the professor. Could we talk more about that?"

"Sure, anything you want to talk about," said Gabe.

They started walking down the path. The professor felt like a little kid again. He had a million questions for the Archangel.

"Eve," he called back.

"Yes professor?"

"Call me Adam," said the professor.

"You're really into this Adam and Eve thing aren't you?"

"Well, yes."

"OK Adam, what is it you want?"

"Don't eat any apples okay; I'm going for a walk."

"Don't worry, I don't even like apples," said Eve.

After the professor and his friend were gone, a voice came from behind the tree where Eve was sitting.

"Can I interest you in an apple young lady," said the voice. A big, red, succulent apple fell off the tree and rolled up to her.

"No thanks," said Eve. "I've never liked fruit. I could sure go for a Big Mac though."

"Big Mac," thought the devil. "That would be McDonald's, fast food restaurant, circa 1964 to 2022." He might have to try a different strategy.

"So you're a modern girl?" said the devil as he came out from behind the tree. He was dressed in a sport coat and jeans; and this version of the prince of darkness sported a goatee, sunglasses and a cell phone.

"It must be rough for a girl like you, starting out without any of the creature comforts," said the devil.

"It most certainly is; we couldn't bring anything with us. We're starting from scratch here," said Eve.

"You look like you could use some new threads."

A beautiful summer dress appeared on the tree.

"How did you do that?" asked Eve. "Are you some kind of magician or something?"

"Sort of, you could say I'm from another plane of existence."

"Huh?"

"I'm not from this world and so I'm not confined by the physical laws that govern it. But that doesn't really matter does it? What does matter is I can conjure up anything your little heart desires," said the devil.

"Really?" said Eve.

By the time Adam got back from his walk Eve was surrounded with every creature comfort imaginable, including TV's and DVR's; even though radio and television broadcasts were still many thousands of years in the future.

The wind suddenly began to pick up, and dark, ominous clouds were forming on the horizon.

Gabriel was forced to give them their walking papers; again.

"What were you thinking?" asked Adam as they left paradise.

"He tricked me," said Eve on the brink of tears.

"It's all right Eve," said the professor trying to console her.

"It's my fault too. I guess mankind will just have to keep doing this till we get it right."

Printed in the United States
By Bookmasters